QUESTIONS FOR THE DEAD

QUESTIONS FOR THE DEAD

A MARTIN RODAK PSYCHIC MYSTERY

MATTHEW PORTER

Identifiers

Library of Congress Control Number: 2026901734

ISBN: 979-8-9945407-0-1 (paperback)
ISBN: 979-8-9945407-1-8 (ebook)

Published by
Ephemeral Industries
PO Box 271167
Littleton, Colorado 80127

www.EphemeralIndustries.com

For Celeste.
You bring joy to every journey.

CHAPTER 1

I swear to God, every time I take Fielding anywhere, he starts screaming about dead people. I suppose I shouldn't complain, because that's pretty much what I pay him for, but still.

"No! No! Turn it off! It's too bright! I can see them! There are so many! Turn it off!"

This all makes more sense if you know that Fielding is a psychic. Yes, they're real. No, I've never claimed to be one, no matter what anyone may tell you. Psychics tend to carry a lot of baggage, and most of them are complete pains to work with. But they can be worth it.

Fielding's deal is that he sees dead people. And they talk to him. This happens whether he wants it to or not, and that takes a toll. He looks every one of his sixty-odd years, but handling him is like dealing with a child. A talented child, useful in working jobs like this latest case for John Harris of Pioneer West Insurance.

Fielding had his long, thin hands up in front of his face, and he looked like he was trying to pull his head down into his tweed jacket.

"Please, turn it off!"

Harris himself stood stunned, one pudgy hand still on the light switch. We were in a small workroom in the basement of a building owned by Vicar and Blake Auctions and Appraisals. This was in the northeast part of Denver, one of many squat industrial blocks across I-70 from the National Western Complex. Outside, the day was bright and brisk, but inside was all dust and darkness. Until Harris went and turned on the light.

Harris had hired me to trace some items stolen from the auction house. Vicar and Blake is an important client for Pioneer West, and Pioneer West is an important client for my bottom line at Martin Rodak Investigations. A one-man operation, not counting help from people like Fielding.

Next to Harris stood William Tucci, the operations manager for Vicar and Blake. He kept his hands deep in the pockets of his puffy jacket, jingling its fancy titanium zippers. He had been short-tempered all morning, and now his eyes were wide as he braced for another outburst from Fielding.

Harris still had not moved. I reached past him, nudged his hand out of the way, and switched off the light. The darkness came back, pierced only by the small flashlight I carried and a bit of sunshine filtering in from a distant window high up on the basement wall.

Harris shuffled back a few steps and brushed at his big walrus mustache. Fielding let out a great sigh.

"I'm sorry," he said. "There were just so many of them. All over. Sometimes the light makes them too easy to see."

As usual Fielding spoke rapidly, his words bumping against one another as if he couldn't apologize quickly enough. He apologizes a lot.

One of his blue eyes peered out from between long gray fingers. "So many. So many."

I put a hand on his shoulder. I felt him tense for an instant, and then relax. Good. I needed him to calm down and do his thing. I couldn't afford to have Fielding's nerves derail this job.

"It's okay," I said. "Take your time. If there's anyone who can help, just talk to them and find out what you can. I'll be right over here."

Fielding nodded. I took one more look at him, then stepped back toward the door. Harris and Tucci had recovered a bit. Harris looked worried. Tucci had his hands out of his pockets, balled into little fists.

"You'll have to excuse my associate," I whispered. "He can be a little sensitive."

Harris took me by the elbow and led me a few steps away from Tucci.

"What's going on?" Harris said. "Is he going to be okay?"

Harris is an old friend, and had seen Fielding react to ghosts before. So he was right to wonder why Fielding seemed even more upset than usual.

I gave what I hoped was a confident nod, but I kept looking at Fielding, alert for another sign of distress.

"He'll be fine," I hedged. "It's just his typical nerves."

"Sure," Harris said. "But why is he even here? This is a property case, not a death case. What'd you bring him for?"

"Not my idea," I said. "As soon as you sent me this case, I talked to Cindy. She said I should start here, and she insisted I bring Fielding."

Cindy is my map reader. She can spot just about anything going on in the state, maybe the country, by looking at the dozens of maps on her walls.

Harris sighed. "Fine." He shrugged his beefy shoulders. "I guess you know what you're doing. But try to keep things low-key, all right?"

"Understood," I said. As I turned back toward Fielding, I rubbed my temples in a futile attempt to stem the pain that was spreading forward from the back of my head. It never failed when I brought Fielding in on a case. A literal as well as figurative headache.

Just then Fielding began darting around in a tight circle, flinching and dodging something only he could see.

"Good God!" he cried out. "No wonder there are so many. They were working, and they had no time."

Fielding's voice echoed down through the empty basement. Tucci jumped back a step, while Harris just closed his eyes and shook his head.

"What's he saying?" Tucci asked. "Who is he talking about?"

I deflected the question with one of my own. "How old is this place?

"Vicar and Blake has been in operation since 1902, when it began as an auctioneer of mining properties and equipment." Tucci's answer seemed well rehearsed, like part of a tour for high schoolers. Then he paused and looked around to assess the building where he stood. "The company first used this location in 1945. Some of the foundation work dates back to a furniture factory that was destroyed during the fire of 1940."

A fire. Great. I was beginning to understand why Cindy had told me to bring Fielding. If anything had happened down here, there were plenty of witnesses. The kind only Fielding could talk to. But what did this place have to do with a theft from V and B's downtown offices?

Fielding had slowed his frantic dodging but was still looking around at random points in the air.

"You were working," he said. "It was too quick. The oil, the varnish. The wood. It was so quick you couldn't get out. Some of you are still trying."

Tucci was starting to look pale. "Who is he talking to?"

"You may not want to know," I said.

Tucci reached up to grab me by the shoulder. His grip was

not very strong, but he seemed to be trying to turn me around to face him, so I obliged.

"Listen, Rodak, I've read about you and your flaky history. If you expect me to —"

Harris stepped forward and interrupted. "Mr. Rodak and his assistants have unusual methods, but I've found that they consistently produce good results."

Tucci looked back and forth between Harris and me, then took a step back.

Fielding started speaking to us again, and he seemed more calm. "They say there is someone new. Someone they don't know. Up ahead."

Harris, Tucci, and I made way for Fielding as he left the small workroom. We followed him down the hallway, moving cautiously through the dim light among old crates and cobwebs, until he stopped by the door to another room.

"In here," Fielding said. "This is where they say the new one is."

"Okay," I said. "But hold on a minute." Something seemed odd about the floor in front of the doorway, so I bent down to take a closer look.

Colorado's Front Range is home to a lot of dust. Old buildings in Denver tend to collect a good amount of it, even if they've been sealed up. And different times of the year have different kinds of dust, from a fine powder of pollen and earth in the springtime to a grittier, almost sludgy dust in the wetter winter months. If you know what to look for, in an undisturbed place, you can examine the layers almost like tree rings.

This was not an undisturbed place. The dust in front of the door was compressed and smudged, with only a little of the fine springtime variety covering the thin spots.

I raised my flashlight to the doorknob. There too the dust showed chaotic smudges where I'd have expected a smooth coat.

"Has anyone from your company used these rooms recently?" I asked.

"Not that I know of," Tucci said, "and I'd definitely know. Why?"

"Because someone has been in this room in the past few weeks. Two months at most. The dust is all messed up here."

Tucci opened his mouth as if to argue, then closed it again. I turned back to Fielding.

"You ready to go in?" I asked. We needed to know what was inside, but I didn't want another of his panic attacks.

"I think so," he said.

I turned the doorknob, reaching around to grip it by the shaft and avoid touching the big round brass knob. When the latch clicked I pushed the door open and moved aside. Fielding took a deep breath and stepped through.

Immediately he gave a shout. "Wait, stop it. Don't do that! Stop yelling at me!"

"What? What is it?" Tucci shouted back.

I held up a hand to quiet him. If Fielding was getting overstimulated, the last thing we needed was someone else yelling at him.

I called out softly, "Everything okay? What do you see?"

There were a few moments of silence, and then Fielding replied calmly, "It's okay, Martin. I found the new one. He was just excited. He started yelling the moment I came in. But there are things here you'll want to see."

I entered the room, followed by Tucci and Harris. My flashlight showed it to be twice the size of the previous one. Along one wall was a stack of shelves littered with cans, bottles, and tools. In the middle of the room stood a tall, flat worktable.

"Fielding?" I said. "Is it okay if we turn on a light?"

"Y-yes. Go ahead."

I flipped the light switch by the door and stepped farther

into the room. Fielding was focused on an empty spot in midair near a back corner. From time to time he nodded and murmured. He turned toward me for just a second.

"He's the only one here," Fielding said. "The older ones are staying away from him. They said he smells wrong."

Harris raised an eyebrow at me, but I just shrugged. Ghosts apparently have complicated ways of detecting one another. Fielding says they can also detect those rare people who can see and hear them.

I turned to the broad table and the papers strewn across it. They weren't nearly as dusty as everything else in the room. And their contents were pretty interesting.

There were floor plans of the main Vicar and Blake building downtown, plus maps of the surrounding blocks and technical spec sheets on security systems. Even printed photos of interior offices. The angles of the photos suggested that they had been taken on the sly.

"At least we know what this room was used for," I said. "Planning the theft."

Tucci made a choking sound and rushed to examine the papers on the table. I put out a hand to keep him from touching anything, and Harris looked over his shoulder.

"I don't understand," Tucci said. "Who would have all this information about our security? And who could have used this building to make their plans?"

"I'm sorry to suggest it," said Harris, "but the obvious answer is someone inside. Someone who works for you."

Tucci straightened up. "You're right, of course. We need to scrutinize every employee at Vicar and Blake. Damn. I can't believe—"

"Joseph," Fielding spoke up.

"What's that?"

"It was Joseph," Fielding said. "He was the man inside. Joseph Vargas."

"Joseph Vargas," said Tucci. "Yes. He worked for us as a handler. Moved things to and from storage, helped with loading large items, preparing them for shipping, that kind of thing."

"He had access to your facilities?" I asked. "Keys, key cards?"

"He did until five weeks ago."

"What happened then?"

"He stopped coming to work. Didn't even give notice, just called to say he'd quit. Really, you think you're doing something good by giving a job to someone like that, and —"

"Someone like what?" I asked.

Tucci rolled his eyes. "Vargas. He was, I don't know. Indian? Hispanic? Anyway, um, you know, he seemed ..."

Tucci stammered and let his tirade trail off. My stare and Harris's sad head shaking may have had something to do with that. I wasn't too surprised to learn Tucci was racist, but at least he had the sense to be embarrassed about it.

"How long had Vargas worked for Vicar and Blake before he quit?" I asked.

"Six years," Tucci said.

"Six years," Harris echoed. "Sounds pretty dependable to me."

"So Vargas disappeared five weeks ago," I said. "When the police were investigating, did you happen to mention that one of your employees had quit suddenly three weeks before the theft?"

"Of course," Tucci said. "The police said they'd follow up on that. But they never found him."

I put my flashlight away in one suit pocket and got my notebook out of another. I made a note to follow up on Vargas's key card and the V and B access records.

Fielding was still in the corner murmuring into the air. Now he turned to speak to Tucci. "Joseph feels bad about that," he said. "About robbing the auction house. He doesn't like you very much, but he did like his job."

Tucci straightened up and faced Fielding. "What are you talking about? Just how do you know this?"

"Joseph just told me," Fielding said.

Tucci and Harris were silent.

"So," I said, "that means Joseph is dead."

That was it for Tucci. He looked back and forth between Fielding and me, and his face took on a satisfying new shade of pale. Then he turned and walked stiffly out of the room. Harris looked at me and then at Tucci's receding back.

"You'd better go after him," I said. "Fielding and I will meet you at the cars as soon as he's done here."

Harris nodded. "Okeydokey." He smoothed his mustache, probably to hide a grin, and followed in Tucci's wake. Sometimes Harris takes a childish delight in the discomfort of people who deserve it.

"So, is Joseph being helpful?" I asked Fielding.

"Yes," he snapped. He had turned to face the corner again. He held up a hand to keep me quiet and returned to his conversation. He nodded frequently, and occasionally asked a question that I couldn't quite hear.

I turned back to the table to examine more closely the papers and photographs. It wasn't the work of professionals, but it reflected a lot of inside knowledge. Joseph and his friends were clearly not master criminals, or they never would have left all of this material behind, but they had pulled together all the info they needed.

Behind me, something changed in the way Fielding was talking with Vargas.

I turned and saw that Fielding seemed to be smiling. For

him, that was much more unusual than a conversation with a ghost.

"What's going on?" I asked.

He held up a hand. I let him have his quiet, but listened closely to catch a few of Fielding's words.

"But how does it work? ... So, what do I have to ... Are you sure? ... Of course, of course ... I won't ... But why did they ..."

I looked at the papers some more, letting Fielding continue his conversation in peace. But then he said a phrase that cut through the steady murmur to get my attention.

"Why me?"

I turned to look at him again. He must have sensed my movement because he held up his hand again to keep me quiet. Finally he nodded several times, mumbled one last thing to Joseph Vargas's ghost, and turned back to me. I stole a glance at the empty spot he'd been talking to. Still empty, of course, though I always expect to see something.

"All right, Martin," Fielding said. "I think Joseph has told me all he can for now."

"Good stuff?"

"I think so. Can we talk about it outside?"

"Of course." I slid a small digital camera out of my pocket. Better for a chain of evidence than the camera on my phone. "You might want to step out of the room for a minute. I need to use the flash."

Fielding nodded and went out to the dark hallway. I took some wide shots of the room to show the layout. I also took a portrait shot of the place where Fielding had been talking to Joseph. Finally I turned my attention to the table. I took close-ups of every paper I could see. I nudged a few things to one side or another with the end of my pen to uncover more of the writing, but I knew better than to mess with things too much or to leave my own prints on anything. Denver PD would not like that. I had gone nearly six months without pissing off the one friend I had left in the department, and I thought it might be nice to keep that streak going.

I finished with the photos and joined Fielding in the hall. We made our way up the stairs and out to the cracked, weedy parking lot, where three cars were parked with their noses together. Tucci paced in front of his silver Escalade. The panic he had shown in the basement seemed to have faded, and now he looked more angry than scared. When he saw us he stopped pacing and glared.

"So, everything all fine now?" He broke into a thin-lipped smile. "Have you two finished your nice conversation with my deceased former employee?"

"Well, we —"

Tucci's fake smile turned to a scowl as his voice rose. "Don't bother. I don't know how many other would-be clients you've managed to take in with this little show of yours, but count me out. I'm not about to believe that you can talk to dead people."

"Actually it's just my associate Mr. Fielding who —"

"Yes, I know. Your 'associate.'" He actually put finger quotes around the word. "That's a nice touch. You don't claim to be anything special yourself, do you? The fact is that you're not anything special, Rodak. You're just another phony. You learn to spot them in the auction business."

"Are you about done yet?" I asked.

Tucci shook off the question. "I don't understand why Mrs. Lansing allowed them to put you on this case. How did you really come by the information we're paying you for? How did you know to come to this building? Maybe you had some inside knowledge? Just what do you expect me to believe?"

I decided to ignore Tucci's accusation.

"What you believe or don't believe is not any great concern of mine," I said. "I completely acknowledge that the methods my assistants and I employ are unusual. But I can assure you that any information we provide will in the end be supported by evidence that will stand up in a court of law. Five years with the district attorney's office taught me the importance of that. And as for payment." I smiled again and nodded toward Harris. "That's up to the insurance company."

"He's right about that." Harris stepped toward us, moving nimbly for a man of his bulk. "Martin Rodak Investigations has been engaged by the Pioneer West Insurance Company. By filing a claim, Vicar and Blake has authorized Pioneer West to conduct an investigation to recover the lost property or identify the parties responsible, using whatever methods our company considers appropriate."

Tucci raised both eyebrows. "Are you telling me you intend to continue —"

"Martin has a dynamite track record. If he says that he has uncovered a promising lead, I'd be crazy not to have him pursue it."

Tucci stared at Harris. Before he could speak, Harris continued.

"I'll be sure to keep you informed of all developments. Mrs. Lansing as well, given her personal interest in this case."

Tucci glared at Harris for a moment and then turned to his car. "I expect daily updates," he said as he got in.

"I'll make sure of it. Talk to you soon."

Tucci wasted no time in starting up the SUV and speeding out of the lot, crushing a trail through the tall stalks of thistle that had broken through the pavement. As he turned the corner and disappeared from view, Harris shook his head and laughed.

"Mrs. Lansing?" I said.

"She's the chair at Vicar and Blake. Majority owner. She was very interested when she learned you'd be working on this case. Seems she read about you in the papers."

Some of my early cases as a PI had gained a bit of questionable publicity, including newspaper coverage and a short profile in 5280 magazine. In general it brought in more business than it kept away, so I took the good with the bad.

"As long as she didn't call me a 'psychic detective,'" I said.

Harris laughed. "No, she seemed to have the right idea. But she did grumble a bit about the 'mentalists and other oddballs' you hang out with."

Harris cleared his throat, then looked around and smoothed his mustache. "So, did Fielding get anything good?" He hadn't said "speaking of oddballs," but the implication was there.

"I don't know yet," I said. "It can take some time to follow up on what he learns."

Harris nodded. Fielding was slumped against the back of my MINI Clubman, on the far side from where we stood next to Harris's Land Rover.

"First, I'll give my friend Jeff Lang at DPD a call. I have to tell them about this place, and about Vargas. Then I'll go back through the claim file and see what I can connect with whatever Fielding can give me."

"What more is there to connect?" Harris said. "If Fielding has already talked to the inside man?"

"Even with Fielding on our side, questions for the dead don't always have straight answers," I said. "All we know so far is who Joseph is, that he was involved in the theft, and that he's dead. Sometimes the information is a little disjointed. We may not know yet who Joseph was working with. And if they killed him, we won't know what happened to the stolen items after that."

"Okeydokey. Fair enough. Just let me know before you spend more than two weeks on this. You're good, but you're not cheap."

"Hey, I've got a lot of mouths to feed. Speaking of which ..." I pointed a thumb back at Fielding. "I'd better find out what's going on with this one."

CHAPTER 2

I 've never been special, and for that I'm grateful.

Don't misunderstand me. I'm good at what I do. I was a pretty good lawyer when I was a Deputy District Attorney, and I've had some success since I left that behind. But anyone who says I'm a "psychic detective" is full of crap, and if they say it more than once they're looking for a fight.

I'm no psychic. Some of my friends have "gifts," and I've seen what it does to them.

Most spend their entire lives running away from their talents, pretending that they are not who they are and can't do what they can do. They end up stuck in lives that look normal from the outside but are pretty much dead inside.

A few embrace what they can do, but that usually means that they end up isolated from every other person on the planet, consumed by their weirdness, broke or crazy or in jail or some combination of all three.

It's a lot like the way "normal" people handle the whole psychic thing. Most deny that psychic talents even exist, and mock anyone who holds an open mind.

Others are quite certain that psychics are out there, and are just as certain that they are agents of Satan or alien invaders or foreign terrorists.

Then there are some who are sharp enough to know that psychic talents are real, and who understand that psychics are just people with quirks.

Finally a few figure out that those quirks are useful, and can help turn a buck. People who exploit psychics to get things done.

I guess I'm in that last group, damn my ass to hell.

Still, I consider Fielding a friend. I pay fair rates to the psychics I use, and try to take care of them as best I can. God knows they need it.

Fielding's home was not far from the old Vicar and Blake building. He lived in a small square house on a block that ended at the fence surrounding one of the oldest cemeteries in Denver. Years ago I'd thought it odd that Fielding would live near a graveyard, but apparently it's a pretty quiet neighborhood from his point of view. The way he explains it, ghosts don't tend to spend any time in graveyards. After all, if a dead guy hasn't moved on it's because he doesn't know he's dead or because he has some unfinished business to deal with. Either way, he's not going to hang around where his body has been planted. He's more likely to be at the place where he died, or a place that was important to him while he was alive.

I pulled up in front of the house and shut off the engine so I could talk to Fielding for a minute. He was usually a bit out of sorts after a job, but he seemed more distant and agitated than usual. Many doctors had tried to figure Fielding out over the years, and most placed him somewhere on the autism spectrum. But today I could tell that something different was going on.

Fielding fidgeted and continued staring out the windshield.

"So, what did you learn from Joseph?" I asked. "Anything else we can use?"

Fielding fidgeted some more and looked down into his lap. "I don't know. He said a lot that doesn't make sense yet. You know how it is."

"I know. I know. Still, was there anything that makes sense? Any information you can give me?"

"Maybe."

"I thought you said you got some good stuff. Did he see who killed him?" I asked.

Fielding flinched. "No. I don't know. I asked him who killed him, but he was confused. He couldn't tell me who they were."

They. So there were more than one.

"Okay, okay," I said. "Someone involved in a robbery gets killed, it's usually because his partners turned on him. But he wouldn't tell you who they were?"

"No. When I asked, he said he wouldn't tell me. Or he couldn't tell me. I don't know if he was protecting someone, or just confused."

"Must have been confused," I said. "Why would be protect someone who killed him?"

"It was all confused. Maybe I'll be able to figure out something by the morning."

Sometimes it does work that way. Dead people don't always think straight, and sometimes the things they say are puzzles that take some time to figure out.

"Okay," I said. "But if you don't have more for us to work with by morning, we need to go back so you can question Joseph again."

Fielding shook his head. "I don't want to go back. That place was too crowded."

"I know," I said, "but we do what the job takes ..."

"Not what's easy," Fielding finished. He nodded, but still squirmed and stared out the window.

I sighed and closed my eyes to think for a second. I needed

to make Fielding happy, because I was pretty sure I wasn't done with him on this case. I had one thing in reserve, so I reached back to the rear seat and felt around until I found a small package wrapped in brown paper.

"Here, I got you something. I think you'll like this."

Fielding's eyes widened when he saw the package, but before he could take it I held it back out of his reach.

"You understand we really need all the information Joseph can give us, right?" I said. "Anything you can get from what he told you today. And going back to see him again if we have to."

Fielding swallowed sharply, but he nodded. His eyes never left the package, and as I lowered it his hands moved quickly to take it and he began opening the paper carefully.

"That's — that's very kind of you, Martin. Very kind. There was no need to — strictly business association — not that you're not a friend — very thoughtful to bring me something ..."

Fielding had made it through the layers of brown paper to reveal a book. It was a small hardback edition of *Robinson Crusoe*. The book dealer who sold it to me said that it was from a small run printed in 1932. I'd planned to hold it for some time when Fielding was especially obstinate. This was not the worst I'd seen him get, but I decided this case was worth the bribe.

Besides, it's nice to see Fielding enjoy something. And there's nothing in life that he enjoys as much as his books.

Fielding's eyes widened farther, as wide as I ever saw them, as he turned the book over in his hands. "Martin, this is wonderful. I don't think I've read this one before. Really, this is so thoughtful. Thanks so much." By the time he looked back up at me, his eyes were wet and shiny.

"Just a token for an old friend," I said. "I saw it when I was in New York and thought you'd like it."

Withdrawn as he is most of the time, Fielding can get

emotional very quickly. I was hoping he'd get out of my car and into his house before he got too weepy on me.

After a few more awkward words of thanks, Fielding got out, clutching his new old book close to his chest, and walked up to his door. Once he had found his key and let himself in, I pulled away.

I drove south toward Melissa Parker's place. She's another of my associates. I believed she could provide some insight, and I was always happy for an excuse to visit her.

On the way I decided to give Cindy an update on what her lead had gotten us. I tapped her name on my cell phone, and she answered on the third ring.

"Hello?"

"Hello, Cindy."

"Martin. Why on earth are you taking Colorado Boulevard at this hour? The traffic will be terrible."

Cindy worries over everyone as if we were her grandchildren. But she was right about the traffic, of course, and I was on Colorado just north of City Park. She could always tell where I was.

"I'm on my way to see Melissa," I said. "Just wanted to tell you that your advice paid off. Fielding and I went to that building over by the stock show, and Fielding made a new friend."

"Oh dear. Is he all right?"

"He'll be fine. A little worn out is all. I just dropped him off at home. Anyway, not much to tell yet, but I wanted to say thanks. You and your maps came through once again."

"You're most welcome, Martin. You take care. And mind that accident near Sixth Avenue."

In my rearview I could see the lights of an emergency vehicle speeding south. Toward Sixth, I was sure. "I will. You be good now, Cindy."

After I hung up, I considered Cindy's advice about the accident. I also thought about the fact that I hadn't eaten all day and was feeling pretty empty. I turned on Colfax and crawled through traffic until I stopped at Itty's Tavern in Greek Town.

Technically Greek Town is still Denver's only officially designated ethnic community, but the banners that had adorned its painted lampposts twenty years ago are long gone, as are several of the Greek diners and cafés whose owners had fought for the area's recognition. Itty's has been there a long time, and while Itty isn't Greek, his place is an anchor of the block.

It was early, so the place was still quiet. Just a couple of guys sitting at the bar and Itty's nephew Jerry behind it, filling peanut buckets.

"Hey, Marty," Jerry said as I walked in. "Long time. You workin'?"

"Yeah. Good to see you, Jerry. Set me up with some of the dark and a steak sandwich."

"No problem."

Jerry gave me a tall glass of Guinness. The tavern was mostly a dimly lit box, but there were a couple of sunny booths near the front window. I carried my drink to one of those, sat down, and pulled Harris's case file from under my arm. I opened to the claim information from Vicar and Blake and the descriptions of the stolen pieces.

There were three lots missing in total. The thing was, they didn't have much in common with one another. One was a collection of late-nineteenth-century photographic equipment. All of it was in good condition, so the lot had been expected to attract interest from collectors. The second was a piece of early-twentieth-century western sculpture, an original bronze casting by Michael Fenn. The last was a set of three small Native American jars.

No connection that I could see. Not the most valuable things in the building at the time. Nor even the most portable, especially the sculpture. Maybe they were just targets of opportunity, the first things Vargas and friends found when they broke in.

Or maybe they had been commissioned to steal specific items? Perhaps a collector didn't want to risk losing out at auction?

Historical photographic equipment is a hot collectible among the latest wave of young tech millionaires. This lot contained some significant pieces, including a well-maintained wet-plate camera from 1853. I suppose I could see someone obsessing over that kind of thing.

The Fenn sculpture had been sold at auction for one hundred ten thousand dollars eight years ago, and had been expected to fetch at least one-forty this time around. Not bad money, but there were other Fenn pieces available around the country. This one depicted a horseman with a rifle, which could describe just about every Fenn reproduction I'd seen in every hotel lobby in the western United States. I doubted anyone would go to the trouble of sponsoring a heist just for that.

The jars were interesting. They had some value, but not enough to make them worth a heist like this. Not much to look at. They were bulbous things ranging from two to four inches in diameter, with small spout-like openings at the top, made of thick brown clay. The thing that made them attractive was their age and pedigree. They were from a people of southern Colorado called the Lacalma, and the jars themselves were estimated to be at least four hundred years old. There seemed to be a lot of academic interest in studying them. Vicar and Blake had expected most bidders to be universities or museums, or wealthy buyers looking to donate the pieces for a tax break and academic gratitude.

Jerry brought my sandwich. I ate with my left hand while making notes and sketches in my notebook.

Okay, say Joseph Vargas and friends had been hired to steal one of these lots. Which one? And what about the rest of the loot? Just picked up because it was handy?

The weird variety of stolen merchandise made me lean toward an independent job by Vargas and company. Either way, an indie job or a sponsored job where they picked up some extra stuff, how had they planned to off-load what they stole?

A lot of questions. I was counting on Vargas's murder to hand me a lucky break.

That sounds awful, I know. So let me be clear about something: I'm basically an insurance investigator. Once in a while I may take a missing-person job, or a background check, or some other consulting work. But I pay my bills from contracts with Pioneer West and a few other insurance companies who hire me to investigate claim fraud, or to retrieve insured property like in this Vicar and Blake case.

A few times a year John Harris sends me a death claim. That's when Fielding comes in handy. Nothing beats getting the victim's own description of a fatal crash or an industrial accident.

An accident is one thing, but murder is different. Generally I don't deal in murder. No private investigator does, because no one hires us for that. Catching a murderer is the most important thing in the world that no one is willing to pay for. So I leave that to the real cops. Serious, underpaid, and sometimes even skilled real cops like the ones I worked with when I was a Deputy DA.

But if I'm going to be honest, finding a murder victim in the middle of a property case might make my job a lot easier.

Of course I was sorry to learn that the theft had led to murder. Naturally. I'm not a monster. But with Fielding on my side, murder could be a pretty easy case to solve. A vast majority of murders are committed by someone known to the victim, and

Fielding is one of the few people who can talk to a murder victim. It seemed likely that one of Vargas's partners in crime had turned on him, and that person might still have the stolen items I'd been hired to find. I should be able to ID the killer, if Fielding could just squeeze the right information out of Vargas.

Information. That reminded me. I still needed to call Lang.

I finished my sandwich, gathered up the file and my note-book, left some money for Jerry, and went back out to my car. Before starting it up I dialed the phone. After two rings a familiar voice came on the line.

"Major Crimes Division. This is Detective Lang."

I've known Jeff Lang for a long time. Worked a bunch of cases with him when I was a prosecutor. He was one of the few cops who hadn't considered me a deserter when I left the DA's office.

"Jeff," I said, "it's Martin Rodak."

"Marty. How's things? You and the superfriends staying busy?"

"Busier than some weeks. I just started a new case for Pioneer West."

"Interesting job?"

"Pretty interesting," I said. "There may be a murder involved."

Lang sighed through the phone. "Okay, keep talking. No, let me guess. Fielding met a dead guy?"

"You got it."

"Marty, you know that doesn't give me much to go on. Until we find a body, or get a credible report from someone ..."

"I know, I know. Just wanted to give you a heads-up. Fielding is right more than he's wrong, isn't he?"

"Well, yes," Lang said. "A lot more."

"So there you go. Anyway, that's not the main thing I needed to tell you now. Who's working the Vicar and Blake theft?"

"Fred Carson, with me on call. And Carson is not a happy man right now. Feds are breathing down our necks about that case."

"Feds? Why?"

"Apparently there were some Indian, I mean, Native American artifacts stolen. Which means the Department of the Interior takes an interest, which means we need to get results or they call the Department of Justice and the case goes to the FBI. That's why it was bumped over to us in Major Crimes, even though it's technically just a property crime."

Lang paused for a moment.

"Wait a minute," he said. "Is that the case you're working for Pioneer West? The V and B thing?"

"Yep."

"Oh great." I could hear Lang's palm covering his forehead. "Fred's going to love that. First feds, and now you messing around."

"Hey, hey. Nobody's messing around. I come with an offering. Fred needs to check out the old V and B storage building up on Brighton."

"Why?" Lang asked.

"Because that's where the thieves planned their job."

I gave Lang a description of the meeting with Fielding, Harris, and Tucci, and what we found in the basement.

"And don't worry, I was good," I said. "I didn't mess with the scene once I realized what we had there."

"I'm sure you were careful," Lang said.

"Tell Carson I'll come by in the morning to give a statement."

"I will. See you later, Marty."

I hung up and started the car. Then I drove to Melissa's place, a nice little garden apartment near Cherry Creek.

I heard her voice as soon as I rang the doorbell. "Coming, Martin."

She opened the door into her bright, cool living room. She was wearing black-framed sunglasses that matched her jet-black hair and highlighted the pale, pretty features of her face. Seeing her smile always made me feel like a weight was being lifted from my head, replaced by a warmth in my chest.

"Hello, Melissa. This an okay time for a chat? I could use some help."

"Sure. I was just watching the Rockies extend another eighth-inning lead."

The TV in the corner was turned off. I knew that it wasn't connected to anything. No cable, no antenna, no power even. But somehow Melissa was able to watch things on it. Which would be remarkable even if she weren't blind.

Melissa led me inside. Besides the television, there was a small sofa and a comfortable chair, and a large drafting table that took up most of the room.

"I was just working on some more card designs," Melissa said. "My publisher is pressing me for new cards for the holidays. Gives me a headache, thinking about Christmas so early in the year."

Melissa works as an illustrator and greeting card designer. Not a typical trade for someone with no sight, but nothing about Melissa is typical. For me, she's a weirdly effective sketch artist. She can't see a floodlight in front of her face, since she was born without the usual connections between her eyes and her brain, but she can detect the history of objects or places and turn those visions into drawings.

"I don't have anything physical for you yet," I said, "but I have some photographs. Here, just a sec."

I took out my camera and switched it to Review mode, then brought up the first picture I had taken of the basement room where Fielding met Joseph. "Here you go. This is the first picture. I've got more too, with more detail. Let's see what you get from them."

Melissa sat down at her drafting table and took the camera. She held the LCD display squarely in front of her face and appeared to stare at it intently, as if she could see it through her black glasses. After twenty or thirty seconds she held the display up to her forehead, then placed it in front of her eyes again.

"I get lots of people. Old people. No, not old. Old-fashioned. People from a long time ago." She lowered the camera. "What kind of case is this, anyway?"

Damn. She was getting interference from the furniture makers.

"Don't worry about it," I said. "Just concentrate. What do you get that's more recent? Maybe the last few months?"

Melissa held up the camera again. "I get ... some people," she said. "Three people. Three men." She held out the camera to me. "Here, show me more."

I took the camera, flipped to the next picture, and held it up for Melissa. After a few seconds she nodded and I flipped to the next.

As I continued the slide show, Melissa's right hand drifted across the table and took hold of a pencil. On the pad in front of her she began to sketch. Slowly at first, but as she continued she picked up speed. By the time I finished stepping through the photos and lowered the camera, she was sketching frantically, tearing sheets off her sketch pad to start new drawings or restart ones that hadn't gone right. All the while she continued staring straight ahead, her empty black glasses locked in front of her, her fine arched eyebrows perfectly still. Only her hands moved as she tried to draw what was in her mind.

No matter how many times I see it, this part always creeps me out.

Finally she stopped. Her brow softened and a slight smile returned to her lips.

"Here," she said. "These are the men."

She pushed the jumble of papers out of her way and spread three sheets in front of her. They were stark sketches, more like artistic portraits than the flat, dead drawings generated by police sketch artists. One man was gaunt, with a thin mustache and wearing a tie and a dress shirt that hung loosely around his neck. Another was stockier, with straight black hair and a worried smile. The third was a bald man with a hard look to his face and a loosened tie at his throat.

"That's great," I said. "Anything more you can get?"

"This is it, except for the old-timey people I mentioned before," Melissa said. "You know I don't do my best work from photographs. Bring me something I can touch and maybe I can do more."

"I know. Thing is, the place is a potential crime scene. The police wouldn't be happy with me carrying off souvenirs."

"Okay. I hope this helps in the meantime," Melissa said.

"You know it does," I said. I leaned over and kissed her forehead. She smelled like roses and vanilla. She smiled.

"You want to know what I know?" she said. "I know it's been weeks since you said you'd let me cook dinner for you."

"That still sounds great," I said. "Sorry, I've just been busy."

"Sure. But you did promise. How about tomorrow night?" Melissa's voice dropped a little lower. "I'll make something delicious." The tip of her tongue played at the corner of her lips.

I had been making my way to the door, but I forgot how to make my feet move. "Yeah, well. That still sounds great. I, uh, I'll let you know about tomorrow night."

Melissa's smile widened and broke into a delicate laugh. "You're blushing, Martin."

"Hey, how would you know? You can't see me."
"But I know you."

CHAPTER 3

When I got home I spent a few hours working on the case. I looked through the rest of the file I'd gotten from Harris, but nothing new leapt out. I made notes on what I would need from the Vicar and Blake employee records, and I added Melissa's drawings to the file. I planned to show them around at the V and B offices as soon as I could arrange a visit. I knew one of the men in the pictures had to be Vargas, and hoped someone could identify the others. I also made some notes about what to ask Fielding in the morning and what to include in my statement for Fred Carson.

When I was done with the Vicar and Blake file, I updated some billing paperwork for my prior Pioneer West case. After that I watched TV over some saltines and spray-can cheese and eventually went to bed.

I DON'T WAKE up very well. It takes a few minutes for me to figure out what's going on, and during that process I'm far too likely to hit something. It's amazing that I don't need to replace my phone once a month.

The phone woke me up around five o'clock. I grabbed it from its charger on the nightstand, then smacked myself in the forehead with it before I managed to position it next to my ear and talk into it.

"Rodak," I mumbled. "What?"

"Martin. It's — I'm sorry — I didn't — it was — after you brought me home, I went out — now the police think —"

"Fielding? What's going on?" I sat up at the edge of the bed. "Slow down. Where are you?"

On the other end of the line, Fielding took a deep breath before he tried to speak again. "I'm at the police station. Downtown. I — I'm under arrest."

"What? What for?"

"The police think I had something to do with killing Joseph Vargas. I swear, Martin, he was dead before I met him. I met him for the first time yesterday."

"Wait, wait. Why do they —"

"They found out I went to the body. I went to it, I admit, but I only knew where it was because Joseph told me —"

"Stop talking," I said. "Do you understand, Fielding? I need you to stop talking now."

Fielding was silent.

"Good. Now you sit tight. I'll be down there as soon as I can. You say you're downtown? Denver police headquarters?"

Pause.

"Um, yes. There's a sign that says 'Major Crimes.'"

The DPD's Major Crimes Division handles murder investigations, among other things. But Jeff Lang had mentioned that they were also working the Vicar and Blake theft, so maybe that was why Fielding had been taken to that division for questioning.

"Okay. You've met my friend Detective Lang. He works there. I'll call him and try to get this straightened out."

After hanging up the phone, I went to the bathroom to splash some water on my face.

"Why do you keep going out of your way for these people?" I asked my reflection.

I knew the answer, of course. Or at least two answers.

Having a team of psychics in my corner helped me close cases, set my name apart from the competition, and brought in more work. That was the mercenary explanation, and the one I was most likely to admit to.

But I also felt responsible for Fielding, and for the others. I liked to think they were better off working for me than not, and I tried to give them help when they needed it. But sometimes working for me could complicate their lives as much as their talents did.

I left the sink, put on the same suit I had worn the day before, and ran out to my car. It was not quite dawn, and the streets were mostly empty as I pulled out. On my way to the station, I dialed Lang's cell phone.

"Rodak, what's going on?" Lang said when he finally answered.

"Fielding has been arrested."

"I know," he said. "I just got a call that he'd been picked up, something to do with the Vicar and Blake case, and that Vargas thing you tipped me about. What the hell did he do?"

"I don't know," I said, "but I'm sure he didn't kill anybody."

I told him about Fielding's phone call. "That's all I know," I said. "I'm on my way to Cherokee Street."

"I'll meet you there," Lang said.

Twenty minutes later I was at the Police Administration Building at Cherokee and Thirteenth, explaining to a desk officer that I was there to meet Detective Lang, when Lang came in behind me.

"Sergeant, I know why Mr. Rodak is here," he said. "I'll take care of it."

Lang signed me in and handed me a plastic visitor badge that I clipped to my dark green lapel. He sent me through the metal detector, then walked me over to the stairway door. Major Crimes was on the fourth floor, so I knew Lang wanted some time to confer on the way.

There was more gray in Lang's red hair than when I had first met him, but he climbed the stairs with ease. He lost no breath even as he talked the whole way up.

"Let's be clear about this," he said as I followed him up the first flight. "I can't give you any special access or any special treatment. I shouldn't even be talking to you. You're the employer of a suspect. You might wind up being a suspect yourself."

"Come on, Jeff," I said. "You don't think that I —"

"Of course not." Lang stopped on the landing and turned to me. "And I trust you when it comes to your people." He shrugged. "But I need to do this the right way. The department has had enough press about bad investigations these past couple of years, and I'm not about to let this be another one."

Lang turned around and started up the next flight of steps. "So, here's the story," he said, "as I got it from the uniforms who picked him up, and Detective Wrigley, who questioned him last night.

"Around twelve thirty the TOP line gets a call from a cabby. He picked up a weird old guy around eleven thirty. Drove him to a private mailbox store, a twenty-four-hour place down Colorado Boulevard. Waited for him about twenty minutes, then drove him back home. Thing is, the guy was acting real nervous, and kept mumbling to himself about a dead body."

TOP is Taxis On Patrol, the DPD's program training cabdrivers to notice and report suspicious activity. No surprise that a guy as nervous as Fielding talking about a body would merit a phone call.

Lang continued. "So a pair of uniforms go to the house where the old guy was picked up and dropped off. They look around, then ring the bell to see who's home. Fielding answers the door, and as soon as they introduce themselves he starts babbling about a dead guy and a body and swearing that he never talked to the guy until after he was dead."

"Ah, damn it," I said. "That doesn't sound good."

"Yeah," Lang said. "Even if it is true. Anyway, he was still wearing the same jacket, with dirt and what might have been old, dried blood ground into the sleeves. Of course the boys cuff him and take him in for questioning. On the way he insists on telling them where the dead guy is. Another unit went to the place he described, by the river, and found a body. We have a preliminary ID as Joseph Wilson Vargas."

I climbed the last set of steps to join Lang by the door to the fourth floor, but I didn't say anything.

"Marty, you admit Fielding is a little weird," said Lang. "No offense."

"No question he's got a few crossed wires."

"And it's more than a little weird that you should tell me yesterday that Fielding says that Vargas is dead, then later that night he knows where the body is."

I let out a low sigh. "Can't argue with that."

Lang was silent for a moment. He shifted his weight back and forth a few times and finally spoke. "So, be honest. Is there any chance that he could —"

"No," I said. "Not at all."

"You sure? Really?"

"I'm sure. Listen." I leaned forward, my voice lowered even though we were alone in the stairwell. "Fielding has a complicated brain. He's fragile, but he's also harmless. There's no way he did this."

Lang held his breath for a moment, staring past me, then let it out in a growl. "Okay. I believe that. But this looks bad. He's been kept in an interrogation room since he was picked up this morning, but soon he could be moved to lockup."

That made me wince. Jail is a bad place for Fielding, for a dozen different reasons.

"We need some information," Lang said. "I'm sure he knows more than he's told us."

"Maybe." I thought for a few seconds, then said, "Let me talk to him. I'll be able to figure out what's going on."

Lang shook his head. "I can't do that. I'm sticking my neck out as it is just having this conversation."

Pain in the ass, but he was right. Unless ...

"I'm his lawyer," I said.

"What?"

"I'm his lawyer. You're not going to deny his right to talk to his lawyer and have him present during questioning, are you?"

Lang smiled.

"Of course you won't," I told him.

I didn't mention that I'd gone inactive with the Colorado Bar around the time I left the DA's office and set up my investigations business. Lang didn't need to know that.

"All right, Marty. I'll buy that," Lang said. "Let's go talk to Fielding. I'll let him know his *lawyer* is here."

Lang led me through the door out of the stairway and into the maze of fluorescent-lit cubicles where the Major Crimes Division lived. A few detectives who had worked overnight were squaring away paperwork and computerized log entries before heading home for sleep or out for breakfast. Alongside them some early risers were picking up messages and flipping through notebooks to plan their days, engaging in empty morning chatter.

As we walked I thought about the assurance I'd given Lang, and whether or not I believed it. How certain was I that Fielding had not been involved in Vargas's death? At the Vicar and Blake building, he'd reacted to their meeting differently than I'd ever seen before. And he'd never done something as suspicious as going off on his own to check out a body.

As harmless as I considered Fielding to be, I knew he could get emotional. And while there was no way he could overpower a fit young man, he was smart and he could be sneaky when he had a mind to. I wondered how Vargas had been killed.

Lang and I crossed to the other side of the floor where the interrogation rooms were. When we walked into the first room, we found Fielding sitting in a metal chair at a long, plain table. The room smelled of sweat and pine-scented cleaner, and the green walls had been painted recently. Fielding looked up as we entered.

"Martin!" he said. He began to stand up, but Lang shook his head and gestured for Fielding to keep his seat.

"Hello, Fielding," I said. "I told you I'd be here as soon as I could to get this sorted out."

"Mr. Rodak tells me he's your legal counsel," Lang said.

"My ..." Fielding looked back and forth between Lang and me, but seemed to calm down when he saw me smile and nod.

"That's right," I said. "I'm Mr. Fielding's lawyer, and I intend to be present during any further questioning."

If Lang wanted to keep things official and formal, the best thing I could do for Fielding was to go along.

Fielding looked at Lang, then me, then back to Lang. "Right. Of course."

I sat down in an empty chair next to Fielding, and Lang sat across from us. Fielding was wearing a city-issued T-shirt and gray sweatpants. I'd never seen him in anything this casual.

He saw me looking at his shirt. "They took my clothes to process. They're looking for edvi ... evidence."

"That's all right," I said. I laid a hand on his shoulder. "We'll get this straightened out."

Lang looked at me with a frown, then turned his attention to Fielding. "Okay, Mr. Fielding, let's go back over what you've told the officers and the other detective about what happened last night."

Fielding looked at me, then back at Lang. "All right. But it's just like I said before. Some time in the evening I went out and took a walk. I went down to the river, and that's where I found the body."

He told it calmly, like a story. It was surprising the way he could turn that on when he needed it, but then he did spend all of his time reading.

"So you did not know that the body was there before you found it?" Lang asked.

"Well, I did," Fielding said. "Not exactly, maybe, but I knew about where it was."

"And how did you know that?"

Fielding looked back at me before he answered.

"Why don't you tell Detective Lang when and where you learned about the body?" I said.

Fielding fidgeted with his hands in his lap, then said, "Yesterday afternoon, when I was working with Martin. At the old building near Brighton Boulevard."

"You were investigating a theft?"

"Yes," Fielding said.

"And you learned something there that made you think a murder might be involved," Lang said.

Fielding looked at me. I knew he didn't want to talk to a police detective about speaking with a ghost, but Lang was setting things up so he wouldn't have to.

I smiled and nodded. "It's okay. You can just answer Detective Lang's question yes or no."

"You learned something at the old building that made you think a murder might be involved?" Lang said again.

"Yes," Fielding said.

"And you learned something that made you think you knew where the body might be," Lang continued.

"That's right!" Fielding said, sitting up a little straighter in his chair. "That's exactly right. That's where he told me —"

Lang cut him off. "So that's where you learned something about where the body might be, but not the exact location."

"That's right, Detective." Fielding sank back down into his chair.

"And you didn't tell that to anyone at that time because you didn't really understand it until later?"

"Um, yes, That's right."

"So sometime last night you figured out where the body might be, and you went to look for it."

"Yes."

"And did you find it?"

Fidget. "Yes."

"Okay." Lang sat back and drummed his fingers on the table. Fielding stared at the hammering fingertips.

"Here's one problem I have." Lang paused and stopped his drumming, then looked up at Fielding again. "Why didn't you call the police as soon as you found the body?"

Fielding stared at Lang for a moment, then turned to me, then back to Lang. "I — I planned to. It was late at night and I planned to call in the morning."

"Is that so?" Lang said.

"Yes," Fielding said. He paused, thinking, then went on. "And ... and I knew Martin would be calling you in the morning and I figured that we could let you know about the body when we told you about the other things we found in the basement." As Fielding continued his speech grew louder and faster, words running into one another.

"Right," said Lang. He smiled at me, then turned back to Fielding. "That does make sense."

Lang got up and went to a small table in the corner of the room. He filled a plastic tumbler with water from a plastic pitcher. He took his time as he brought it back to place it on the table in front of Fielding. Finally he settled back into his chair and got back to his questions.

"You know, Mr. Fielding, I don't think you had anything to do with the death of that man you found by the river."

"I didn't," Fielding said.

"But you have made a few mistakes that have made things harder for us here," Lang said.

"I know. I'm sorry."

"One is the fact that you didn't call us right away. You find something like this, you really ought to call us right away. Or call Martin and you can contact us together."

"I will. I'm sorry." Fielding took a drink of water, then dropped his hands back into his lap.

"Another thing is the fact that you touched the body. You did touch the body, didn't you," Lang said.

"Yes. I'm sorry."

"Why did you do that?"

"I — I wanted to make sure it was — I mean, I wanted to see if the person needed my help."

"But the person you found was dead, isn't that right?"

"How could I know that?" Fielding shouted, and rose in his

chair, putting his clenched fists on the table. Lang sat straight up.

"How could I have known that he was dead?" Fielding said. "You assume that just because I can ... I mean, how would anyone know he was dead until they looked? I just wanted to know if he was dead. I mean, I wanted to know if he needed any help."

This was the hardest part of working with Fielding. I never knew what would set him off. I laid a hand on his arm and he relaxed a little, but he was still clearly angry.

"It was pretty clear that he was dead," Lang said. "He'd been there for at least a week." Lang closed his eyes and wiped his hands across his face. "But okay. You checked on him, and you found that he was in fact dead."

"Yes, he was dead," said Fielding. "He was entirely dead before I ever touched him. Before I got to Joseph, he was already dead."

Lang relaxed a little and nodded. "Just one more question, Mr. Fielding. Did you find anything on or around the body when you, uh, checked to see if he needed help?"

"Like what?" Fielding said, his eyes narrowing.

"Like anything. Our men found that he still had cash and ID on him, but I want to know if there was anything else we might have missed."

"I don't think you missed anything. I don't know if you missed anything. All I did was check to see if he was dead. All I did was check to see if he needed help."

"Why did you then decide to go to the mailbox place in the middle of the night, right after you found the body, before you called anyone?"

Fielding looked at me, then back to Lang. "I have a mailbox there. I was looking to see if I had any mail."

"In the middle of the night?"

"I — I was expecting a check. I can use the money. I thought there might be a check in there. There wasn't. If there was, I could have used one of those machines to deposit it and not wait for the bank to open. I was out anyway."

Lang raised one eyebrow at me, then looked back to Fielding. "That's a long way to go in the middle of the night."

Fielding sighed and looked around the room and up at the ceiling. "Okay, you're right. I did hope there was a check, but that wasn't the only reason."

Lang leaned forward and lowered his voice a little. "You need to understand, Mr. Fielding, that it's important that you tell us everything that happened. We can't understand your story if you leave anything out, okay?"

"There's another reason why I went out," Fielding said. "I had ordered a book, and I hoped it might have been delivered."

Fielding looked up at me. "I'm sorry, Martin. It's not that I didn't like the book you gave me today. I like it a lot and I can't wait to read it. It's just that I knew the other one might be in the mailbox and I was upset about the body but I didn't want to call anybody in the middle of the night and I couldn't decide which one to read and I thought that if I went and got the other book I could look at them both and maybe I could —"

"Hey, hey, it's all right," I said. I placed a hand on his shoulder, not too tight, in the way I knew calmed him down when he got wound up like this. "It's okay. Detective Lang just wanted to know why you went to the mailbox at such an odd hour."

I looked up at Lang. "But it sounds like he had a good reason. Right, Detective?"

Lang sat back and closed his eyes. He opened them a moment later, but still didn't look at Fielding or me. He stared at the ceiling for a few seconds, then got up and went to the door.

"Wait here," he said as he left.

I knew Lang had gone to have a talk with his Captain, so we

might be waiting for a while. Fielding fidgeted with his hands in his lap. Occasionally he stole a worried glance at me.

"I'm sorry to bring you into this, Martin," he said. "There was nobody else I could call, and I was afraid that this would interfere with the new case."

"It still might," I growled. Fielding looked pained, so I tried to soften my tone a bit. "But don't worry about it. I'm glad you called me."

Sooner than I'd expected, Lang came back into the room. "Well, Mr. Fielding, here's how it is. You haven't been formally charged with anything, and I don't think we need to charge you."

Fielding looked up from his lap to stare at Lang. His eyes were growing wet. "Thank you! Thank —"

Lang cut him off. "This is not to say that you haven't done anything wrong, or that there's nothing we *could* charge you with. Tampering with a crime scene, failure to report a body, those are pretty serious."

"I'm sorry, Detective, I just —"

"You just need to be quiet for a minute now, okay?" Lang said.

Lang sat back down in his chair before he continued. "We're not going to charge you with anything at the present time, but we do expect your cooperation in this case. We may need to question you again, and personally I'd like your word that if you ... 'think of' anything else that may have to do with Joseph Vargas's death, you will let me know immediately."

Lang made air quotes with his fingers around the words "think of." The gesture seemed out of place from a Denver cop in his fifties.

"I understand, Detective," Fielding said.

"Now, Mr. Rodak," Lang said, looking over at me. "As Mr. Fielding's lawyer, and his employer, can you assure me that he will remain in town and will be available if we need to talk to him again?"

"Absolutely," I said. "I'll keep an eye on him."

"Okay, then," Lang said. "You can go now, Mr. Fielding."

"What about my clothes?"

"Your clothes we need to keep. You can have what's left when the lab is done with them, and when we're done with you."

CHAPTER 4

We walked back to my car in silence. Fielding continued to stare at his fidgeting hands once he was seated.

"I'm sorry, Martin," he said.

"It's okay," I said. "But I'm worried about you. What were you thinking, going off like that alone and not telling anyone? Not telling anyone about finding a dead body, for Christ's sake?"

"Like I said, I was going to tell you in the morning. I didn't know the police were going to come get me in the middle of the night."

"Yeah. Well," I said. I never could decide how angry to get at Fielding when he did stuff like this. Not that he had ever done anything quite like this before.

"Now I just made a promise to Detective Lang that I'd keep an eye on you."

Fielding looked up. "Martin, I can take care of myself. I just —"

"You seem pretty agitated," I said. "And I'm not about to break a promise to Lang because you wig out again. Really, I've never seen you like this."

Fielding looked back down at his hands, but now they were

pale, scrawny fists. "Well, maybe I am like this. Maybe I'm like this when the police come to my house and bother me and make me come with them in the middle of the night just because I waited to —"

"Easy, easy," I said. "I know, this is all stressful. But you do need to calm down."

I knew Fielding had plenty of reason to be upset. He could still be in some serious trouble with the police, and apparently there was a murderer wrapped up in the case and still at large. That no longer seemed like the lucky break I'd thought it was. But at this point the best thing Fielding could do was stay calm and stay out of trouble. I wanted to add "and stay out of my way," but that wasn't really an option.

"I think you should stay at my place for a couple of days," I said. "You need to not be alone for a while."

Fielding took a minute to think about that, then let out a sigh. "Okay," he mumbled.

"Let's stop by your place, get some clothes and stuff, then go over to my house," I said. "I want to shave and change out of this suit."

WE GOT to Fielding's house around ten o'clock. The day was warming up and there were a few kids down the end of the block running around under the trees that spread their branches over the cemetery fence.

"I just need a few things," Fielding said as he unlocked the door. "I don't want to keep wearing these jail clothes. And I need to get some books."

Fielding's living room smelled old but clean, and had nice northern light coming in through a big picture window. There were two soft stuffed chairs, a polished wooden coffee table, and two walls of bookcases. It felt like the reading room of a posh private library that had long gone to seed.

Fielding went back into his bedroom. "I'll just get my clothes. I want to get out of these prison clothes," he said again.

"That's fine. I'll wait here."

I strolled over to one of the bookcases. It was packed tight, and the cases on the other wall were almost full as well. There were hundreds of books.

Every one was a copy of *Robinson Crusoe*. Different editions, different printings, different ages. Few of them looked alike. Many were paperbacks produced over the years for classroom use or cheap sale. Some were rare volumes that would probably be worth thousands to a book dealer.

It was the only book Fielding ever read. He read every different edition he could get his hands on, and it always seemed like each one was a brand-new book to him.

I looked at the book collection for a while. The copy I'd given him the day before was sideways on top of the right-hand bookcase, not yet incorporated into whatever library system Fielding used. Then I checked my phone for messages. Nothing new.

Soon Fielding came back. He was wearing khaki trousers, a light jacket, and a checked shirt, and carrying a small suitcase.

"I just need to figure out what books to bring," he said. "I don't think I'll bring the new one you gave me. I want to enjoy that once things have settled down more."

He turned to scan the bookcases with a sharp gaze. "Hmm. I've got a comfortable Puffin book from the eighties that I haven't read in a while. I'll need some others as well. And — Oh no!" Fielding turned to me with a look of concern.

"What's wrong?" I said.

"I'm expecting a new book. It might be delivered while I'm not here."

"I thought it was being delivered to your other mailbox."

"What?" Fielding looked up at me, his forehead stretched in confusion. Then he took a breath and shook his head. "No, that was a different book."

Fielding put down the suitcase, wrung his hands, and looked around the room. Then he seemed to calm down and looked back at me.

"I know," he said, "I'll talk to my neighbor. She's right next door. Lucille. I'll leave a note for the UPS man and ask if they can leave any deliveries with her."

"Okay," I said. "You can stop by and talk to her on the way out."

"I'll go over right now. Can you take this bag out to your car for me?"

"Sure."

Fielding was out the door before I could pick up the suitcase and carry it out to the back of the Clubman.

A MINI Clubman is a ridiculous car for me to be driving. Fine for a caterer, maybe, but not the image I'm going for as a private investigator. But Melissa likes it, partly because the color is called "Hot Chocolate."

I leaned against my dessert-colored car and watched the kids play until Fielding returned.

"Lucille says she'll be home all day, and tomorrow too, so she doesn't mind getting the new book for me from the UPS," he said. "Wait just a minute, though. I need to write the note and get some books."

He disappeared back into the house. A mom across the street called the kids in, and the block got quieter. A little while later Fielding came out and taped a note next to the doorbell. He carried a small backpack, sharp bulges in the blue nylon revealing the corners of heavy books.

I got in the car, and Fielding sat in the passenger seat with his bag of books in his lap. He closed his eyes and let out a loud sigh.

"You all set?" I asked.

"Yes," he said. "Let's go."

He didn't say any more for the rest of the drive. There was enough midday traffic that it took us a good half hour to get to my place.

I own a small house down near the University of Denver. Not fancy, but thanks to jobs from Pioneer West and a few other generous clients, I manage okay. I pulled into the driveway and went to get Fielding's suitcase from the back of the car while he scrambled out with his books.

When we went inside, it occurred to me that we had been lucky. The cleaning service had been in just two days before, and I'd been too busy with the Vicar and Blake case and then with Fielding to make much of a mess.

I brought Fielding's bag to the spare bedroom. In one corner a bass guitar gathered dust on its stand next to a small amp. Under the window stood a computer desk with my old Macintosh.

"There's no bed," Fielding said after he followed me into the room.

"No, see, there's this futon. The frame folds down to make a bed." I bent down to give the futon a pat, and the old wooden frame creaked a little.

"So, that's like a bed?"

"Yes, it's just like a bed," I said. "Just not as squishy. It's kind of firm."

"Firm. Well. I might like that. Might be good for my back."

"Great. Try it for tonight, and if it's no good you can take my bed and I'll sleep in here."

"Oh no, no, no, no. This will be fine."

"Okay, good. Let me know if you need anything else."

Fielding nodded.

"There's one other thing I should tell you about," I said. "Just so you're not surprised."

Fielding looked up. "What is it?"

"Next door, a woman died about two years ago. Her name was Helen McGinnis. She was about eighty years old."

"Oh dear," He looked at the window as if expecting to see something outside.

"She had a heart attack, and from what I've heard it was pretty quick. The thing is, when she died she was waiting for her daughter to arrive on a visit from Santa Fe. From what you've told me, that kind of thing can lead to, well ..."

I paused, looking carefully at Fielding for a reaction. "I mean, it sounds like the kind of thing that might have led to Mrs. McGinnis hanging around the neighborhood."

Fielding was quiet as he continued to look out the window. Then he spoke up.

"Yes, that is the kind of situation that can make them stay," he said. "But I haven't seen anyone since we got here."

"That's good to hear," I said. "Just didn't want any surprises for you."

"Thanks, Martin. Very kind."

I cleared some room in the closet, and Fielding hung up the jacket and few shirts he had brought with him. Then he started pulling books out of his blue backpack and laying them out on the futon. Seven different copies of *Robinson Crusoe*, including one that looked older than the one I had given him just the day before. He studied them carefully, muttering to himself.

I left him to his choices and went out to the front room. It's supposed to be a combination living and dining room, but the dining area is the closest thing I have to an office. The big oak table, usually covered with folders and papers, is the one place the cleaners know not to touch. In the corner is a locked file safe where I try to remember to keep anything sensitive.

The safe also contains my Ruger LC9. The handgun, along with classes, range time, and help with the paperwork for my concealed carry permit, had been a gift from Jeff Lang when I left the DA's office and set up shop as a PI. The only time the Ruger ever left the safe was when I joined Lang at the shooting range twice a month.

I sat down at the table and started looking through the case file again. There was still a question about what was the real target of the robbery. The items were all so different, but one of them must have been the key. And I was absolutely sure that Fielding knew more than he had said so far. Of all the times Fielding has spoken with dead people, this was the first time he'd ever gone out of his way to find a body. In the past he had just left that kind of thing for me to deal with. He seems to consider the problem of corpses unimportant. So what was different about this one?

I needed more information from Vargas. But before I resorted to dragging Fielding back to the old Vicar and Blake building for another chat, I needed to pull out of him anything he had already learned.

First I had to let him calm down a bit more. Enough that it would be useful to talk to him, and enough that he wouldn't do anything else crazy and get himself into more trouble.

I cleared a space on the table and started a list of research topics. I couldn't find my black notebook, and I was too tired to go get it from the jacket pocket where I must have left it, so I used a yellow legal pad.

I hadn't been working long when my phone rang. The number told me the call was from the Police Administration Building.

"Rodak," I said.

"Martin Rodak. I understand that Detective Lang let you go home with my witness, maybe my prime suspect?"

I recognized Detective Fred Carson's Texan drawl. His scowl came clearly down the phone line.

"Well, you know Jeff. He can't say no to a former prosecutor with a nice smile."

"I've seen your smile, Rodak. It ain't that nice."

"Yeah, well. Sorry about your witness. You okay with this?"

The last thing I needed was Carson to insist I bring Fielding back in. But unlike Jeff Lang, Fred Carson hadn't looked too kindly on my leaving the DA's office to become a private investigator. He might not turn down a chance to make my life difficult.

Carson let me hang for a while in silence; then finally he grumbled and spoke.

"The record from Detective Lang's interview with him is good," he said. "For now, I'm okay with it."

I turned away from the phone for a second so he wouldn't hear my sigh of relief. "Thanks, Detective. I appreciate that."

"But I may want to talk to him myself later," Carson said. "By the way, the first word from the lab backs up some of what Fielding told you and Detective Lang. There was blood on his clothes, a type match for Vargas, but it was ground into the fabric when dry. At least a few days postmortem. Consistent with Fielding finding the body last night like he says."

"That's good news."

"Yeah, I guess. But that's just the preliminary testing and an eyeball judgment from the lab guy. And anyway, I didn't call just to chat about your friend."

"Uh-oh."

"I hear you found where my art theft was planned," Carson said. "You gonna come talk to me about that at some point? If you're not too damn busy?"

"Aw crap. Sorry, Detective. I was supposed to come in and give you a statement this morning. Then this whole thing with Fielding —"

"Yeah, yeah. Excuses. I want a statement from you, and I want it today. Be here at one o'clock."

I looked at my watch. Almost twelve thirty. "Okay, but can we make it a little later? Maybe two thirty, three o'clock? I need to make sure Fielding is safe and settled."

I could hear Carson grumbling on the other end of the line. Then he exhaled into the receiver. It sounded like a grizzly deciding not to eat me after all.

"Yeah, okay," Carson said. "I'll see you at two."

I hung up and shook my head.

I was a little worried about Fielding. I wasn't sure what I was supposed to do with him while I went back to Cherokee Street. But he was a grown man, I supposed, and it was the middle of the day, so he should be all right. I settled him on the sofa with a sandwich, a glass of milk, and one of his books, and went out to talk to Detective Carson.

I spent about an hour giving Carson the simple version of what Fielding and I had seen and done. I left out the part about Fielding seeing dead people and talking to Joseph. Lang was okay with how I did things as long as I didn't give him any details. Carson, on the other hand, was one of those who couldn't bear the idea of people with abilities he considered unnatural.

I got home to find Fielding right where I had left him. The milk glass was empty, the sandwich was half gone, and Fielding was about a hundred pages into another copy of *Robinson Crusoe*.

"Hello," he said, not looking up.

"Hi, Fielding. Enjoying the book?"

"Yes. I'm rereading this one again." He held up a chunky school edition hardcover.

"Yeah, I remember that was one of your favorites. Was the sandwich okay?"

"Yes. But you don't have a reading chair."

"What?"

"You don't really have a reading chair," Fielding said. He was still sitting in one corner of my small sofa.

"Yeah, I guess not. I suppose I read in different places."

"And where are your books? I don't see books in your house. Not many."

"Ah, yeah," I started. "I've got plenty of books, but most of them are still in boxes in the basement from when I moved in."

Fielding shook his head and turned back to his own book. "Martin, you can't read them if they're in boxes."

"These days I mostly read e-books," I said.

Fielding looked up, eyes narrowed. "What?"

"Electronic books, I buy them online and read them on my phone."

Fielding's eyes grew wide, and his mouth dipped into a horrified frown. He stared at me for what felt like a long minute, then turned back to his book. He bent down so that his nose was just inches away from the page.

"No, you don't," he said.

"What's that?"

"You don't. You don't read books on your telephone. A book is a book, and if it's not a book it's not a book." Fielding started rocking slightly as his eyes scanned the page.

I admit I smiled a little; then I felt bad about it. "You're right, of course. Sorry, I got confused."

Fielding said nothing, just continued reading.

Damn, I thought. Sometimes I'm not sure whether I say things like that because I'm an idiot, or because I'm mean and want to upset him.

I had gone into the kitchen to pour a drink when my phone rang. It was Melissa.

"Hello again, Martin," she said. "Just wanted to remind you about tonight. Seven thirty okay for you?"

"Yeah, uh, about tonight. I'm not sure that's going to work after all."

"Martin! You've canceled on me twice before. I'm not accepting any more excuses."

"Melissa, I'm really sorry about that. But something's come up."

"Oh? What?"

"I'm kind of looking after Fielding for a few days. He's staying at my place."

I gave Melissa a quick summary of my day. One day? It felt like it had been a week long.

"I see," she said after I had finished. "I'm sorry to hear about all that. You're sure Fielding is going to be all right?"

"Yes, I think so. He's a little shaken up, and to be honest I'm worried. Going out on his own to find a body in the middle of the night? That's not like him."

"Well, why don't you just bring him along to my place tonight?"

"What? I mean, I don't think —"

"I insist," Melissa said. "Besides, I've already started cooking. I'll admit it doesn't sound like the kind of evening I had planned, but it'll be good for you both. Better than sitting around your place all night."

I smiled at that. "I'll have you know my house is a perfectly pleasant place to spend an evening."

"I'm sure it is," Melissa said, with an extra little trill in her voice. Then she laughed. "But I'll bet the dining table is covered in papers."

"Now, how on earth do you know things like that?" I asked.

"I told you, Martin, I know you."

CHAPTER 5

Dinner is generally not a big thing for me. For lunch most days I'll get something at someplace like Itty's if I'm out and about, or have a peanut butter sandwich if I'm at home and busy, or just skip it entirely. Dinner is more often a beer and some Ritz crackers than anything an average person would call a meal.

In short I have a pretty awful diet. Only the fact that I don't eat much of it keeps me from getting fat, especially since I quit boxing soon after I got out of college.

If I let Melissa cook for me on a regular basis, I'd be in trouble, because I'd never stop eating. She's an amazing chef. Dinner started with a delicious minty salad, followed by roast pork with a spiced, fruity glaze. Every bite was incredible, and not just because I hadn't eaten all day.

Melissa is as good at conversation as she is at cooking. As she, Fielding, and I sat around her dining table, we talked about baseball, music, and local news. Fielding was pretty quiet, but livened up a bit when Melissa turned the conversation to books.

"I've been reading a very interesting new book," he said.

"Really? I'd love to hear about it," Melissa said.

"I do think you would enjoy it," Fielding said. "It's about a man who becomes shipwrecked ..."

Fielding then offered a ten-minute version of *Robinson Crusoe* that was actually pretty good. Melissa listened intently, her black glasses staring straight ahead across the table. She sipped her coffee and asked brief questions at all the right times.

"Well, that sounds like an amazing book," she said when Fielding had finished. "I'd like to read it sometime."

"I have it at home," Fielding said. "Or rather at Martin's house now. I could let you borrow it, if you like. If you promise to take very good care of it, that is. Then you could ..."

Fielding's voice trailed off and he looked down at his dessert before he spoke again. "Oh, of course you couldn't. Read the book, I mean. Since you can't see, and ... I'm sorry, I didn't mean to ..."

Melissa laughed. "Nothing to worry about. I very much enjoyed your description. I almost feel as if I've read it myself already. You seem to know the book so well, and you have a marvelous way with words." She reached out toward his voice and gave him a light pat on the arm. "I do look forward to reading it sometime. I'm sure the library has a braille copy."

Fielding looked up again. He seemed to be blushing slightly, and he actually smiled a little. That was a rare sight, and I was especially happy to see it after all he had been through these past two days.

"This coffee was wonderful," I said, "and I'm greedy enough to ask for more. Do you mind, Melissa?"

"That sounds great," Melissa said. "I'll get some from the kitchen." She rose carefully, pushing her chair back from the table with a precise motion, then walked to the kitchen with graceful, measured steps.

"I'll help you," I said, and followed her into the next room.

Melissa's kitchen is a clean place. I don't mean *Good Housekeeping* kind of clean. I mean it looks like a place where they manufacture microchips for space stations. It was plain white — floors, ceilings, countertops, cabinets. The appliances were white. So was every box and canister I could see, and these were arranged in precise rows along the backs of two of the counters. It would seem a little creepy if it weren't for the wonderful smells that lingered from dinner. Beside the aromas, the only sign that Melissa had just prepared such a feast was a roasting pan soaking in the sink.

"Thanks," I said.

"What for?"

"For being so nice to Fielding. I'm glad we came tonight."

"Me too," Melissa said. "But he's a sweetheart, really. I'm glad you told me about that book, by the way, or I'd have been a little confused."

"Yep. He is an odd one," I said. "But I think something is still bothering him."

"I know. I haven't talked with him often, but he seems even more quiet and nervous than he did before."

"Exactly." I stared at the coffeepot for a moment, not really seeing it. What was it that didn't seem quite right with Fielding? Granted, he'd had a hell of a time the past couple of days, including being taken in by the cops, but still there was something else.

Then Melissa spoke again and snapped my attention back to her. "I'm glad you could come, but I will admit that it's not the evening I had planned."

I gave her a little hug — a hand lightly on her shoulder so she wouldn't be surprised, then a gentle squeeze. "Well, we'll have to do something about that. I'm thinking Saturday afternoon."

"And what would you be thinking about, Mr. Rodak?"

"I'm thinking ... lunch in the park, then a concert."

Melissa smiled. "That's a nice thought to think. Now, the concert — it's not one of those noisy electronic things you like?"

"Not at all. It's an alt-folk duo from San Francisco, playing at the Bluebird."

Melissa's smiled even wider. "You got tickets to Mackerel Smack? That's terrific!"

It was my turn to smile. "I hoped you'd like that."

"Oh, I will," she said. "You know," she continued, one eyebrow rising above her glasses, "a person could mistake this for an actual date."

"Yes, I suppose they could, if they weren't careful." I kissed her on the cheek. "For now let's have some more coffee, and then Fielding and I should head home."

We went back into the dining room, where Melissa poured coffee. I sat back down across from Fielding as Melissa went to return the coffeepot to the kitchen.

"She's a very nice person," Fielding said as he scraped up the last of his cheesecake.

"Yes, she is indeed."

Melissa returned to the table and resumed sipping her coffee. "This is more company than I've had in a long time. Thank you both for coming."

"You're welcome," said Fielding. He looked up at Melissa briefly.

"Thank you for such a wonderful dinner," I said. "You are a marvelous cook, Melissa."

"I am, aren't I? Maybe I can persuade you to visit more often."

"Maybe you can at that."

We chatted a little more, but I noticed Fielding starting to nod. He must have been pretty tired. Apart from an hour's nap at my house, he hadn't slept much in the past two days.

"I think we should be heading out soon," I said.

"Wait, before you go." Melissa stood and walked to her drawing table in the living room. "You forgot this when you were here yesterday. One of your notebooks." She returned to her seat, then reached across the table to me, holding one of my little black books with the elastic strap.

She had reached halfway across the table, then stopped. "That's weird."

"What?"

"This is your notebook, right? I could tell it's not one of mine."

"Yep, that's mine."

Her brow furrowed. "Is it a new one?"

I thought for a moment. "No, I've been carrying that for a few days."

"Hmm. It's not —" She handed me the notebook and sat back in her chair. "Never mind."

"Thanks," I said, putting the notebook in my pocket. "If I'd realized that was gone, I'd have started panicking."

Fielding and I stood up and got ready to go.

"Are you sure we can't stay to help with the dishes and things?" I asked.

"No!" Melissa said. "Absolutely not. You'll put something away in the wrong place and I won't find it again for days."

"Okay, if you say so. Thanks again for everything."

At the door I put my hands on her shoulders and she leaned up to give me a little kiss. Then she gestured toward Fielding with her head. I guided her to him, and she put a fingertip on his chin and gave him a kiss on the cheek. He turned red.

"Okay. Bye," he said.

During the drive back to my place, Fielding looked out the window. "I think she likes you."

I smiled, but kept from laughing. "I think so too."

"Do you like her?"

"Yes, I do," I said. It made me happy to say so. "I like her very much."

"That's good," Fielding said. He seemed relieved, as if some question had been settled.

When we got into my house, Fielding went right to his book, and the corner of the sofa he had claimed as his own all day.

"I'm dead," I said. "Going to bed. Aren't you exhausted?"

"No," Fielding said. He already had his book open and was scanning the page where he'd left off. "I'm going to stay up and read some more."

"Okay. Let me know if you need anything. See you in the morning."

I went into my bedroom and got undressed. I was asleep within minutes.

———

WHEN I WOKE UP, it was still dark. I fumbled for my phone. It wasn't ringing, but it did tell me that it was nearly 1:00 a.m.

One a.m., and the phone wasn't ringing. What the hell had woken me up?

"Fielding?" I said, not too loud in case he was still sleeping. I got no answer. I got up and pulled my blue-checked robe from the hook behind the door. As I shrugged it on, I stepped out into the hall.

"Fielding?"

The door to his room was open, and he wasn't there. And he wasn't still on the sofa with his book.

Where had he gone now?

As I moved into the living room, I heard something. It came from outside. I went to the window and parted the blind with one hand to look out.

In the edge of the streetlamp's circle of light, I saw Fielding. He was looking across the hedge into the neighbor's yard, staring at a spot about a foot higher than the top of his head. He was talking intently into empty air.

Goddamn it. Must be Mrs. McGinnis.

I was about to go outside and pull Fielding back into the house when he moved away from the fence. As I watched he walked to the front steps and bent down to pick something up. He had his back to me, so I couldn't see what he had, but whatever it was he held it up in front of him for a few seconds, then put it in his pocket.

He walked back to the edge of the yard where he had been standing before. He stood still for a moment, shoulders tensed as if he were getting up the nerve to do something. Then he looked up and out across the fence to where he had been staring when I first saw him through the window.

He didn't start talking again. Instead he began looking around. He craned his neck and looked this way and that around the hedge, as if he were searching for a missing cat.

After a few minutes of this he stopped. He stood still for a moment. Then he turned and walked back toward the house.

The light was dim, but I could tell that he was smiling.

I moved away from the window, but I didn't leave the living room. I heard Fielding at the door. He opened it slowly and carefully with as little noise as possible. He paused to slip off his shoes and leave them in the entry hall, then opened the inner door and stepped into the living room in his stocking feet. I waited until he was in the room before I spoke.

"Okay, Fielding. Time for you to tell me what's going on."

Fielding exploded into a panic when he heard me speak out of the darkness. He slammed his back up against the door and started shouting. "What? What? Who's that? What? Stop! What —"

I switched on a light and help up my hands at my sides as I walked toward Fielding. "It's okay. It's just me. We need to talk."

CHAPTER 6

Fielding brought his hands down from in front of his face. "Martin! It's you!"

"Yes, it's me. Want to tell me what you were doing out in my front yard at one in the morning?"

"I — I was looking. I was just looking around."

"What were you looking at?"

"I was just looking around."

I let that hang there for a moment until Fielding started talking again

"I was —"

He stopped talking and sat down on the edge of the sofa, wringing his hands. "I was looking at Mrs. McGinnis. The old lady who died next door. You told me about her."

I sat in the chair across from him. "Yes, I did. Why did you go out to talk to her?"

"I — I don't know."

Again I let that sit. Fielding hates quiet when he knows I expect him to say something.

"I — she — she called out. She said she had something to say to me."

"And what then?"

"Then." Fielding swallowed and clutched his hands more tightly. "Then she started screaming at me. She screamed awful things. Things about her daughter. Things about me — she said I must be the reason her daughter was so late. She had been waiting for so long and she was so ... angry."

I closed my eyes for a few seconds, and sighed. I was exhausted, but fortunately my standard Fielding headache had not yet arrived.

"That sounds rough," I said. Fielding takes the brunt of a lot of unresolved pain when dead people find out that he can hear them. "Tell me, did she ever leave her yard?"

"No. She said she had to stay home and wait for her daughter. That's one of the things that made her angry. She said she couldn't go anywhere until her daughter arrives."

"So ... did you tell her she was —"

"No!" Fielding cut me off. "I did not. I've told you, Martin, if they don't know they're dead, they almost never believe me. If I tell them, it just confuses them. For Mrs. McGinnis, I just know it would have made her even more angry."

"Okay," I said. "You know best. It's not your job to go around explaining things to people."

"Thank you," Fielding said.

"Just one other thing I want to know about."

Fielding glanced at me from under his wispy eyebrows and then looked away. "What?"

"I want to know what you put in your pocket."

"What? Nothing. There's nothing in my pocket. I didn't put anything there. There's nothing in my pocket."

"Fielding, don't lie to me."

"What? I'm not lying. I didn't do it. Nothing in my pocket." Fielding still wouldn't look at me, but he was starting to raise his voice.

"I saw you, Fielding. You put something in your pocket. What was it?"

"Nothing."

Now it was my turn to raise my voice. "Damn it, Fielding, I saw you pick something up off the porch, put it in your pocket, and then go back over to the fence. You were looking for something. *What did you put in your pocket?*"

Fielding stopped fidgeting but kept staring at his hands. "A thing."

I closed my eyes and massaged my forehead with one hand. I try to be patient with Fielding, but Jesus, sometimes ...

"What kind of thing?"

"Just a thing I found."

I took a deep breath and let it out slowly before I spoke again.

"Listen," I said, "I stuck my neck out pretty far for you today. I kept you out of jail, promised to make sure you don't get into any more trouble. Promised to keep an eye on you."

Fielding glanced up at me, his brows in a knot, then looked back at his hands.

"I didn't just make that promise to my friends in the police," I continued. "I made that promise to you. I want to make sure you're all right. So will you tell me what you put in your pocket?"

Fielding bit his lip. Then he reached into his pocket. "This," he said as he placed a small object on the coffee table.

It was a small Ziploc bag. Inside the bag was a little clay pot, about two inches wide at the middle, with a narrow, flared neck on top. A small cork was stuck into the spout at the top, and the inside of the bag was streaked with some kind of oil.

"Oh crap," I said. "Is that what I think it is?"

"Maybe. I think. Yes." Fielding did not look up.

I went to the dining table and picked up the Vicar and Blake case file from the insurance company. As I carried it back to the living room, I flipped through the file until I found the auction catalogue listing for the Native American jars. I put the photo down next to Fielding's plastic bag.

The jar in the bag looked like one of the three jars that had been stolen from the auction house. The catalogue photo did not show any cork, and under my living room lamp the color of the pottery looked a little darker than in the photo. But it was clearly the same object. It appeared to be the smallest of the three jars.

"Where did you get this?" I asked. I kept my voice calm and level. It wasn't easy.

"I found it."

"No, you didn't. Don't lie to me, Fielding. I'm asking you again, where did you get this?"

"I don't know."

That didn't even get a response from me.

"Joseph gave it to me," Fielding said.

"Joseph Vargas?" I asked.

"Yes. He gave it to me."

I leaned forward and spoke quietly. "Joseph Vargas is dead."

"Right. Joseph Vargas gave it to me."

I closed my eyes again and gripped my forehead. When I opened them, Fielding was looking at me with wide eyes. He seemed to be shaking a little.

"I may not talk to dead people," I said, "but I know that they can't give things away. They can't pick things up, they can't hand things over, and they can't sign contracts. So tell me. What do you mean when you say that Joseph Vargas gave you this jar?"

Fielding wrung his hands some more before he spoke. "He told me where it was, and he said I could have it."

"And where was it?"

"He left — it was in — it was in a mailbox."

"It was in ... wait," I said. "It was at the same mailbox store as your box?"

He thought for a second. "Yes."

"Do you even have a mailbox there?"

He paused again. "No, that was a lie. I'm sorry."

I took a deep breath. I was getting angrier, but I needed to focus on getting information. "So, how did you know where to go?"

"Joseph told me. He told me where the jar was and where the key was. He told me I could take the jar and that I could keep it."

"Why did he do that?" I said.

"Because I could talk with him. He said that made me special. He said the pot was like medicine and he knew I could use it."

I sat back and thought for a minute. I closed my eyes. "Do you understand," I said, "that a dead person can't legally give away anything?"

"No," Fielding said. "And anyway, that doesn't make sense. If it was his, and he can talk to me, why can't he give it to me?"

"Okay, let's put that aside for a moment. Do you understand that this jar is stolen property? That means even if he was still alive he couldn't legally give it to you. Thieves are not free to give away the things they steal, and you are not free to take them from them."

"Oh," said Fielding in a quiet voice. "I didn't think about that."

"No," I said, "you didn't think about much here, did you?"

I sat for a minute, considering what I'd learned. Bad as the situation was, I had a feeling I had missed something important. "Wait. Did you say Joseph gave you a key?"

More hand wringing.

"Fielding?"

"Yes," Fielding said. "He did."

I sat up again. I had a rotten feeling that I knew where this was going. "And how does a dead man give you a key?"

"He, um, he had it on him. He told me where I would find his body and where he had the key. He said that I could have it. It was in his shoe."

Great. This was just great. I couldn't sit still anymore. I stood up and stomped across the room and back. "So not only did you find a dead body and not tell the police, but you took something from the body and didn't tell the police. Or me."

"Yes," Fielding whispered. "I'm sorry."

"You're sorry." I continued pacing across the room and back. "I'm glad to hear that you're sorry."

Fielding was in very deep. And I was probably in deep enough with him that I might not be able to help much.

Meanwhile Fielding was starting to panic. "I'm sorry, Martin. I'm sorry. I didn't mean it. Okay? I said I'm sorry. I'm really sorry. I'm —"

"All right!" I shouted. My voice was loud in the small room, and it rang off the dark windows. "I *know* you're sorry. That's *great*. Now let me think about this and figure out what the hell we can do now."

I resumed my pacing. When I turned back around, Fielding was shrunk back in his corner of the sofa, his head pulled back, wide eyes following me around the room. I stopped next to him.

"I didn't mean to yell at you," I said, trying to keep my voice soft and even. "This is just some pretty important stuff, and I need to think about it a little, okay?"

Fielding nodded.

More pacing. More thinking.

I thought about the charges Fielding might be facing. At the very least, interference with a police investigation. Tampering with evidence. But the real problem was explaining how Fielding knew about the key. Carson was already suspicious about how Fielding had found the body. Not to mention —

"Tell me, how did you bring the pot home from the mailbox place? Why didn't the police find it on you?"

Fielding just looked at his hands.

"Did you hide it someplace?"

Fielding shook his head slightly.

"What, then?"

Silence.

"Goddamn it, Fielding —"

"I mailed it."

"What?"

"I mailed it to myself," Fielding said. "Or rather I sent it by courier. I didn't use the actual United States Postal Service, so I can't really say that I mailed it. When I got it out of Joseph's mailbox at the mailbox store, I wrapped it up and sent it from there."

I thought about that for a second. Damn devious, that was. Like he expected to get caught. "But wait, when did you get it? You weren't home all day except when I was there."

Fielding started tapping the arm of the sofa, not looking at me. "I sent it to my neighbor. Lucille."

I had to sit down again to think about that. That meant —

"You're kidding me. You mean that when you went to see your neighbor today about your book delivery, you were really picking up this thing? While I was there? Right under my goddamn nose?"

"Yes," Fielding said in a small voice.

I closed my eyes for a minute. Good God, I felt tired. "You know, Fielding, I kind of thought we were friends."

"We are friends, Martin. We are friends. I'm your friend. We are. We're friends, right, Martin? Please, are we still friends?"

Fielding's voice got higher and faster as he got more agitated. I held up a hand to stop him.

"Yeah, yes, we're still friends," I said. "I'm your friend. And as your friend I can tell you that I am angry and very, very disappointed with you. You lied to me. You tricked me. You had things that you *knew* were important, and you didn't tell me about them."

Fielding shrank back into the sofa and stared at his lap, shaking his head.

"Not only did you not tell me, but you took tricky little steps to hide things from me."

"I'm sorry, Martin," Fielding whispered.

"I know," I said, more quietly. "I know you're sorry. I just want you to know that I expect better things from my friend in the future. Got it?"

Fielding looked up at me and nodded. "Yes."

"Okay. Now, here's what we're going to do. First, we're going to get some sleep. Then in the morning we're going to go to the police station and talk to Detective Lang. And you are going to tell him the truth. About the body and the jar and everything."

Fielding was quiet for a moment. "Then what's going to happen to me after that?"

"I don't know."

CHAPTER 7

I lied to Fielding. About getting some sleep. I sent him to his bed, and I stayed in the living room. Much as it pained me, I couldn't trust him not to go off on some nighttime journey, so I wanted to be between him and the front door.

I lay there on the sofa most of the night and thought about what we were going to tell Lang and Carson, and what would happen to Fielding. In the short term, police custody seemed possible, seeing as he had knowledge of the Vicar and Blake theft, contact with Vargas's body, and possession of some of the stolen property. Lang might do what he could to keep him away from murder charges, but Carson never did like me that much. And ultimately it wasn't up to the police. They'd make recommendations, but the DA's office would decide what charges to pursue.

I remembered what it was like in that office. Connecting Fielding to the murder itself would be a slight reach, based on what I knew so far, but it would be a tempting career move. Though maybe not the kind of headline a serious politician would like. "Psychic Detective Charged with Ghost Murder!"

Not that Fielding is a psychic detective, or any other kind of detective. But that wouldn't stop the headlines. Or an eager prosecutor.

And what about me? I couldn't ignore that question. Whatever they went after Fielding for, I was all set up for an accessory charge. And Carson might push all the way back to the start of the Vicar case and try to get me for messing with the crime scene in the basement. Even if I beat any charges against me, if things went bad for Fielding, my business would suffer and I'd lose my PI license.

By the time morning came around, I hadn't gotten much sleep. But I had decided one thing: first thing I had to do was call Liz.

Elizabeth Duncan is a tough lawyer. A good lawyer. And she works exclusively in criminal defense. "White collar to pay the bills, blue collar to keep things interesting." She handed my head to me once on a case I prosecuted, and I'd consulted with her a few times since I left the DA's office. I was hoping she would find Fielding's case interesting enough that she would help him out.

I got up, made coffee, and woke Fielding. By the time I had shaved and showered, it was eight thirty. I figured that was late enough to try Liz at her office.

I explained to Fielding that I was calling a lawyer friend of mine, who would help him explain things to the police.

"She can't guarantee anything," I said. "You need to understand that. But Liz will do everything possible to help things turn out okay."

"I understand," Fielding said.

He sat down and tried to read his book while I dialed the phone. A bright and serious-sounding receptionist answered. "Law offices of Duncan and Lewis."

"Good morning, this is Martin Rodak. I'm calling to speak with Mrs. Duncan."

"Certainly, Mr. Rodak. I'll see if she's in. May I say what this call is in regard to?"

"Just tell her it's me," I said, "and that I want to talk about a new case."

At least Liz's firm had snappy hold music. A western tune. I listened to about a minute of it, and then Liz came on the line.

"Martin Rodak. What the hell have you been doing with yourself since you stopped loitering in courtrooms?"

"Hi, Liz. You know, I just realized one day that I couldn't keep up with lawyers like you. Decided to quit while I was behind."

"Ha! Now, that's a day's load of bull. I read the paper. You've been a busy man. Denver's psychic detective."

I ground my teeth at that, but only for a second. It was hard to stay mad at Liz Duncan for long. She carried herself like the heir to Molly Brown, and she played the role well.

"I'm no psychic, Liz. I just have interesting friends. Speaking of whom, I'm calling because one of those friends needs some help."

"Well, that sounds hard to pass up," Liz said. "Defending one of Martin Rodak's psychic friends. Something to do with a case of yours?"

"Yeah, something like that. The police think one of my associates may have gotten a little too involved."

"Hmm." I heard the sound of Liz tapping a pencil against her desk. "Your friend is in luck. I expected to be in court all week, but managed to swing a deal yesterday. Come up to my office. We'll talk and decide if I can help."

"Thanks, Liz. We'll be there in an hour."

I hung up and turned back to Fielding. He was watching me over the top of his book. I sat down facing him across the coffee table.

"I just spoke to my friend Liz," I said.

"She's a criminal defense lawyer," Fielding said.

"Yes, that's right. She's good at representing people in court, but she's just as good at seeing that things don't come to that. Now it's time for us to go to her office so you can talk to her about what happened."

"Okay. Will we be coming back here?"

"I hope so. But I'm not sure when. We may have to go talk to the police after we talk to Liz."

Fielding bit his lip. Tears crept into the corners of his eyes. His voice trembled when he spoke. "Will I have to go to jail?"

Fielding had spent a little time in jail when he was younger. Not the best place for anyone, but it was a special kind of hell for a high-strung guy who had to listen to dead people.

"I hope not. Liz will do everything she can to keep that from happening. You do understand that you made some big mistakes."

Fielding nodded, and his lip wobbled. I put a hand on his arm, and he settled down a bit.

Fielding closed his book and looked down at it in his lap. His fingers fidgeted along the edge of the green leather binding. After a moment he looked up and nodded. "Okay."

I made some Pop-Tarts while Fielding selected books for his backpack. We ate in silence and drank coffee, then made our way downtown through the late-morning traffic.

Liz had her office in the Tabor Center on Seventeenth Street, where we parked in the underground garage. Fielding hummed nervously as we rode the elevator to the tenth floor. When the doors opened, we stepped out into a cool lobby decked out in frosted glass and black lacquer. A beautiful red-haired receptionist sat behind a wide desk, and when she spoke I recognized her voice from the telephone.

"Good morning. May I help you?"

"Martin Rodak," I said. "We have an appointment with Mrs. Duncan."

"Certainly. If you'd like to have a seat, I'll —"

"Never mind that, Annie." Liz's voice rang out from behind me. I turned to see her emerge from a door at the back of the lobby. She was tall, with a dark red suit and well-coiffed hair mostly turned to bright silver.

"I'll take care of these gentlemen," she told the receptionist. She raised her mug toward Fielding and me. "You boys want some coffee?"

"No, thanks, Liz," I said.

"Well, then, come on in here." Liz led the way into a small conference room off the lobby. The room had a frosted glass wall facing the hallway, and one broad window looking out across lower downtown toward Coors Field and the mountains beyond. In between was a round oak table. Liz put down her coffee, took a legal pad and felt-tip pen out of a drawer in the sideboard, and sat down. I motioned Fielding into another chair and sat down next to him.

Liz looked up at me. "Wait a minute, Marty. I think you'll need to wait outside."

"Liz ..."

"You want your friend here to waive privilege on everything he tells me? If I'm going to be his lawyer —"

Liz stopped herself to give Fielding a motherly pat on the arm. "I'm not saying I can do that yet, dear," she said, "but I want to make sure we don't make any mistakes."

Then she turned back to me. "If I'm going to be his lawyer, our communications have to be private or they're not covered by attorney-client privilege."

I waited to make sure she was finished. "Cocounsel."

"What?"

"Cocounsel. I'm also serving as Mr. Fielding's attorney."

"Bullcrap."

"Why not? I'm still a lawyer." And a real attorney again as of an hour ago, I thought. Before leaving the house, I'd paid my bar dues online and brought myself back to active status.

Liz glared and grumbled.

"Either that, or you can represent us both," I said.

Liz narrowed her eyes. "What's that, now? Are you mixed up in this as well?"

"Not as much as Detective Fred Carson will want to think I am. But yeah, the whole thing is wrapped up in a case Fielding and I were investigating."

Liz tapped her pen on her legal pad, making a pool of little blue freckles on the yellow paper. "Well, then," she said, "you can't very well represent your pal Fielding here. That's a huge conflict of interest, you being involved in the incident, maybe looking at charges yourself. I'm surprised at you, Marty. Thought you'd know better than that."

Damn. "You're right, Liz."

"Then you get your ass out of my conference room. Get a cup of coffee, make yourself comfortable in the lobby." Liz shooed me out of the room with a wave of her hand.

"And don't you go distracting Annie," she added. "She's got work to do, can't spend all morning flirting with you."

Annie was looking up when I went back in the lobby. She shook her head and smiled as she looked back at her computer screen. I guessed she'd heard Liz's warning.

I made my way to the kitchen, then spent a few minutes puzzling over the coffeemaker. It was a sleek, complicated thing that made individual cups from little packets like paper shotgun shells. There was a shelf with fourteen different types of coffee and tea to choose from. I picked something that sounded simple and watched as the machine forced my coffee into a narrow white mug. After all that, I still hadn't killed much time before I went back into the lobby.

I sat down in an overstuffed cube of a chair near the reception desk and read the front page of the *Wall Street Journal*. After that I started thumbing through the day's *Denver Post*.

A trio of young attorneys emerged from the elevator and greeted Annie as they passed on their way down the back hall to their offices. When they had gone, Annie spoke up.

"Mr. Rodak?"

I looked up. "Yep?"

"I'm sorry to disturb you, but I just had to say how remarkable I find your work."

"Um, thanks. I appreciate that."

"What's it like being a psychic detective?"

"I'm not a psychic," I said. "I'm just an investigator."

"But your agency, then ..."

"I do have some talented friends," I said.

Annie nodded. "So you really did help the police find that little boy up in Evergreen? You and your ... friends?"

I put down the paper. "Yes. That we did."

"It was such good news, the way you were able to save that boy."

"It was."

"But it was sad how things turned out for his brother."

"Yes. It surely was."

Not much more to say about that. It had been early in my days as a PI when Jeff Lang asked me to consult on the kidnapping of two boys. "A mixed result" was one description of the outcome. One boy had been killed, but thanks to Fielding he was able to lead us to his younger brother in time. I didn't like to think about it much, and I definitely didn't like to talk about it. Annie seemed to sense as much, and I think we were both relieved when she turned to answer the phone.

I tried picking up the paper again, but couldn't concentrate on reading. I checked my phone and found an email from John Harris asking for an update. Damn — I hadn't told him about

Fielding, the jar, or any of what had happened since the scene at Vicar and Blake. I sent him a quick reply promising to call him later in the day.

After about forty minutes Liz and Fielding emerged from the conference room. Fielding looked shaken, darting his head left and right until he spotted me. Liz looked serious, the way I remembered seeing her in court.

I stood up and went over to them. "You okay, Fielding?"

"Yes, Martin, I'm fine."

I turned to Liz. "Can I talk to you a second?"

"Sure," she said. "Nothing about the case, though."

"I know."

Liz ushered me back into the conference room. Before closing the door, she turned to Fielding. "You just relax for a few minutes, dear. Let Annie know if you'd like a cup of coffee or anything else."

"Okay, Ms. Duncan. Thank you."

Liz shut the door and sat on the edge of the table. "Quite a guy, your friend Fielding."

"Yes indeed. I knew you'd be a good person to work with him."

"I'm a good person to work with in general, but thanks." Liz gave me a half smile. "Now what else do you want to talk about?"

"It's about Fielding," I said. "I'm sure you know by now that he's, well, a special person."

"You mean he's a goddamn psychic," she said.

"Not the words I'd use, but sure."

Liz looked down at the table and shook her head. "Son of a bitch," she muttered. I had heard her use that phrase enough to know it wasn't about anyone in particular. She took a breath before looking back up.

"Okay, let's assume I believe in that crap," she said. "What do I need to know?"

I sat down in a nearby chair. "First is what you've already noticed. Fielding's gift makes him a bit high-strung. He's a very nervous guy."

Liz barked out a laugh. "I just spent an hour with the guy. I know that much."

"Okay, here's another thing," I said. "It's pretty important that he stay out of jail."

Liz sighed. "Jesus Christ, Marty, that's a high priority for every person who walks into my office. Stop wasting time and tell me what's on your mind."

I thought for a second before I responded. "Here's the thing. Every jail in a town like this, somebody died there at some point."

"Yeah ...?" Liz raised an eyebrow at me.

"And somebody dies in jail, it's usually not under the best of circumstances."

"Yeah, yeah," Liz said. "That's a given. What are you getting at?"

"That's a problem for Fielding. Being in places where people died, and especially where people died in a bad way."

"Aw jeez ..."

"He reacts badly," I said. "Sees things. Gets excited. It would be a bad scene for him, for the sheriff's department, for everyone involved."

"Come on, Marty. You know I'll do everything possible to keep him out of custody, but there's no way I can tell a judge that he has to give my client release to pretrial services because otherwise he'll see dead people and flip out. I'll make the usual arguments. Fielding comes across as pretty harmless, so our chances are good. But I can't make any guarantees."

"I know. I just want you to know what's at stake. This case'll be weird enough without surprises."

Liz sighed again. "All right. I appreciate the heads-up."

She picked up her phone and flicked through a few screens. "Why don't you and Fielding wait in here for a bit while I call our old friends at the DA's office, then Detective Carson? I'll arrange a proper, low-key walk-in for Fielding."

Liz opened the door. Fielding was drinking a cup of tea, and telling Annie all about *Robinson Crusoe*.

"Come on in here, dear," Liz called to him. "You sit with your friend Marty while I make some phone calls."

Fielding nodded. He took his tea, made a polite excuse to Annie, and came back into the conference room. He sat down at the table and gripped his tea mug with both hands.

"She's nice," he said. "Rough, but nice. Thank you for bringing me to talk to her."

"You're welcome," I said.

We sat in silence. I read a magazine I found on the sideboard. Fielding sipped his tea, turning to look out the window from time to time.

Liz returned about a half hour later and sat down next to Fielding. "Okay, here's the thing, dear."

She glanced at me for a moment. I expected her to kick me out again, but she just shrugged and went back to talking with Fielding. "I spoke with Detective Carson, and with someone at the district attorney's office. Carson and a Deputy District Attorney are going to meet us at the courthouse later this afternoon. You are going to turn yourself in —"

At that Fielding stiffened. Liz put a hand on his arm to calm him. "You are going to turn yourself in, and you are going to give the police the object. Then they will ask you more questions. You have to be very, very careful to make sure you answer their questions honestly and completely. Just take your time. If there is any question I don't think you should answer, I'll speak up before you can start talking. You understand?"

Fielding looked up at her and nodded, still clutching his mug.

"If you cooperate with the police, they should have no reason to keep you in custody. I expect that by this afternoon you'll be able to go back home with Martin."

Fielding nodded.

"Though I suspect Marty's place is not all that much better than a jail cell," Liz said. She slapped Fielding on the arm with the back of her hand.

Fielding actually smiled a little at that. It was a thin, sad smile, but it was better than panic. "He doesn't have any books."

"Well, that's hardly civilized, now, is it?" said Liz.

CHAPTER 8

Liz ordered in lunch for Fielding and me. When we'd finished our sandwiches, she ushered us down to the parking garage. She insisted on driving Fielding there herself, and wanted me to take my own car. Still trying to keep me at arm's length. I could understand that, and I recognized that the way things were going, it was actually better for me than it was for Fielding. But I made sure she understood that I would damn well be in the courtroom or anywhere else Fielding was taken.

The Lindsey-Flanigan Courthouse is a relatively new building in downtown Denver, all glass and white stone and steel. The atrium looked huge and bright, especially compared to the old building where I tried my first cases. The courtrooms inside were just as fancy, but we weren't going there. I met Liz and Fielding near the security checkpoint, and once we passed through we went to the third floor, which contained offices and meeting rooms.

I hoped we wouldn't need to go down to the basement where the holding cells were, or through the tunnel to the detention center on the other side of the Justice Center Complex.

Fred Carson met us in the hallway. His brows were lowered

over his stony eyes. He was six foot five inches tall and almost as wide, and he wore a dove-gray suit.

"Rodak. I wish I was surprised about this. Lang isn't wrong about much, but it figures he'd be wrong about you. After what I've heard —"

"Absolutely none of which is relevant to Mr. Fielding's case, Detective." Liz cut him off with that glassy growl of a voice she used in the courtroom when dealing with a hostile witness. This was the Liz Duncan I remembered most. This, and that nice Mrs. Duncan who charmed any jury she got near.

Before Carson could answer, the door next to him opened. A young man with short dark hair and a crisp department-store suit looked out.

"Detective," he said, recognizing Carson. He turned to Liz and Fielding. "Ms. Duncan. And ... Mr. Fielding?"

Fielding nodded.

"I'm Craig Peterson, Deputy District Attorney," the young man said. "Come on in so we can talk."

Peterson held the door while Carson walked into the room. Then he seemed to notice me for the first time. "And you are?"

"Martin Rodak," I said. "I'm Mr. Fielding's associate, here to assist in any way I might be able."

"Martin Rodak ..." Peterson chewed over my name for a moment, as if trying to remember where he'd heard it. Apparently he did, because after a few seconds his eyes widened a bit. "Um, Mr. Rodak, it's not entirely appropriate for you to —"

"Don't worry yourself, Counselor," Liz cut in. "Mr. Rodak may be helpful under the circumstances, and I'll be the first to shoo him out if he poses a problem."

Peterson sighed. "All right. Come in, please."

We followed Peterson and Carson into the small bare conference room. Liz, Fielding, and I sat down on one side of the narrow table, and Peterson and Carson sat opposite us. On the table next to Peterson's files and legal pad was a small remote control. He pushed a button to activate the room's video and audio recorder. He stated the date and time, and asked each of us to speak our full name, before he started in on his questions.

"Mr. Fielding," Peterson began, "I understand the reason you are here relates to the death of Joseph Wilson Vargas."

Fielding nodded.

"Can you please answer audibly, Mr. Fielding?" Peterson said. "As agreed by your attorney, Ms. Duncan, we're recording this conversation."

"Yes," said Fielding.

"According to the police report of your statement, you found Joseph Vargas's body the night before last."

"Yes."

"And you made a statement to the police about that."

"Yes. After ..." Fielding glanced at his lawyer. Liz looked back at him from under raised eyebrows, and Fielding stayed silent.

Carson didn't. "He made a statement to Denver PD officers who picked him up and brought him to police headquarters."

"My client is not necessarily agreeing with any of Detective Carson's accounts," Liz said. "The fact is that Mr. Fielding is here of his own free will, and is prepared to cooperate with the police investigation in any way he can."

"I, uh, appreciate that, Ms. Duncan," Peterson said. "But your client's involvement raises a number of issues, and may be cause for some serious charges against him. Of course Mr. Fielding's cooperation will be given due consideration, but we need everything out on the table." He made a gesture like he was fanning out a hand of cards, but it was small and tentative, as if he'd just learned about it from a book on public speaking. "We need to know everything Mr. Fielding knows about Joseph Vargas and his murder."

"I don't know anything about his murder," Fielding said. "I don't. He didn't tell me."

Peterson raised an eyebrow.

"Jesus, here we go ...," grumbled Carson.

"Who didn't tell you?" asked Peterson. "Who did you speak to about Mr. Vargas?"

"Um, no one. Nobody. I mean, I just mean I don't know anything about the murder. Any murder. You said I should tell you what I know about his murder, and I'm just telling you that I don't know anything about his murder."

Here we go indeed. Fielding was speaking more and more quickly. Getting wound up again. Now was not the best time for it.

"Okay," said Peterson. "Let's leave that aside for now and move on to something that may be more important."

He glanced at Carson before he went on. "I understand that you have something in your possession that may be related to Joseph Vargas or to another open criminal case."

"You mean the ..." Fielding began. He broke off and looked at me, his eyebrows knit.

"Go ahead," I said. I looked at Liz and she nodded.

"Show them what you have," I told Fielding.

Fielding reached into the pocket of his jacket and pulled out the plastic bag containing the pottery jar. He put the bag on the table and pushed it toward Peterson and Detective Carson. "Here," he said in a small voice.

Peterson looked at the bag carefully, then glanced at Carson before looking up at Fielding. "And what is this?"

"It's something I found."

"And where did you find it?"

"I found it ... It was ... I found it in a mailbox."

"Your mailbox?"

"No. I mean, not exactly. I mean, it wasn't a real mailbox. It was one of those private mailboxes. That you can rent at a kind of mailbox store."

Peterson sighed. "And was this in a mailbox that you yourself had rented?"

"No."

"Whose was it?"

Fielding looked down at his fidgeting hands. "I think it was Joseph Vargas's."

Peterson made a note on his legal pad. "And why do you say that?"

"Because Joseph Vargas — because — because of the ..." Fielding looked up at Liz Duncan.

"We can stop this at any time, dear," she said to Fielding.

Peterson snorted softly. "I really don't think that is a practical option for Mr. Fielding at this point."

Liz fixed him with a cold stare. "It's an option at every single minute we're here. I just want to make it absolutely clear to my client and to you that his cooperation at this point is completely, one hundred percent voluntary. You have not arrested him, and I believe that's because you really don't want to. Either way, Mr. Fielding is here of his own free will and I accepted your assurance that this would be given all possible consideration in how you pursue this case. If that is no longer true, I will have to consult with my client as to how we wish to proceed."

Peterson had shrunk visibly in his seat. He cleared his throat and slid back upright. "Very well. Mr. Fielding," he said, "I do appreciate your cooperation. But I do need you to answer that last question. Why do you say that the mailbox where you found the item belonged to Joseph Vargas? And how did you get access to it?"

Fielding took one more look at Liz, and at me, before he answered. "Mr. Vargas ... he ... Mr. Vargas gave me the key. He told me where to find it and he said that I could have it."

Carson coughed and rolled his eyes.

"Maybe you can explain that to me," Peterson said. "Did you have any contact with Mr. Vargas when he was alive?"

"No, I didn't." Fielding looked down at his lap. "Just at the auction house basement."

"I think what my client is trying to convey is that based on what he discovered in the auction house basement, he believed that Mr. Vargas wanted whoever arrived at that information to have access to the mailbox and to take possession of what was inside." Liz looked at Fielding. "Is that about right, Mr. Fielding?"

"Yes."

"But that doesn't —" Peterson began.

"But then I realized that Mr. Vargas was dead," Fielding said, "and that the thing he wanted me to have was not his, so I knew I had to come here and give it to the police."

Nice. Liz had coached him on that point.

Carson gave a barely audible grumble. Peterson still looked confused. "But if you say you had no contact with Joseph Vargas before he died, then how could you possibly say that he wanted you to ..."

Peterson's voice drifted into silence. He started at me for a long second, then at Fielding, then back at me. He seemed to be remembering something, probably something he'd read about me and my associates. Then he shook his head and gave another little snort.

"Oooohhh kayyyyyy," he said slowly, "let's put aside the question of why you believed Vargas wanted you to have the jar. I do acknowledge that you came in voluntarily and you did voluntarily return this evidence."

"What's all the oil and crap all over it?" Carson asked.

"I was making it work. Um, I mean ... I was trying to fix it," Fielding said.

Peterson and Carson exchanged a pained look but did not respond to that.

"Okay, Mr. Fielding," Peterson said then. "I think we understand each other. But you must understand that failure to report a dead body is very suspicious,"

Peterson kept his narrowed eyes on Liz Duncan for a few seconds before turning back to Fielding.

"The facts that you interfered with the body, took the key, and went to the mailbox and took this object, those are much more serious."

Fielding looked down at his lap again, where his fingers were twitching.

Peterson opened the folder in front of him and scanned down the first page. "I also see from your record that this isn't the first time you've been in trouble. You have had a few run-ins with the law in the past. Disorderly conduct. Interference with a police officer. More than a few things like that."

"Yes," Fielding said.

"But I also see that your record has been good for several years."

"Yes. Since I met Martin again and started working for him sometimes."

"Exactly," Peterson said.

Peterson closed his folder and pushed it aside. He leaned into the table and looked across at Liz, Fielding, and me. Detective Carson pulled a paper evidence bag from his pocket and put the jar inside, still in Fielding's plastic sandwich bag. He sealed it up and made some notes on the label with a Sharpie that he produced from another pocket.

"Okay, let's lay it out," Peterson said. "I don't know that you had anything to do with the actual death of Joseph Vargas."

Fielding nodded vigorously. Carson grunted and shifted in his seat next to Peterson.

"But clearly, Mr. Fielding, you know things about this case. Some of those things you have shared with me and Detective Carson and Detective Lang already. And some things ..."

Peterson looked nervously at Carson before he went on. "Some things you may have ways to discover in the future. I know about you and Mr. Rodak, and about his other associates. I know that you have certain ... avenues of information that may have led you to Mr. Vargas's body and to his mailbox."

Now we were getting to it. Peterson knew about me, and about Fielding, and apparently he believed in Fielding's talent. So if he had leverage to pressure Fielding into helping him find a murderer and score a conviction, he was sure as hell going to use it.

Fielding glanced at me and then nodded.

"Here's what I'm prepared to do, Mr. Fielding," Peterson continued. "Given that you have come in voluntarily, and given the fact that you do not seem to represent any danger, and given that Mr. Rodak seems to exert a positive influence upon you, an influence that I suspect we can thank for your appearance here today, I am going to recommend that you be released to his care."

Fielding nodded again.

"You need to understand, you are being charged with a crime. More than one crime, in fact. Today you will go before a judge for what is being called an advisement hearing, where the judge will discuss the charges and the deal we're offering. We're not really interested in putting you away. We're more interested in finding the person who killed Vargas."

"And recovering the property stolen from the auction," Carson added.

"Yes, that too," Peterson said. "If you promise to help us, we will ask the judge to put aside the charges against you and, as I said, release you into your employer's care."

Peterson looked at me. "Assuming this is acceptable to you, Mr. Rodak."

"Sounds fine to me," I said.

Peterson turned back to Fielding. "If you help us with our investigation, by continuing to provide whatever information you might have, from ... whatever sources you might have available, then when all is said and done we will drop the charges against you for the interference you have committed so far."

Peterson tried tapping on the table for emphasis, but stopped when Liz chuckled.

"But you need to understand," Peterson continued, "that if you do anything to hinder our investigation, if you keep anything from us, if you fail to provide help that you can provide, then we'll pursue those charges to the fullest."

Fielding nodded. "I understand. I'm here because I want to cooperate and I'll tell you anything I know that will help your investigation because I'm sorry I took the thing from Mr. Vargas's mailbox even though he said I could have it and from now on I'll tell you anything I —"

Fielding was winding up again, getting nervous and letting his speech run away from him. I put a light hand on his arm.

"It's okay," I said. "Take a breath."

Fielding swallowed and nodded. Peterson looked like he was suppressing a smile. Carson was glaring at Peterson under his bushy eyebrows.

Liz Duncan tapped her pen on the table, loudly. "I want a copy of this recording for my file. I want a record of the representations that have been made to my client in exchange for his cooperation."

"Of course," Peterson said. "I'll have a copy ready for you to pick up tomorrow morning. And of course I'm willing to formalize our agreement with your client. But now" — Peterson checked his watch — "we have about twenty minutes to catch

Judge Carp in Courtroom Six. He agreed to handle the advisement this afternoon. I'm perfectly willing to make the recommendations I described, based on our agreement in principle."

"Fair enough," Liz said with a faint smile.

Liz hadn't said much during the meeting. Clearly she had set up this deal with Peterson by phone before we ever left her office.

"Come on, dear," she said to Fielding. "Let's go talk to the judge and then get you out of here."

CHAPTER 9

As we got up from the table, Carson took out his handcuffs.

"You've got to be kidding me," Liz said. She shot a disgusted look at Carson, then peered down at the cuffs and back up.

"That's really not required, Detective," Peterson said. "I don't think Mr. Fielding is a threat to anyone, do you?"

Carson looked a Peterson, then down at the cuffs, then shrugged. "I don't know what he is. But okay." He put the cuffs away, then took Fielding by the arm.

"You are under arrest for interference with evidence of a felony and obstruction of justice," Carson said. Then he recited Fielding's Miranda rights, which seemed theatrical considering how much Fielding had already said voluntarily, and the fact that he had his lawyer next to him.

"This is a formality, Mr. Fielding," Peterson said. "If you continue to cooperate in our investigation as we discussed, the arrest and all charges will be dropped from your record."

Fielding was taking the whole thing remarkably well.

"You doing okay?" I asked him.

"I'm all right, Martin," Fielding said. "Like Mr. Peterson said, I was arrested a few times before. This one isn't so bad."

Peterson led us out of the room and down a back hallway. When we reached a small lobby in the rear of the building, he used a key card to call an elevator marked for authorized personnel only. We rode down to the second floor in silence. Once there, we followed a short hallway until we came to a side door to Courtroom Six.

Carson poked his head in and said a few words. A moment later a uniformed bailiff joined us in the hallway.

"I hope this pays off as well as you think it will," Carson told Peterson. He nodded to Fielding, Liz, and me and then walked away, back down the hall toward the elevator, taking with him the evidence bag with the little oily jar.

Fielding rubbed his arm where Carson had been holding him. He had seemed pretty calm through the whole ordeal so far, but as he watched Carson leave, his brows knit and his fingers began to fidget again.

The bailiff led us into the courtroom. It looked like a very modern wedding chapel, all polished wood and good light. Up on the walls hung discreetly framed display screens for showing videos or presenting other electronic evidence. As we filed in, Liz led Fielding to the table on the left side of the room, while Peterson took his place on the right. I took a seat at the front of the empty gallery area behind Liz and Fielding.

Judge Harold Carp sat at his bench, leaning over to talk to his clerk, who sat shuffling papers at a broad desk to the judge's right. The judge's bald head shone in the light from the room's high windows. As we took our places the judge looked up.

"Mr. Peterson! So good to see you again on this fine day. And I understand you have something interesting for me." The judge's eyes sparkled through his round eyeglasses, and he

drummed on the top of the bench with the end of an unsharp-
ened yellow pencil.

"I believe I do, Your Honor," said Peterson. "I've given Bailiff
Quintana the most recent documents related to this matter, and
of course I'll file copies with the clerk's office downstairs this
afternoon."

The bailiff handed the papers to Judge Carp's clerk, who
looked them over briefly, made a small note on a corner of the
first page, and handed them to the judge. As the judge read the
papers he mumbled quietly to himself, occasionally raising his
eyebrows or blowing puffs of air through pursed lips.
"Hummmmm. Hmmm. Okay."

The judge looked up. "So, Mr. Peterson, you're asking to
defer any charges against Mr. Fielding at this time, based on his
agreement to assist with your investigation of the ..." Judge Carp
looked down at the sheet. "The, uh ... this Vargas matter."

"That's correct, Your Honor," said Peterson. "We are encour-
aged by Mr. Fielding's offer of cooperation, and we believe he
may be of significant assistance in the investigation."

The judge read some more from the sheet. Then he looked
up over his glasses, scanning across the line of us from right to
left until his eyes found me. "And you are Martin Rodak," he
said.

"That's right, Your Honor," I answered.

"Well. I wondered if you'd end up in my courtroom one of
these days. Not that I'd have predicted these circumstances."

"Actually, Judge, I had the honor of trying a case before you
a number of years ago," I said. "Back when I was with the district
attorney's office."

"Is that right? Really? Well, then, my apologies for not
remembering. So many come through here." Judge Carp looked
down again, then back up at me as he thought of another question. "Did you win?"

I chuckled and shook my head. "No, Your Honor. Ms. Duncan here cleaned my clock."

"Ah yes." Carp smiled at Liz and raised an eyebrow. "You I know, Ms. Duncan."

"It's a pleasure to see you again, Your Honor," Liz said.

"Okay, then," the judge said. "To business. It says here that Mr. Fielding will be released into the care of Mr. Rodak while your investigation is ongoing."

"That's right, Judge," Peterson said.

"And, Mr. Rodak, this is okay with you?"

"It is perfectly fine with me, Your Honor," I said.

"What is your connection with Mr. Fielding, again?"

"He's a part-time consultant to my private investigation practice, Your Honor."

Judge Carp put the documents aside. "Well, then, I don't see any problem here," he said. "Ms. Duncan, you are okay with this, and you explained the situation to your client?"

"Yes indeed, I have, Your Honor."

"And, Mr. Fielding, do you understand the situation you are in?"

Fielding jumped a little when the judge said his name, and his voice trembled a bit when he answered. "Yes, sir. Ms. Duncan explained things to me, and I want to help the police."

"And you understand that there are still some serious charges that can be pursued against you? These charges have not yet been dropped, and will be dropped only after you assist with the Vargas investigation."

"I do understand, Your Honor."

"Okay, folks. That's all I need to hear. I'll sign off on this, and you can — Mr. Fielding, are you all right?"

The judge had stopped to look at Fielding, who was half-turned to look at the gallery. He was looking over my shoulder, though there was no one else back there. He was saying something in a low, hissing voice that I could not make out.

"Mr. Fielding?" the judge asked again.

Liz took Fielding's elbow in her hand and gently turned him toward the front of the room.

"What? Yes? Oh. Yes, sir," Fielding said. "I'm okay. I'm sorry." Fielding spoke to the judge, but he kept trying to glance behind him again.

"Well, then, Mr. Peterson, I'll agree to sign this order, if you'll then file a copy —"

"*Stop* it! Leave us alone!" Fielding had turned around again and was glowering at the empty air behind him.

"Come on, Fielding," I said in a low voice. "Just stay calm a little while longer."

"I'm sorry, Martin," Fielding said. He turned toward me, but I could tell that his attention was still on something else.

Judge Carp tapped his pencil a few times. "Ms. Duncan, is there some problem with your client?"

"No. No, Your Honor." Liz took a sideways glance at Fielding, but spoke with confidence.

"We're perfectly fine, Your Honor," she said, "and Mr. Fielding looks forward to being able to help with the investigation. I apologize on his behalf for any breach of decorum. Mr. Fielding does have some special needs, which will be well managed under Mr. Rodak's care."

Judge Carp raised his eyebrow again, but then he signed the last page of the papers Peterson had given him and handed the whole thing down to his clerk. "Okay, I think we're done," he said. "Have a good day, gentlemen. And lady."

As the judge leaned down to speak with the clerk, Peterson turned toward us.

"We'll give you a call first thing tomorrow, Mr. Fielding," he said. "Rodak, I presume we can reach him at your office number?"

"That's right," I said. "We'll talk to you then."

Peterson walked toward the side door we had come in. Fielding was pulling at Duncan's sleeve and looking again into the gallery behind me.

"He's been doing it ever since we came in here. He won't stop ... he won't stop."

Liz put a hand on Fielding's arm. "Come on, dear you can go home with Martin now."

"Shut up!" Fielding shouted. He pulled away from Liz and tried to lunge over the rail into the gallery. "You shut up! Stop saying that! Just stop it!"

I tried to put my hands on his shoulders to stop him. As he pulled away from me, he flung his left arm behind him, and his elbow smacked Liz in her sternum, sending her stumbling back toward the defense table.

"Shut up!" Fielding was still saying. "Don't ask questions like that. Just go away. I don't have to talk to you!"

I finally got a hold of his shoulders and gripped hard. Judge Carp was calling loudly to his bailiff. "That's enough, Fielding!" I said. "That's enough!"

"He's been back there asking these awful questions ever since we got here he's just awful and he won't stop —"

"It's okay," I hissed "Let's just calm down and go home."

"But he *won't stop! Shut up!*"

Fielding pulled out of my hands and tried again to lunge over the rail to get at his invisible tormentor. But he didn't get far. Quintana, the bailiff, had crossed the room and grabbed one of Fielding's arms. He pulled Fielding back, turning him around toward the table. As Fielding's body was spun, his arm twisted behind his back. The bailiff kept his grip on the arm and pushed

Fielding forward and down until his head smacked against the table's pale wood surface.

"*Mr. Fielding!*" Judge Carp shouted. When he saw that Fielding had been restrained, he addressed Peterson. "Mr. Peterson, is this the kind of behavior the court can expect from someone who you seek to have released in spite of serious criminal charges?"

"Your Honor, I assure you this defendant's outburst is as surprising to me as to anyone."

"Surprising and extremely troubling," said the judge. "And this kind of behavior in my courtroom also raises the possibility of additional charges. The assault on Ms. Duncan —"

"Your Honor," Liz said, "I'd hardly call that an assault. Mr. Fielding was just excited by the —"

"I know you're a good lawyer, Ms. Duncan," the judge said, "and no doubt you will continue to aggressively represent your client's best interests. But in this situation it's not clear to me that your client's best interests include allowing him the freedom to act out violently. If he is capable of doing this in a courtroom, I must pause to think what he might do out in the community."

"I'm sorry, Your Honor." Fielding's muffled voice came from the surface of the defense table, where the bailiff still had one hand pressing down on the side of Fielding's head.

"Let him up, let him up," said the judge.

The bailiff eased up on Fielding's head and pulled him to his feet. He kept Fielding's wrists pinned behind his back but let him stand up and face Judge Carp.

"I'm very sorry, Your Honor," Fielding repeated. "I'm just excited by everything that happened today. I started thinking about an old memory."

"Who were you talking to?" asked the judge.

"I was, I mean, it's, well, myself, really."

"You do understand the importance of what's going on here?"

"Yes, sir."

The judge turned to me. "Mr. Rodak, I do understand that you have some experience in helping Mr. Fielding through difficult times. You have seen this kind of thing before?"

"I have, Your Honor." I was stretching the truth a bit, as I had never seen Fielding so violent before. Something had changed ever since Carson left us and we entered the courtroom. "I understand the court's concern, but I believe that as soon as we let him get some rest he will be fine. I assure you I will keep a close eye on him."

"And you, Mr. Peterson? Are you still confident that this man can be released safely, and will be of assistance with the state's investigation?"

"Ah, I do, Your Honor," said Peterson. I'd expected him to waver once the judge started expressing doubts, but he seemed read to stand by the deal.

Judge Carp sighed and drummed his pencil on the bench in front of him. "Very well. Bailiff, please escort Mr. Fielding, Ms. Duncan, and Mr. Rodak to the elevators."

The bailiff nodded. He let go of Fielding's arms and placed a hand gently on his back to guide him toward the door, following Liz. The bailiff's other hand was on his belt — near his Taser, I was glad to see, and not his gun. I came around from the gallery to join them.

We were more than halfway to the door when Fielding suddenly twisted away from the bailiff, back toward the gallery. *"Shut up! Shut up! Shut up!"*

Fielding launched himself headfirst over the rail. His hands were fixed like claws, thrashing away at the air in front of him. He was nearly over the first row of seats when his foot caught the railing and he was sent sprawling. His chin slammed into the back of one bench, and his lower ribs into another. Blood sprayed from his mouth. Still, he screamed and slashed out at something only he could see.

The bailiff lunged and grabbed one of Fielding's arms. He pulled Fielding up and out of the gallery. With one swift movement he turned Fielding around and pushed him down against the table. With his other hand he flipped his handcuffs off his belt and snapped them shut over Fielding's wrists, binding them tight behind his back.

The side door of the courtroom banged open and two more bailiffs ran in. A few steps into the room they stopped to survey the scene.

"Stand by, Officers," said the judge. He or his clerk must have signaled for more help when Fielding lost it.

"I'm sorry," murmured Fielding. I didn't know who he was talking to — the judge, me, Liz, himself. Everyone. There was still blood in his mouth, bubbling out and slurring his words. He must have bitten his tongue when he hit his chin on the gallery bench.

"Ms. Duncan!" said the judge.

Liz looked up, away from the frightening mess of Fielding down against the table.

"My training is in law, Ms. Duncan, not in medicine or psychology, but it is clear even to me that your client's condition is far worse than anything that was revealed to me in this afternoon's proceedings."

"I understand, Your Honor, I just —"

"I have very little choice in the matter at this point," said the judge. He turned to Peterson. "Mr. Peterson, surely you do not still argue in favor of releasing Mr. Fielding in his current condition?"

Peterson looked nervously at Fielding, me, Liz, and back to the judge. "I must admit, Your Honor, that Mr. Fielding's condition is far more serious than I had been given to believe," Peterson said. "For his own sake as well as that of the people, I recommend that at the very least Mr. Fielding should be held for psychiatric evaluation."

The judge nodded and began making some notes.

"If I may address the court?" I said.

Judge Carp looked up. "Yes, Mr. Rodak?"

"Your Honor," I said, "I understand that Mr. Fielding's behavior here this afternoon has been ... well, let's say, extreme."

The judge nodded with a wry half smile.

"But having known Mr. Fielding for quite some time," I said, "I can tell you that I have never seen him in such a state. And I believe that it is just the current environment that has led to this unfortunate outburst. I am sure that if I can get Mr. Fielding home, and allow him to get some rest, he will quickly recover and will be able to provide the assistance he so readily offered to the DA and the Denver Police Department."

Judge Carp's half smile faded. "Oh? And what is it about the environment of my courtroom that has provoked this uncontrolled, violent behavior?"

"Nothing about your courtroom, Your Honor. I didn't mean to suggest that. It's just that Mr. Fielding has a unique —"

Something to my right caught my eye. I glanced over and saw Liz shaking her head. It was a small movement, but the glare that shot from her lowered eyes showed me how serious she was. I got the message: don't mention any psychic stuff.

"What I mean is," I continued, "um, is that Mr. Fielding's nerves are particularly sensitive to situations like this."

"I can imagine." The judge looked over some papers from the back of the stack Peterson had provided. "And as I understand from his record, Mr. Fielding has had prior occasions to suffer this 'sensitivity' to the justice system."

"That is true, Your Honor. However —"

"Unfortunately, Mr. Rodak," the judge cut in, "and Ms. Duncan, and Mr. Fielding, any sensitivity that leads a suspect to a violent, dangerous outburst in a courtroom is one that must be handled carefully."

I looked down at Fielding. His eyes were tight shut. From the way he grimaced, it seemed like he was trying to block out some awful sound, to ignore something painful. I figured the ghost was still talking at him.

Judge Carp continued. "This is especially true in this case, when the person in question is accused of crimes including interference with a murder investigation."

Peterson spoke up. "I understand, Your Honor. I assure you I had no —"

"All right, Mr. Peterson," the judge snapped. "I know you were focused on the best interests of the people and of your investigation. But although your department has broad discretion as to how to handle cases and when to pursue them, as a judge I too have discretion, and considerable responsibility, as to the handling of suspects who are arrested and brought into my courtroom."

Peterson nodded. I glanced over at Liz but could read nothing on her face.

"I can't in good conscience allow Mr. Fielding's release at this time," the judge continued. He reached a hand out to his clerk, who gave him the paper he had signed minutes earlier. The judge crossed out the signature block on the last page and made a notation in the margin. "I am going to order that Mr. Fielding remain in custody pending further proceedings on a charge of criminal contempt, and whatever other charges the DA might proffer. But my main aim is to require that Mr. Fielding undergo psychiatric evaluation. I believe this is necessary for his sake, and for the safety of the people of Colorado."

"Your Honor," said Liz, "if Mr. Fielding is released he will report for psychiatric evaluation or counseling, daily, or on whatever schedule the court may require. In the meantime, freedom of movement will allow —"

"I'm sorry, counselor, but we're talking about someone who is accused of some very serious crimes interfering in the pursuit of justice in an apparent case of murder, and who is also subject to uncontrollable violent behavior." Judge Carp's voice was growing louder, and he had leaned forward in his chair. The earlier sparkle was gone from his eyes, and a red color crept up his face toward his high, round forehead.

"I am simply not going to release Mr. Fielding into the public," he said. He turned toward Peterson and continued. "The Denver Police Department and Colorado's prosecutors have successfully secured convictions for murder and other crimes without the assistance of potentially violent ... that is, without the help of outside consultants like Mr. Fielding, and I'm sure they will perform admirably in this case with or without him."

The judge sat back in his chair and let out an explosive breath. "As I said, this court orders that Mr. Fielding undergo psychiatric evaluation. After that, and depending on the results, the court will consider the disposition of the other charges against Mr. Fielding, including the contempt charges stemming from today's events."

Judge Carp directed Quintana and the two other bailiffs to take Fielding into custody and deliver him to the holding facilities maintained by the sheriff's department in the building's basement levels. The judge would file the order for psychiatric evaluation within the hour.

And just like that, Fielding was gone.

CHAPTER 10

We spent the next fifteen minutes arguing with Judge Carp and with Peterson. Liz actually did the arguing. I just stayed out of her way and tried to figure out what or who had so freaked out Fielding.

Maybe some beat reporter from the *Denver Post*, or the old *Rocky Mountain News*, who died but couldn't give up the job?

Still, this was a fairly new courthouse, and I hadn't heard of any reporters dying in the place since it was opened. Maybe the ghosts had moved from the old courthouse to the new one, right along with the judges and the staff.

Eventually Liz got terms from the judge and from the prosecutor that she knew were the best she'd get. Chief among these were that no new charges would be filed against Fielding at least until after the psychiatric evaluation was complete.

Peterson gathered up his papers and disappeared. Liz and I left the courtroom in silence and walked to the public elevators. Once we were alone in the elevator, Liz wheeled toward me. "What in the living goddamn hell was that?"

I just shook my head. "I don't know, Liz. I mean, I do know — and so do you. But I never saw it that bad, or that violent."

"So, what does that mean? He saw a ghost?"

"Ghost, dead person, spirit, whatever you want to call it. Sounds like someone was asking him a bunch of nasty questions, and he snapped. Probably a reporter."

That finally got a smile from Liz, but there wasn't much amusement in it.

"A reporter," she said. "I've had some pretty extreme reactions myself, when it comes reporters."

She backed up a step and sighed.

"How long have you known Fielding, again?"

"Years," I said. "Long enough, I thought. He'd had some problems before we met, but this was something else."

Liz and I parted in the lobby. I went to my car and drove toward Fielding's house.

Another of the accommodations Liz had wrangled was that I would be allowed to stop by Fielding's place and pick up a few things for him — a book, his toothbrush, a change of clothes for when he was released — and bring them to the facility in Littleton where he would be held for his psych eval.

Fielding's toothbrush and a change of clothes I could get from the things he had left at my house. But I needed to stop at his place for a book. Fielding had attachments to particular books — that is, to particular copies of his one and only book — and he liked certain editions for certain times and places. He had brought a few hardcovers to my place, ones he was willing to travel with, but I didn't think he'd want anything so nice in the psych facility. At his house I'd probably find some old paperback editions, maybe even something he had multiple copies of. He might not worry so much about something happening to one of those.

The short Denver twilight had come and gone by the time I got to Fielding's place. The neighborhood was dim and quiet as I pulled up in front of his house. The cemetery beyond the fence at the end of the block was a black pool, dotted with the dim light from the few lampposts that camped beside its old narrow walkways. Out in the cul-de-sac a streetlight glared off my windshield and off the black paint of a sedan parked across the street.

TV light flickered from the window of Lucille's house next door. Fielding's place was dark, except for a single light in the window of the front room. He must have a lamp on a timer, I thought.

Then the light moved, swinging up and around toward the window before pointing back down.

A flashlight. Someone was in Fielding's house.

I quickly stepped to the side of the yard, toward the edge of Fielding's small front lawn and out of view of the front window. A few more quiet steps and I was up at the corner of the house, out of the cone of the streetlight.

I squinted into the shadow along the side of the house, impatient for my eyes to adjust. Staying close to the house, and under the window, I crept toward the front door. I went up the brick steps to the small porch and then crouched out of sight next to the door, listening for noise or voices from inside. I heard noise, all right — heavy avalanches of books being thrown to the floor, scrapes of moving furniture, distant crashes from the kitchen in the back.

I heard a muffled, angry voice giving some kind of instructions, and the activity inside became more gentle, but still it continued. Someone was looking for something.

As I listened, I pulled my phone out of my coat pocket and thumbed two short text messages to the 911 Emergency Communications Center. First was just Fielding's address, as that should send a nearby police unit to check it out as quickly as possible. Then:

Break-in in progress - at least 2 intruders -
notify det carson & det lang DPD.

Two seconds later I got a string of canned replies:

Police are on the way.

Are you in danger?

Please STAY AWAY from any dangerous
situations, but tell me what you see now

I glanced at the message, then went back to listening. I didn't have to listen very hard, as the thuds and thumps from inside continued.

I hated to let this go on. They were destroying the place. How soon could the police get there?

I crept up to the doorway, trying to think of some way to distract the people inside without scaring them off before the police arrived.

As I got up to the door, the opening bars of the theme from *Rocky* erupted from my shirt pocket. Loud. I had slipped my phone in there after texting the police, and like an idiot I hadn't set it to silent mode. I tried desperately to grab it from my pocket to turn it off, but it slipped out of my hand and banged against the door before it landed on Fielding's rubber welcome mat.

The noise from inside stopped. Then one of the voices: "Someone's there!"

The door in front of me open and someone charge past, shoving me out of the way. I slid sideways on the brick steps and tried to grab the metal handrail, but it was no good. I was aware of two dark shapes running down the steps past me and toward the black car, but that's all I could see before my feet went out from under me and I went headfirst down the steps. Soon the car I'd seen across the street was rounding the corner and then was gone.

Fifteen minutes later I was slumped in the entryway of Fielding's living room, just inside the front door, and a Denver PD officer was leaning over me. His name tag said "Garvey."

"Wake up, guy. Come on. You okay?"

I tried to nod, but the motion turned into some kind of crazy skull-bobbing. The back of my neck felt like a big knot of fire, and there were floating pinpoints around the edges of my vision, bright dots against the dark room. Apparently I'd hit my head on the bottom step as I slid down the steps.

Flashing lights from a police unit out in the street played in through the window, making the place look like some bookish goth disco. I knew the police wouldn't have moved me with a head injury, so I must have crawled up the steps on my own. I couldn't remember doing that.

I found my legs and pushed upward, trying to stand.

"Hey, hey, take it easy," said Officer Garvey. He started to put a hand on my shoulder to keep me seated, but then he gave up and helped me up to a standing position.

His partner, tagged "Toomey," was less helpful. He stood in the living room a few feet away, gun drawn but low at his side.

"You want to tell us who you are, and what you're doing here?" he said.

"Rodak," I croaked. "Martin Rodak." I felt a little better standing up. "I'm the citizen who called it in."

"Okay, Mr. Rodak," said the first cop. "You mind telling me what happened here?"

"No," I said. "No, I —"

I began to feel wobbly again. "Just let me sit down a sec."

With the cop's help I stumbled to Fielding's sofa and sat down heavily. Somewhere behind us the other cop found a light switch and turned it on.

Light leapt from the ceiling fan and revealed the mess that used to be Fielding's library. Books were scattered everywhere. Great heaps on the floor, a pile in the stuffed leather reading chair. One bookcase was pulled away from the wall and half-toppled into another. Some larger books had been damaged, covers roughly torn off and pages splayed and pulled out of their bindings, but most of the volumes had just been dumped and scattered. The few cabinets that didn't contain books were open, their contents jumbled and spilling out.

Jesus, I thought. Lucille must watch TV pretty damn loud if she didn't hear this from next door.

My head was already starting to feel a little better. I had a sore spot on my left temple, and what felt like a growing knot in the back. I reached around behind me. It hurt like hell to touch the lump at the back of my skull, but it was small and I didn't feel anything wet. Could have been worse.

The cop with the drawn gun returned it to its holster, then went back to the center of the room and looked around at the damage.

"So," he said, "you want to tell us what you were looking for in here?"

I raised an eyebrow at him. "Remind me again," I said, "which one of us fell on his head? I told you, I'm the one who called it in. I didn't do this."

"Then who are you?"

"Still Martin Rodak. I'm a private investigator."

"Really."

"If you'll contact Detective Lang as I texted to the ECC ..."

"It's not Lang's case," said another voice with a deep Texan drawl.

Detective Fred Carson loomed in the front doorway. When he stepped forward I could see another plainclothes officer following in his wake.

Carson looked to the two uniforms, who were now both standing in the middle of the room. "You two clear the rest of the house?"

"We did, Detective," said Garvey. "No one here except Mr. Rodak."

"There was a black sedan out front," I said. "Black, or at least dark. Looked new. Across the street."

"Not when we got here," said Toomey.

"You're making me get a jump on my work, Rodak, coming out at night like this," Carson said to me. "That'll look good on my performance review."

He paused and turned to the other plainclothes officer. "Steve, take these two and check the rest of the house. See if it all looks like this." He looked around at the mess surrounding him. "Somebody wanted to find something pretty bad."

"That's a remarkable deduction, Detective," I said.

Carson ignored me. He looked back at the other detective and the two uniforms, who were still standing there. Toomey had a half smile on his face, but quickly doused it and followed Detective Steve toward the back rooms. Carson shook his head, then turned back to me.

"I was going to be here in the morning anyway, Rodak," he said. "I've got a warrant to search this place."

"What? Why?"

"Oh, come on. Your pal Fielding happened to find a dead body no one was looking for, which happened to be connected to a case he was working with you. And he withheld evidence. And he went apeshit in a courtroom in front of a judge while being given a sweet deal to help the cops figure out the whole mess. You don't think we're going to take a close look at your guy?"

Carson took a few steps around the room, then looked back at me. "And be honest, Rodak. You really sure he wasn't involved in the thing at the auction house? He seems like an avid collector."

Carson looked around the room to emphasize his point.

"Only of books," I said. "And no, I don't think he had anything to do with the auction house or Joseph Vargas."

Detective Steve and the two uniforms came back in.

"The rest of the house is a mess, but not as bad as this place," said Steve. "Drawers, cabinets, all dumped. Looks like they were only halfway through with the kitchen."

"So they were interrupted. Maybe they didn't have time to find what they were looking for," said Carson. "Maybe we got lucky."

He turned to me with a twisted smile. "Maybe you can explain to me what they would be looking for in Fielding's house, if Fielding had nothing to do with any of the crimes?"

"No, Detective," I said. "I have no idea."

"Maybe more of the stolen merchandise." Carson looked around the room again and gave some instructions to Detective Steve.

As Steve and the uniforms mapped out their plans to search the place, Carson invited me to get the hell out of his way. By that time an EMS unit had rolled up. The paramedics insisted on checking my head, but agreed that it wasn't too bad. They gave me an ice pack, let me sign a waiver, gave me strict instructions to see my own doctor first thing in the morning, and let me go. They wouldn't let me drive, so I got my phone back from Carson, who had found it at the bottom of the front steps, and hailed a ride.

As I got into the car, I noticed Lucille peering out from her front window. I guess the noise and lights had finally gotten her attention.

CHAPTER 11

Once I got home I sat on the sofa with my notebook and my ice pack, planning to figure out what I could do next to help Fielding. Instead three days with barely any break finally caught up with me and I fell asleep.

I woke up to my phone ringing. It was still dark outside. I found my suit jacket in a pile on the chair next to me and fished my phone out of the pocket. The screen said it was 9:15 p.m.

"Rodak," I answered.

"Martin, it's John Harris. I heard about Fielding. What happened?"

"Fielding had a bit of a breakdown in court."

"A breakdown?" Harris said. "I heard it was, well, dramatic."

"Can't argue with that," I said.

I got up and carried the phone into the kitchen so I could get a drink.

"Apparently Fielding saw someone," I continued. "Don't know who yet, and it doesn't really matter. Bottom line is that he panicked, got a little violent. The judge ordered a psychiatric evaluation."

Harris said, "How long does that mean they keep him?"

"Technically the eval period is seventy-two hours," I said. "But the system is so backlogged he could remain in custody longer."

"Is he going to be all right?"

"Hard to say. We hope so."

"Well, he's in our thoughts, me and Sharon," Harris said. I'd gone to dinner with John and his wife, a few times.

"Thanks," I said.

I filled a glass with water and took it back to the dining room. The table was still strewn with papers and folders from prior cases, plus the case file for the Vicar and Blake job.

"Also, I, uh, called to tell you something else," Harris said. "I was going to tell you in the morning, but now that we're talking..."

"Oh? What's that?"

"I'm sorry to tell you this," he said. "It wasn't my idea. But we have to take you off the V and B case."

"Oh, come on," I said. Somehow I'd expected this, but it still made me angry after everything I'd been through. "You can't be serious. We identified one of the thieves right out of the gate, not to mention discovering that there was a murder involved. You've got to let me stay on this case."

Even as I argued the point, I knew the decision made sense. I certainly would have fired me.

"Like I said, this isn't my idea," Harris said. "It's from my boss. His boss, really."

"I see."

"And we really have no choice." He stopped to clear his throat before he continued. "I know you and I know Fielding, but not everyone does. And now Fielding is in jail, maybe facing charges involving the robbery you're investigating. And a murder besides. We need an investigator who's not personally involved."

I thought about that for a second, then sighed. "I know. I can't blame Vicar for wanting me off the case, given what happened with Fielding, and his association with me."

"Vicar and Blake?" Harris said. "It's not them, it's the higher-ups at Pioneer West. Frieda Lansing herself called my boss this morning to make sure you would remain in the case. Gave him hell about taking you off it."

"I don't get it," I said.

"Rich people. Who knows what they're thinking?"

I thought about that for a minute. "I suppose I should finally meet this Frieda Lansing and thank her."

"Good luck," Harris said. "I hear she doesn't go out anymore. Or see people. But anyway, since Pioneer West is on the hook, Pioneer West gets to investigate however it sees fit. Whether or not she agrees. And whether or not I agree."

"I understand. So, who is taking over?"

"I don't know yet. No decision's been made."

"Well, get someone right away. Don't let this go cold."

"We won't. And be sure to submit your bill for the work you've done so far. I'll make sure it gets paid quick."

"Thanks, John."

I moved my water glass aside and took another look at the files on the table in front of me. "You know," I said, "I can't just leave this whole thing alone. Like you said, Fielding's in jail and my reputation is tied up in this."

"I know, Marty."

"But I guess you'll be needing the case file back."

"Yes, I suppose we will. But anytime tomorrow is fine. And if it falls into a copier or something on the way, I don't think that would be a problem."

I let out a laugh. "Stranger things have happened."

"One thing, though," Harris said. "Explain it to me again.

Why can't you just ask Cindy where the stolen sculpture is? Or the Indian jars, or the camera?"

"Cindy's talent is peculiar," I said. "She can pinpoint actions, but not things. She led me to that basement because I asked her where someone planned an art theft. That's an action. An action is like a ripple, she says. But a stolen piece of artwork, that's just a thing."

"Just a thing," Harris murmured.

"It's like she can see verbs but not nouns," I said. "She can't find Colonel Mustard or the monkey wrench, but if he uses the wrench to brain someone, she can find that pretty easy."

"Okay. I guess that makes as much sense as anything."

"I asked her to monitor the state for someone trying to sell the stolen items. Nothing yet, but maybe we'll get lucky."

"Good idea. Thanks, Martin."

We said our good-byes, and I stuffed my phone back into my pocket. Then I picked up the Vicar and Blake case file and brought it into the spare room. Fielding's bag and his books were still there, carefully arranged on the neatly made futon. I went to the desk where a fax/printer/copier stood next to the computer. I took the first few pages from the file, put them in the sheet feeder, and pressed the button to start making copies.

As the first few pages emerged I pulled them out and started reading them again. They were the original claim information submitted by the auction house, with William Tucci's signature at the end.

I still didn't know the main motive behind the robbery. One of those old Native American jars had gotten Fielding into a lot of trouble. Maybe that's what got Joseph Vargas killed. But were they the primary target of the thieves? The camera equipment was probably worth more than the jars, and would be a lot easier to sell. The sculpture was also worth a lot, but hard to move.

The next few pages of the file were copies of Vicar and Blake consignment paperwork, submitted to Pioneer West as support for the insurance claim. They listed additional details about the stolen items, including the names of the owners who had consigned them for sale. After that there were attachments to the attachments — copies of documents certifying the pedigree and condition of the materials to be sold. Some information was provided by the seller, and some was from Vicar and Blake's experts on authentication and valuation. An expert named Max Wells had signed off on the authenticity of the Michael Fenn sculpture, a Professor Quinn from Colorado State University had authenticated the camera, and the jars had been accompanied by what seemed like a jumble of authenticating paperwork.

I needed to know who might want to steal each of these things. I needed to know what made them valuable, or better yet what made them interesting. I could learn some of that from the file, but I knew I could learn more from the previous owners.

The copier fell silent as it finished with the stack of papers. The file wasn't all that big. I hadn't had a chance to add much to it before Fielding was arrested and everything started going to hell.

I carried both copies of the file back to the dining room, stopping in the kitchen on the way to get a can of diet soda and a handful of crackers. I pulled a large express mail envelope from the box of office supplies under the table, stuffed the original file into it and sealed it up. Then I sat down with my copy and my black notebook.

The Michael Fenn sculpture had been consigned by James McKelvie, a lawyer from Fort Logan. He used to own an inn up there, near the college, but had shut that down ten months ago and was selling off a bunch of artwork he'd had on display.

The statue might make sense as the main target of the heist.

It was big and heavy, so it was not likely any thieves would pick it up as a bonus while they were there to steal other things.

And if the Fenn was the target, then the thieves probably had a link to a buyer ahead of time. No one would steal a bronze, horse-shaped albatross if they didn't have a way to off-load it.

No one from the police, Pioneer West, or Vicar and Blake had been able to contact McKelvie since the theft. I made a note to try again, to find out more about the statue if no other leads turned hot. I also made a note to look into who might have been able to fence a piece of artwork like a Fenn sculpture.

The camera equipment was also promising. It was to have been sold on behalf of a woman named Karen Poole. Poole was the founder of High Fire Industries, a video game company based up near Boulder. The documents indicated that the camera collection had been purchased by a Roger Andrews for sixty thousand dollars. Since then ownership had been transferred to Poole. Times must had been hard, since the reserve on the lot was still only sixty grand. Karen Poole might be worth talking to.

The history of the camera collection prior to Roger Andrews was a little odd. Andrews had purchased the entire lot from a specialty antiques dealer who had assembled the pieces from a few different sources. But the centerpiece, the wet-plate camera, had changed hands eleven times in the last nine years. No owner had kept it more than a year, and many had sold it at a loss.

Then there were those damn Indian jars.

I had never dealt much with Native American issues. Not the kind of thing that came up when I worked as a prosecutor in Denver, or in my private work. But I knew that the sale and purchase of Indian artifacts was a pretty delicate issue. Plenty of sales, claims, and auctions from past decades had been invalidated through suits by Indian tribes to reclaim their heritage artifacts. So it was pretty unusual for something like these jars to be offered for open auction at a place like Vicar and Blake.

I looked over the pedigree information. According to one affidavit, the jars were at least four hundred years old. Some reports attached to the consignment claimed more than six hundred years.

That might explain the sale. At that age, there wouldn't be a current, recognized tribe or nation with a claim to the jars. Most likely they were found in an archaeological dig sometime in the past hundred years.

Then I read further, and discovered that I was wrong. The Lacalma still existed, as a federally recognized tribe. And the Lacalma were the ones who had put the jars up for auction.

According to the file's historical summary, the jars, or ones just like them, had been in the possession of the Lacalma since at least 1756, when a Spanish captain named Fernandes, serving under Don Juan de Onate, mentioned them in his account of a meeting with native elders in the area of the Rio Grande Valley and the San Juan Mountains. Even at that time the jars had been regarded by their owners as very, very old, artifacts from the Lacalma's ancestors who lived in an age long past.

The biggest mystery to me was, why would the Lacalma Tribe auction off such an important part of their history? Some extraordinary circumstance, or some really good persuasion, must have affected that decision.

I flipped a few pages back to reread the consignment paperwork. It was signed for the tribe by someone named Andrew Twofires Gregory, who was identified as a member of the Lacalma Tribal Council. I was surprised to see that Gregory's business address was in downtown Denver, at Seventeenth and California. The modern Lacalma had a relatively small reservation in the southwest part of Colorado and northern New Mexico. This placed them geographically, as well as economically, in between the struggling Ute Mountain Ute tribe and the larger, better known and substantially wealthier Southern Ute.

I looked back at my phone to see the time. It was almost ten o'clock in the evening. I made a note in my book to go see Gregory in the morning. I hoped that he kept regular hours on a Thursday.

Thursday. Already? It was almost —

Damn. Saturday. Melissa.

I picked up the phone again and dialed Melissa's number.

"Hello, Martin!" she answered. "What's cooking with you?"

"Hello," I said. "Sorry, I've got some bad news."

"What's wrong?" A note of sharp concern replaced the playfulness in her voice.

"Fielding is under arrest."

Melissa took in a quick breath. I explained what had happened, starting with Fielding's weird behavior out in my yard after our dinner at her place, right up through the ruckus in Judge Carp's courtroom and the break-in at Fielding's place. I left out the part about me getting knocked on my head.

"That's just awful," Melissa said. "Are you sure Fielding will be all right?"

"I'm absolutely not sure of that," I said. "Jails, hospitals, none of these are very good places for him."

"What are you going to do?"

"Liz Duncan is doing everything she can to make sure Fielding gets treated okay and gets released as soon as possible. The only thing I can do is move forward on this case. Find out who was behind the robbery and the Vargas murder, or at least find out something that will prove Fielding wasn't involved."

"Well, let me know if there is anything I can do."

"I will," I said. Then I remembered the jar. "Damn."

"What is it?"

"Remember the little jar I described, the one that Fielding

says he got from Vargas's mailbox? I should have brought it to you before I took Fielding to Liz and turned it over to the police."

"Hmmm." Melissa hummed thoughtfully into the phone. "Would that have been legal?"

"I really don't know. Wouldn't have cared much," I said. "We wouldn't have gotten Fielding into any more trouble than he's already in, and I bet you could have given us some more information to help him."

"I'm sure that's so," Melissa said. "If you find anything else interesting, you be sure to bring it to me. Anything at all."

"I will," I said. "Hey, tomorrow I'm going to be pretty busy with this, and I expect Saturday will be as well. I don't know if —"

"Martin, don't you say another word. Getting Fielding home is more important than any date."

"Thanks. I'm just sorry about your fish slappers —"

"Mackerel Smack." Melissa's laugh was a beautiful thing to hear. "And I'm sure they'll play Denver again soon. And the park will still be there for a picnic after Fielding is safe and sound in his own home."

CHAPTER 12

First thing in morning I called Craig Peterson at the DA's office, but he was out at a hearing. Next I called the sheriff's department to get information about Fielding. He was in a place called Causeway House. That was in Littleton, a bit south of Denver, but it was the nearest facility with any openings certified to handle court-ordered psychiatric evaluations. Better to have Fielding there than in the state hospital down in Pueblo. When I asked about visiting Fielding I got bounced around from the sheriff's jail division to the public information division and back to an "active case liaison" and learned very little in the process other than that the Denver Sheriff's Department was "operating in accordance with the court's orders and all applicable laws."

Not much comfort, that. Fielding was "in the system." It was up to me and Liz to find a way to get him out. When I called Causeway House directly, the caseworker there told me that for at least twenty-four hours Fielding would be allowed no visitors other than his attorney.

I made a quick call to Jeff Lang and asked him to keep an ear out for any news about Fielding. I didn't bother calling Detective Carson.

Next I called Andrew Twofires Gregory's office.

"Shard Peak Development," answered a receptionist. "How can I help you?"

"Good morning," I said. "My name is Martin Rodak. I'd like to make an appointment to speak briefly with Mr. Gregory, sometime today if possible."

"I see. One moment please." I heard the click of computer keys through the phone. "May I ask what this is regarding?"

"Just some business I would like to discuss with him."

"I'm sorry, Mr. Rodak, but given the demands on Mr. Gregory's schedule, I could not possibly schedule an appointment for him without some idea as to what it is about."

"I'm a private investigator. I'm looking into a matter that I believe is of interest to Mr. Gregory, and I think he and I may be able to share some information about it. I promise I won't take up too much of Mr. Gregory's time, but it is very important that I speak with him soon."

There was a pause while I heard more keyboard clicking.

"I see. Can you please hold for one moment?"

"Sure."

The line switched to some surprisingly good music, but only for about thirty seconds.

"Mr. Rodak?" the receptionist said. "I'm afraid that Mr. Gregory's schedule is booked all morning and for much of the afternoon. However, he can be available for a meeting at four thirty."

"Four thirty. Okay. I'll see him then."

"And do you know our location?"

"Seventeenth and California, is that right? Eleventh floor?"

"That's correct, Mr. Rodak. Mr. Gregory will see you at four thirty."

"Thanks again," I said.

After hanging up I flipped through my notebook, deciding what to do until four thirty.

I reread my notes about the stolen camera equipment, and about Karen Poole. It might be a mistake to focus on those Lacalma jars while ignoring the other items. Even if the jars were the reason Vargas was killed, the other merchandise might shed some light on the thieves and the reason they got onto that job.

A trip to Boulder would give me a chance to talk to Poole. It would also give me a chance to ask someone I knew up there about the Fenn sculpture.

I took a shower and put on a fresh suit. Not too many people wear suits in Denver. Not even lawyers, unless they're in court. But I still have a bunch of them from when I worked in the DA's office, and wearing them has become a useful habit. It lets me blend into a lot of places. Add a tie or not, wear the jacket or leave it in the car. Best of all, I don't have to think about clothes when I have other things to think about.

When I picked up my phone I saw I'd missed a call from Mark Baxter. Mark was another of my peculiar associates. A perpetual student, with two graduate degrees and All But Dissertation for two more. And as if his brains weren't talent enough, he had a remarkable ability for communicating with animals. These days he owned a pet shop and worked as a groomer and dog trainer in Castle Rock.

Mark was a good guy, but I really didn't have time for any four-legged drama, so I decided not to call him back. Instead I put on a pot of coffee and stared at it while it brewed, letting the back of my brain come up with questions to ask at my upcoming meetings. When the coffee was done I poured myself a travel mug, grabbed a granola bar from the jar on top of the fridge, and went out to the car for the drive to Boulder.

My car wasn't there, of course. It was still at Fielding's house, where I'd left it after the break-in. So I hailed an Uber and ate my granola bar while I waited. Forty minutes later I was back in my Clubman and headed out of Denver.

I stopped at the post office to drop off the envelope with the case file I was sending back to Harris. By the time I got onto the Boulder Turnpike, I had waited out most of the morning traffic. I started driving north and west out of Denver, through Westminster and on past the suburbs, parks, shopping centers, and small farms that line the highway.

I was just past Broomfield when my phone rang. It was already plugged into my car stereo, so I poked at the screen to answer it.

"Rodak? It's Jeff Lang," It was a lousy connection, with lots of background noise.

"Jeff? What's up? And where are you calling from?"

"I'm calling from the last damn pay phone in town," he said. "Didn't want to use my own phone, but I needed to call you about Fielding."

"Oh Jesus. Okay, hang on a minute."

I was coming up to an exit, so I got off the highway. Near the bottom of the ramp was a derelict Sears. I pulled into the parking lot and stopped the car. "All right. What's happened? Where is Fielding?"

"He's at a place called Causeway House in Littleton," Lang said.

"I know that," I said. "Is he okay?"

"He's fine, as far as I know, though I don't know much."

"Then what?"

"Carson searched Fielding's place."

"Yeah, I was still there when he started, but he kicked me out. Did he find something?"

"Yes. A bunch of papers."

"What papers?"

"Maps of the auction house," Lang said. "And Joseph Vargas's ID badge from Vicar and Blake."

"What? You're not serious."

"I don't get it either. This is all pretty messed-up."

I just sat there, staring at the steering wheel.

"Listen," Lang said. "I know what you said when we first picked up Fielding. But seriously, do you know this guy? I mean, do you really know him?"

"I know him, Jeff."

"Yeah, yeah. But I mean, look at this mess. It's looking a hell of a lot like he had something to do with the Vicar job. And if he was involved in that, and with Vargas, then —"

"He didn't have anything to do with either one," I said. "He's being set up, Jeff."

"By who?"

"We don't know yet. Vargas couldn't tell us anything about who killed him."

"And how do you know that?" Lang said. "Because Fielding told you? Pretty convenient for him, if he was involved."

I thought about that for a moment. "If Fielding were covering up the murder, why tell us anything at all? Why not just fail to mention the contact with Vargas entirely?"

It was Lang's turn to spend a few seconds in silent thought. "Okay, that's a good point. Anyway, I wanted you to know what was happening. You used to put away bad guys for a living. But this friend of yours, well, I don't know. If he blows up, it won't be a good idea to be standing too close."

"Okay, Jeff. Thanks for letting me know. And I'll keep this call between us."

"Right. Talk to you later."

I jabbed the screen on my phone to end the call. Then I sat for a few seconds, staring at the little winged MINI logo in the middle of the steering wheel.

Then I hammered on the wheel four or five times with the side of my fist.

This made no sense at all. There was no way Fielding could have been involved with Vargas before I pulled him into the case.

Was there?

I knew Fielding had been through some bad times in the past. When I first met him he was facing criminal trespass and stalking charges. But those made sense, considering who Fielding was and what he lived with. But art theft? Murder?

Those were impossible. But then why did he have maps of the auction house in his home? And Vargas's ID?

Maybe I didn't know Fielding as well as I thought.

Had Cindy known something else about Fielding when she said I should bring him with me to Vicar and Blake?

I sat for a few more minutes, deciding what to do. Going back to Denver would be pointless — there was no way I would get to talk to Fielding, and it wouldn't be very productive if I could.

I had to clear Fielding's name. That was his only chance. Mine too. A solo practitioner private eye who hires felons is likely to see his license revoked. And if I ever wanted to go back to practicing law — which I absolutely did not — the state bar would not look kindly upon the situation.

The best thing I could do for myself, and for Fielding, was to keep working the case. Find out as much as I could about the burglary, Vargas, and the murder. Then hand Carson and the DA a better target before they decided to hang it all on Fielding.

CHAPTER 13

I pulled out of the parking lot, got back on the highway, and continued toward Boulder.

About fifteen minutes later I was up at the north end of the tech corridor that flanks the turnpike as it approaches the city. I followed my phone's GPS directions into an office park about a mile north of the highway, one of a dozen or so that had sprouted in the late nineties only to remain half-empty once the first internet boom fizzled. Now they were filling up again with low-tech service start-ups, consultants, and little companies like High Fire Industries.

I looked at each of the low, identical signs until I found the right low, identical office building in the cluster that surrounded the maze of parking lots and access roads.

High Fire occupied floors two and three of the four-story building. I took the elevator up one flight, and when it opened I found myself gazing across a wide lobby to a large industrial-looking desk made of black stained wood and strips of diamond plate steel. Behind the desk sat a young man with brown hair gathered into a bun at the back of his head. His broad, muscled shoulders were encased in a tight black T-shirt that looked like it might have cost as much as my suit. As I crossed the lobby's polished stone floor, he typed erratically on a black wireless keyboard.

"Good morning," I said. "My name is Martin Rodak. I'm hoping you can help me out with something."

"What can I do for you, sir?" The receptionist hit a button to pause the game he'd been playing and looked up. The nameplate that had fallen down on the top of his desk said "Kliff."

"I'm here to speak with Ms. Poole, but I'm sorry to say that I don't have an appointment. Do you think there is any way I might get a few minutes to speak with her?"

"Hmm." The young man looked back down to his screen. "I really don't know. She doesn't take very many meetings, and her calendar tends to fill up quickly."

I smiled. "What does it fill up with, if she doesn't take meetings?"

The young man gave a snort. "Damned if I know."

"So, what do you say?" I said. "Shall we give it a try?"

"Let me call Karen's assistant and see what's up."

I looked around the lobby while Kliff dialed a number. The dark industrial theme was carried through the room. Lots more brushed steel and black-stained wood. One corner of the room held a seating area, while the other had a metal spiral staircase leading up to the next floor. Around the walls were TVs, most of them showing video loops of High Fire's game demos. One of them appeared to involve professional wrestlers with marshmallow heads and weapons made of chocolate. Another TV was tuned to *CNBC*, and the last in the row showed a live video stream where the host and a panel of experts — experts in something, I presumed — lounged on a virtual reality beach while engaged in a fierce debate.

"Hi, Cheryl," Kliff said into his phone headset. "Yeah. Yeah.

No. Yeah, listen. There's a guy here who wants to talk with Karen. Martin Rodak."

Kliff turned from the phone to give me a questioning look. I smiled and nodded to confirm he'd gotten my name right, and he went back to his conversation.

"What? I don't know. No, I didn't. I just forgot. Yeah, okay. *Okay.* Just hang on a second, okay? Jesus."

He looked up at me and smiled. "Mr. Rodak? May I say what your visit is in regard to?"

"I'm a private investigator," I told him. "I'm working on a stolen property matter that I believe may be of some interest to Ms. Poole, and I'd just like to ask her a few questions."

Kliff returned to staring at nothing in particular and talking to Cheryl through his earpiece. "Did you hear that? Good. Okay. So, should I — Okay, let me know."

He jabbed a button on his desk phone to end the call. "Mr. Rodak?" he said, "Karen's assistant is checking to see when she might be available. You're welcome to have a seat in the meantime."

I nodded my thanks and wandered over to the square of bulgy black sofas a few feet away. I didn't bother sitting down. I just watched the updates scroll by on the CNBC screen.

Five minutes later I heard a clattering on the spiral staircase. I turned to see a woman in black jeans and a red top making her way around the final curve at the bottom of the steps. She was a little plump, and her dark, wavy hair bounced prettily as she clacked across the lobby. She gave a quick wave to Kliff, then held out her hand to me.

"Rodak? Martin Rodak?" she said.

"That's right. Ms. Poole?"

"Right, I mean, Karen. Call me Karen. It's a pleasure meeting you."

She raised an eyebrow and examined my face carefully. "You are the same guy I read about," she declared finally.

"I suppose so," I said. "I was hoping you might have a few minutes to talk?"

"Absolutely. Here, let's find a place to sit down."

She led me behind Kliff's desk, down a short corridor, and into a small break room with a vending machine, three round tables, and an expensive-looking espresso machine. At one of the tables sat two young men with bagels and packets of cream cheese.

"Frank? Nagi? Scoot," Poole said. "Take your bagels. I'll bring you some coffee later."

A soon as she had spoken, the two men gathered up their snacks and hustled out the door.

Poole bounced into a chair by a table away from the door. "Sorry, but I hate our conference rooms. Have a seat."

I took the chair across from her.

"So," she said. "This is pretty cool. What does a psychic detective want to talk to me about?"

"I'm not a psychic detective," I said. "I'm just an investigator. I'm looking into a theft from the Vicar and Blake Auction House. I understand that some of the stolen items were there to be sold on your behalf."

"Oh, that. That's right. A bunch of old camera equipment. I kinda got into that thanks to my ex-boyfriend, but when he moved out I decided I didn't want to have it around."

"I noticed from the insurance company paperwork that you weren't necessarily expecting a profit," I said.

"Yeah, I guess," she said. "I didn't care that much. Really, I just wanted to get it out of my house."

"So, if you don't mind my asking — you weren't selling because of some financial issues?"

"Ha!" Poole laughed and tapped out a short drum solo on the tabletop. "No way."

She stopped her drumming and leaned toward me a little. "I shouldn't really laugh, I guess. A few years ago I was pretty close to selling anything I could, just to raise some cash."

"Things weren't going well with the company?"

"Things were downright crappy. We'd just released an online title that wasn't selling, my business partner had just quit, and no investors were willing to kick in more money to fund another project. I was deciding between going into hock to keep the company going, and just shutting it down."

"So, what happened?"

"Ad-supported games happened!" Poole bounced up in her seat again. "While things were still pretty grim around here, I and a couple of the developers who hadn't jumped ship started writing a new game for mobile. Now we've got that and five others in the app stores, and they're selling like crazy. Our latest game cost about a tenth what it cost us to develop that online roller-coaster game that flopped, and so far it's made eleven hundred times as much."

I gave a low whistle. "So the game business is looking up again?"

"It is for now." Poole smiled but shook her head. "Who knows about next year? None of us are becoming billionaires this month, but we have some breathing room. We've been able to keep the doors open, hire back some people overseas, and start work on still more games."

"Congratulations," I said.

"Thanks." Poole looked over her shoulder at the espresso machine on the counter. "You want some coffee?"

"No, thanks," I said. "So, about the antique camera."

"Right. Not much else to say. It was cool, but it was big and ugly and reminded me of that dipshit I'd been living with. I wanted it gone."

"Still, that seems like a lot of money for an old camera."

"Yeah," she said. "That stuff has been kind of popular lately, especially with computer geeks."

"Why?"

"Cameras in those days, eighteen sixties, eighties, nineties, they were a lot like computers were in the early hacker days, before I was born. It was a new technology, and everything was wide-open. Being a photographer meant being a hacker. Figuring out the best equipment, the best chemicals and materials, modifying everything to work just the way you wanted. Spreading the word about what you discovered. Or keeping your discovery a secret, figuring out how to sell it, and making a fortune."

"That does sound pretty cool," I said. "Where did you get those antiques in the first place?"

"I didn't," Poole said. A sneer returned to her face for an instant. "The dipshit, Roger, bought it. Got it from a shop in Denver, a place down on Broadway. Near all the other antique shops. Specializes in antique scientific and medical things. I can get you the name later if you need it."

"Thanks. That would be helpful," I said, though I was pretty sure I knew the place she meant. Made the mistake of mentioning it to Melissa once. The very idea of a store filled with antique medical devices gave her the gibbering creeps. She didn't want to touch anything, not even in her own apartment, for half an hour after I'd changed the subject.

"Do you know of any other people in the area who collect that kind of thing?" I said.

"I'm sure there are some," Poole said. "I don't really know anyone myself. Like I said, that was Roger's thing." She said

"Roger" with a curled-up lip. "That's why I handed it off to Vicar and Blake. I didn't want to deal with it."

"I can understand that," I said. "Didn't Roger want to take any of it with him when he left?"

"No. I don't know why, since he's the one who bought it in the first place. But in the end he hated all of it. Especially the camera itself. He started acting weird a little while after he bought it. He sure as hell didn't want to take it with him."

"Weird?" I asked. "In what way?"

"At first it was just the camera," Poole said. "He would stare at it for hours. Then a few weeks later he threw out all of his other cameras. Real cameras, like an expensive Leica he used to take pretty good photos with."

"That is weird."

"It got worse," Poole said. "When I found him trying to destroy all of my photo albums, I decided we were done. Then before I could get him out, he tried to destroy the antique. I stopped him, and he signed it all over to me when he left."

I made a few more notes in my notebook. "How did you get hooked up with Vicar and Blake when you wanted to sell?"

"My brother told me about them. His company bought some art from them last year. Some sculptures or something. Turns out they're the best place in Colorado for buying and selling high-end stuff."

I looked down at my notebook, quickly scanning the notes I had made. "I might need to talk to Roger. Can you tell me where I could reach him?"

"Yeah," Poole said. "For what it's worth. He works for the IT department at CU, since he went loopy and left his cushy CTO job. But if you call, don't tell him it has anything to do with me or he'll act like a dick and hang up on you."

"I'll remember that," I said. I took a business card from the pocket in the back of my notebook and handed it to her. "If you think of anything else about the camera, or who might have wanted it, or anything about your dealings with Vicar and Blake, please give me a call."

"I sure will," she said. Then she patted the back of my hand. "Now it's my turn. I answered your questions, so now you answer some of mine."

I smiled. "I can see why you're a success. You like to turn things into games."

Poole laughed. "Everything's already a game! I just like to figure out what the rules should be. And that's what I want to talk to you about. Have you ever thought about working on a game?"

"That's really not my thing," I said. "I wouldn't be the least bit of use."

"Oh, I don't mean *working* working," she said. "It's not like you'd be writing code or designing levels. No, I'm thinking of a mystery game. We use your name, you work as a consultant to help write the mystery and help us with the details about crimes and psychics and things."

Poole started bouncing in her seat and staring out over the top of my head. "It would be great! We could do online purchases. A whole series of cases, all by the real-life psychic detective Martin Rodak."

"As I said before, I'm not a psychic detective. I don't think —"

"I know, I know, I know," Poole said. "So you said. But come on, that's how everyone knows you. You were on the home page of the *Westword* website. 'Martin Rodak, Psychic Detective.'"

I closed my notebook and got ready to leave. "Sorry, Ms. Poole, but you've been misinformed. I can't help what is in the papers, but I'm not a psychic detective. I'm an insurance investigator."

"Yeah, but —"

"I just happen to have a number of associates who have unique abilities that can be of help in my work."

Poole stayed silent, staring down at the table. I thought I'd finally gotten her off the subject, but then she looked up. Her eyes looked a little crazy.

"That's it!" she said. "That's perfect! You play as a detective, but you get to collect psychics to help you solve mysteries! You gather your bunch of psychics. Each has a different ability."

She looked up from the table and drummed on it with her fingertips. "You can have dozens of different types," she went on. "Then you can connect with other players online and trade psychic friends. Get rid of your duplicates and pick up the ones you missed. We can offer new characters as downloadable content. It'll be like mystery Pokémon for grown-ups."

Now I'd had enough. I leaned forward to make sure Poole would understand me and looked her in the eye. "You're talking about my friends. I do not collect them. I do not trade them. I damn well do not buy and sell them. And there is no way I'm letting you turn them into a game."

Poole leaned back. "Okay, all right. Crap, I was just —"

I don't know what else she said because I was already out of the room, stomping past Kliff the receptionist and back out to my car.

CHAPTER 14

Back in the Clubman, I sat and stared at the steering wheel for a few minutes, trying to take deep breaths. Then I took out my phone. Another missed call from Mark Baxter, but no messages I felt like returning.

I sat still for another minute, thinking about Karen Poole and her stupid game idea.

Goddamn ...

I didn't treat them like that. Of course I didn't.

Finally I shook my head and started the car. I had no more news from Lang, and I didn't want to risk trouble by calling him, so I might as well stick to my plan. Time to talk to Duds.

Harold Dudsen ran a used book and junk shop a few blocks off the Pearl Street Mall in Boulder. I suppose he and his neighbors would prefer to call it a shop for antiquarian books and furnishings. It was Duds who had gotten me in touch with the dealer in New York who sold me that old copy of *Robinson Crusoe* for Fielding.

I first met Duds when he was in a slightly different line of work. He had been selling used stuff back then as well, mostly expensive tools and business equipment, without the permission of its previous owners. As a fence he'd moved millions in stolen goods all over the front range from Fort Collins to Colorado Springs. He was one of the few crooks I'd actually helped put away back when I was in the DA's office, and he got out of prison around the same time I got out of that job.

I parked in the strip mall lot and walked into Duds's shop, in between a dry cleaner and a nail salon. The window display for Duds's place had been recently redone, but the inside of the shop was dusty and gray-looking. One corner was filled with cheap laminate furniture, packed together more like the inside of a moving van than a retail display. The rest of the shop was a warren of plain wooden shelves stacked in sections with tools, housewares, and clothes, mostly jeans and flannel shirts. The wall behind the counter was covered with pine shelves bending under the weight of used books.

Duds stood hunched over the counter in the back of the shop, twisting a pencil in his fingers. He glanced up, saw that I wasn't carrying anything to sell, and went back to working a puzzle in the newspaper spread out in front of him.

"Feel free to look around," he grumbled. "Let me know if you got any questions."

"Got any of those high-tech German socket wrenches?"

Duds looked up sharply, his eyes narrowed. As I got closer and he got a good look at me, his crumpled mouth became a jagged grin.

"Martin Rodak," he croaked. "It's been a while. What do you want?"

"Oh, you know, Duds. Stopped in to see an old friend. Happened to be in the neighborhood."

"Bullcrap," said Duds. "If you had your way you'd surround Boulder with razor wire and hippie repellant."

I laughed at that, but didn't disagree.

"Seriously, what brings you up here?" Duds asked.

"Let's go get a cup of coffee and talk about it," I said.

"It's the middle of the business day, Rodak. Some of us are trying to earn an honest living."

"And the rest of us appreciate the effort."

I glanced around the empty shop. "Doesn't look to me as if you'll miss out on too many sales if you take a short break. Come on, and I'll buy lunch as well."

At that Duds folded up his sheet of newspaper, tucked it along with his pencil into the pocket of his denim jacket, and stepped out from around the counter. We left the shop, pausing to let Duds set the "We'll Be Back at ..." sign and lock the door, and went to the coffee shop at the end of the strip mall.

I bought a double espresso for myself, plus a huge latte, a turkey sandwich, and two donuts for Duds. We sat down in a corner booth and Duds started unwrapping his sandwich.

"So, Duds," I said. "Business good?"

"Not so bad," he said. "Slow right now, but I make more than half my money the two months a year when classes are starting up at CU. Kids buying textbooks and furniture."

Duds took a bite of his sandwich before he went on. "I was worried about those ebooks for a while. But a lot of kids don't like them, which is good for me. Kids want paper books so they can sell them to me. So I can sell 'em back to them."

I gave that a chuckle as I sipped my coffee. "You sell anything else?"

"Oh, I sell a bunch of secondhand crap for their apartments or dorm rooms. You saw the shop."

Duds paused for a gulp of his latte, then looked at me from under his bushy eyebrows. "Everything I sell these days is on the level. If that's what you're getting at."

"Oh, I know, I know," I said. "But I do figure that a smart guy like you might still know what's going on in the old business."

Duds smiled and drank more of his coffee. "Could be I do."

"If someone were looking to move some art, who might he want to talk to?"

"Art?"

"Sculpture," I said. "Fine art, but not too high-end."

"Well," Duds said, "speaking as one who is not involved in any illegal business himself, I'd say that person should try talking to Johnny Tom. Has a baseball card shop down in Colorado Springs. Used to have a pretty good book of clients for art in Denver and New Mexico. I hear if he can't move something here, he can get it to the right people in LA. If anything special is moving in or out of the state, he'd know about it."

"Johnny Tom. Thanks."

"Glad to help. Insofar as I am not actually getting involved in whatever shit you're digging around in."

"Absolutely understood."

"You'll need a reference to get Johnny to talk to you. Tell him you talked to Lou Franz."

"Who's Lou Franz?" I asked.

"Never mind," Duds said. "I'll square things with Lou. And don't mention my name to Johnny Tom, or he'll shut right up."

"Got it. And I appreciate that the average guy wouldn't go out of his way to help the lawyer who put him in prison."

Duds gave another grunt that sounded almost like a laugh, then finished the last bite of his sandwich. "Yeah, you put me inside. Reason enough to be pissed for a good long time. But I did sell those tools and copiers."

Duds took a bite of donut and washed it down with coffee before he continued. "You sent me down for selling stolen goods, but you didn't let me go down for murder. I know I looked good for it, and most lawyers in your place would have been happy to rack up the bigger conviction. But somehow you knew I didn't kill that guy in Wash Park, and you refused to ding me for it. So you're okay."

"Thanks, Duds." I took another sip of my coffee. Duds's case and a few others like his were a big part of why I wasn't with the DA's office anymore. I never was focused on the conviction scorecard.

"As long as you're in such a helpful mood, let me hit you with another question," I said. "Any idea where a person might try to move some rare artifacts? Old American Indian stuff?"

Duds looked up from his donut and coughed.

"Or have you heard anything about that kind of thing coming on the market recently?" I said.

"No fucking way," he said. "I do not mess with old Native American stuff. Not me."

"Come on. What's the big deal?"

"What's the big deal." Duds snorted. "Curses and shit. That's the big deal. Old Indian stuff, at least any that's worth much, you never know what comes along with it. Especially if it's stol — Especially if it's, uh, changed hands through unusual means."

I raised an eyebrow. "You believe in curses? A down-to-earth guy like you?"

"Damn right I do," Duds said. "You try handling merchandise like I did for thirty years. Hell, you try just running a shop full of secondhand God-knows-what like I do now. You'll know the stuff people own carries things with it. Things you can't see."

I thought of Melissa and her gift for knowing where things have been. "Yeah, I think I see your point."

Duds finished his donut silently. "I guess this all has to do with something you're working on."

"Yeah," I said. "Just a boring insurance case, but I need to track down some items. Thanks for the help."

"Thanks for lunch."

I left Duds back at his shop, after he gave me a few more tips about contacting Johnny Tom. I asked about the antique camera, but he had no leads on that. So I got into my car and headed back toward Denver for my meeting with Andrew Twofires Gregory.

———

IT WAS STILL MIDAFTERNOON, but the traffic down from Boulder was already starting to build. It took an hour and a half to get back to Denver and navigate through downtown to Seventeenth Street. I parked about a block away — expensive, considering that I wouldn't be there long — and walked to Gregory's building.

The plaza in front of the building was nicknamed "The Jedi Memorial," as it was ringed by lighted translucent columns that looked an awful lot like giant *Star Wars* light sabers. At the corner a guy was busy hitching his closed-up burrito cart to the back of an old Chevy Suburban. There were a few people scattered among the outdoor tables, reading, drinking coffee, talking on cell phones.

I went inside through the revolving doors, through the giant lobby of beige marble, and up on the elevator.

To one side of the elevators on the eleventh floor were doors and signs for a number of small offices. To the other side were a set of large frosted-glass doors and a copper sign reading "Shard Peak Development Corporation." Gregory's company appeared to occupy half of the floor.

Inside, I found a reception area decorated with more copper and expensive glass. Behind the reception desk sat a woman in a sharp beige suit. A nameplate on the desk in front of her said "Joan Hall."

"Good afternoon," I said. "My name is Martin Rodak, and I have an appointment with Mr. Gregory this afternoon."

"Oh yes," Joan said. She looked up and smiled. "Welcome, Mr. Rodak. We spoke this morning."

"Yes. I understand that I'm a bit early, I just thought I might —"

"Actually your timing is just fine. Mr. Gregory's prior appointment wrapped up early and I'm sure he'd be happy to speak with you in a moment."

Joan got up and walked away down a hallway past a large conference room. I could see three people inside standing around a table, poring over large sheets of shiny paper.

Joan returned a moment later. "Follow me please."

She led me down a hallway with red and turquoise carpeting, to a back corner office. She knocked once on the open door and took a half step inside. "Mr. Rodak is here, sir." She stepped back out and gestured me inside.

Andrew Twofires Gregory was a tall, broad-shouldered man with sleek black hair, graying at the sides. I knew that he was nearly sixty years old, but he moved with the energy of a man much younger.

"Mr. Rodak," he said, "please come in." He came out from around his large pine desk and took two steps toward me. He extended a ruddy hand and regarded me with a smile.

"It's a pleasure to meet you, Mr. Gregory," I said as I shook his hand. "Thanks for your time."

"It's Andrew, please," he said, leading me toward a comfortable set of chairs in the corner across from his desk. "And the pleasure is mine. I've heard interesting things about you, Martin. My friends in the Denver legal world tell me you've managed to cultivate celebrity and mystery simultaneously."

"I can't say I've actually cultivated either," I said. "But I do have a job right now for which I'm hoping you might be able to provide some information."

"I'll be happy to help if I can." He poured us each a glass of water from a tall pitcher on a side table. As he moved I noticed the glint of a wristwatch with a face the size of a hubcap. It was probably worth more than my car, hubcaps and all.

"It's about the theft of items from the Vicar and Blake Auction House. They included some pieces consigned for sale by the Lacalma Nation."

"Yes, indeed. Very disappointing," Gregory said. "That house had such a solid reputation. I really expected better."

He shrugged, palms to the ceiling. "Still, I guess things happen. I know the auction house is insured, and the council's lawyers are dealing with things on our end."

He paused, narrowing his eyes as he thought. "For whom are you investigating this? Are you working for Vicar and Blake? Or for their insurance company?"

"I was engaged by Pioneer West Insurance to look into this," I said. I didn't volunteer the fact that I had been unengaged less than twenty-four hours ago.

"In that case, I'm sure you understand that there is a limit to what I can discus without the tribal attorneys present. And that I can speak only for myself, not on behalf of the Lacalma Nation or its council."

"I understand that completely, Andrew. I'd like to talk to you today to get some general background about the missing items. There's no way to tell what bit of information might help lead to the eventual recovery of the artifacts — which is, I'm sure you agree, what everyone wants."

"Of course, of course," Gregory said. "So, what can I do to help?"

"First off, what can you tell me about the jars that were consigned for auction?"

"They were quite old, of course. Others could provide more detail than I, but we Lacalma have stories that suggest that jars like these were important to the tribe at least five hundred years ago."

"That's a long time. Why sell them now?"

"That was a decision of the council."

"And was that a unanimous decision?"

"I really can't go into the details of any council proceedings," Gregory said. "Our proceedings are confidential with respect to nontribal citizens."

"Of course," I said. "Still, it's very unusual for a tribe to sell any artifacts, let alone ones that are so old and important. How about you? Were you in favor of the sale?"

Gregory hesitated for a breath and then answered with confidence, "I was all for it."

"Why was that?"

Gregory paused again before he spoke.

"It was the best thing for the tribe," he said finally. "It would bring in significant revenue, as well as help establish a relationship with the academic community and much-needed attention to the tribe and its history, and its current living conditions."

I said nothing, just nodded. Gregory seemed to have gotten onto a subject he liked talking about. His answer seemed well rehearsed, but I wanted to see where he would go with it.

"We did not decide to sell those artifacts on a whim," he said. "There were at least two universities and one museum that were interested in acquiring the pieces for study and preservation. The time was right. And I believe that a sale of these artifacts to a reputable institution would bring not only academic interest in our tribe's ancient heritage, but also interest in assisting our development in the here and now. Greater educational opportunities for our children, for starters."

"But why now?"

"A new wave of academic interest." Gregory took a long sip of water and put his glass back on the side table with a faint clack. "A publication last year by a University of Colorado professor raised the suggestion that the tribe, and the artifacts we hold, may not be as old as previously thought. I don't know that I believe that, but I'm happy to let the academics argue about it, while my people take advantage of the publicity."

"And what were the jars, exactly?" I said.

"A typical ritual item," Gregory said. "Used in ceremonies. Every people in this part of the continent had their own thing. Ours was special jars of oil."

"And what about the rituals? Don't your people carry on those traditions?"

Gregory smiled and waved a hand as if to brush aside my question. "Sure, sure. Some carry on with the chanting and the dances. It's important to many people. Some tourists like it too, though not so many these days. But we can make more pots. The rituals can go on, if that's what people want."

I took a sip from my water while I thought about that. "You don't sound like you approve of traditional Lacalma practices."

"I absolutely approve! But I'm not obsessed like some are."

Gregory sat back in his chair and gave me a look up and down. "Where are you from, Martin?"

"I was born in Philadelphia."

"Yes, but your people, your family." He looked me over, examining my dark hair and square head. "Italy? Eastern Europe?"

"My father's father was Czech."

"Czech. Yes. A good people. Strong. And are you proud of your heritage?"

"Sure, I suppose. As much as anyone. I know a few words of the language thanks to my grandddad."

"That's wonderful. Very fine. And Prague is such a beautiful city."

"So I have heard," I said. "I'd like to see it someday."

"You should go," Gregory said. "So much history, but such a smart, modern city."

He nodded in thought, then looked up at me again. "But how do you feel about the beliefs of your old European ancestors? Fairies? Black magic? Burning suspected witches?"

Good question. Charges of magic and witchcraft might have applied to half the people I work with. But I understood his point.

"I suppose most people would say that times were different then," I said. "Science had not yet taught us very much."

"Very well. But what if you met someone who held those same old beliefs today?"

"I really don't know."

"I think that most modern people would consider them pathetic at best. Am I right? And at worst, they would be considered dangerous."

"Yes, I suppose they would."

"So you understand my position, Mr. Rodak. I am proud of my people. Proud of the things we have accomplished, and proud of the things we have endured. I want us to be a great nation. But our identity as a nation should not require us to hold on to ignorance and superstition just because that was the way of our forefathers. I want my people to be a nation of the twenty-first century, not the sixteenth."

"Okay," I said, "but don't your rituals still have historic importance? Cultural importance?"

"As I said, those can still go on. And we have very skilled craftspeople who can continue to make the pottery, the costumes, and other things they require. And that is good. That is important. It is right that we hold on to those traditions. But those particular jars? Their only distinguishing feature is their age. That is, their possible age. And that is much more valuable in the hands of scientists."

"About that," I said. "Is it normal for universities or research institutes to purchase these kinds of artifacts? I thought they would make arrangements to borrow them for study."

"In many cases they would. But Mrs. Lansing at Vicar and Blake persuaded me — persuaded us, I mean, on the council — that there was an unusual degree of interest in these artifacts, and that presented an opportunity to raise significant funds. She assured me that the final sale price would be unprecedented."

My phone began to vibrate in my jacket pocket. I reached in and pushed the button to send it to voice mail while Gregory went on.

"Do you want to know what the money from this sale would have done?" he asked. "It would have allowed us to expand our schools. And our library. A computer for every student in our school, and six more for the library. Internet access for anyone on the reservation who wants it. And more."

"You expected the jars to sell for that much?" I said.

"I had hopes," Gregory said. "Mrs. Lansing had knowledge of several institutional buyers who would pay very much indeed for access to the jars. Some who would even donate the jars back to us for our own museum once they had completed their studies. She could not guarantee anything, of course, but her auction house and its contacts presented an opportunity too good to pass up."

"Sounds like you had big plans. Did anyone disagree with them?"

Gregory took another drink of his water, then stared into it for what seemed like a minute.

"Of course there were differences of opinion on the council," he said finally. "But as I said, I can't really go into the details of our proceedings. Those are a tribal matter and I'm not going to share them to help an insurance company avoid a payout."

"There's more at stake here, Andrew," I said. "A man is dead, and it might be connected with that sale."

Gregory's hand jerked, spilling water into his lap. "What?"

"A man is dead. A former employee of the auction house was found dead three nights ago, and he may have been involved in the theft."

Gregory was silent, staring down into his lap. When he looked up, I spoke again. "I'm not asking you to tell me any details of your tribal council's deliberations. I'm just asking you to let me know if there is anyone else I should talk with."

"Shouldn't the police be investigating this?"

"They are," I said, "but I don't think they're looking in the right direction. Anything I find out I'll share with them. Discreetly, of course."

"I understand you used to be on their team."

"And I'm still on their side."

Gregory paused for a few seconds. "Wilson Warner," he said then. "*Former* tribal council member Wilson Warner was dead set against selling those jars."

Gregory cleared his throat and blinked tightly, apparently embarrassed by his choice of words.

"Anything else you can tell me about Mr. Warner that might be important?"

"He's not a happy man," Gregory said. "And he is powerfully old-fashioned in my view. I don't know how important that is, but there you have it."

"What reasons did he give for disagreeing with the sale of the jars?" I asked. "Any in particular?"

"Oh, just the very things you echoed a few minutes ago. The importance of the jars to heritage and ritual."

Gregory put down his glass and began gesturing forcefully as he went on. "He honestly believes that those are the original jars. The same jars that the Spanish saw five hundred years ago. Even though it is clear that those jars are nowhere near as old as

Warner says. Clearly we Lacalma made new jars once, probably many times. And we can do so again."

"That's odd," I said. "The paperwork filed with the auction house said that the jars were between four hundred and six hundred years old. A few minutes ago you mentioned five hundred years. Are you saying now that they've been re-made over and over?"

Gregory closed his eyes, and his mouth twisted briefly into a grimace.

"Never mind," he said after he opened his eyes again. "I'm sure that the affidavits are correct. My point is, our people still know how to make jars. If we sell these, we can make more."

"Though now there will be nothing but the insurance payments," I said.

Gregory glared at me for an instant; then he shook his head. He stood up and began to pace across the room. Gone was the friendly, charming businessman I'd met a few minutes ago. "That bastard. That bastard Wilson Warner called me a traitor to our people. He wishes he could turn back the clock a few centuries. Or just keep things the same. No change. Even if that means another generation of our boys and girls grow up without a chance to succeed in the modern world."

"I can see that would be hard to accept," I said. "I've got to say, though, you've been quite successful, haven't you?"

"I got lucky," Gregory said. "Very lucky. Met some kind people. Got a chance to get out. See some of the world. Get a real education."

He stopped pacing and sat down on the edge of his desk. "Yes, I'm successful. But I'm a fluke. But if I have my way, then for the kids we're raising today, my kind of success will be perfectly normal."

Gregory stared out the window for a long moment, then shook

his head briefly and turned back to me with the same broad smile I'd seen when we first met. "Well, Martin, that's a subject I hadn't intended to get into. But it's dear to me, so it should be no surprise."

I put down my glass and got up to leave. "Thanks again for your time, Andrew. And for your insights. This has been very helpful."

"You're quite welcome. I hope I was of some help. Especially considering that there's a death involved." Gregory held up a hand. "Not that I want to know more about that right now. I trust you and the police to do your jobs."

"I appreciate that."

"And I also trust that you will be discreet about our discussion?"

"Of course," I said. "But I will need to contact Wilson Warner. Any idea where I might reach him?"

"I believe he's working with some community group in Colorado Springs," Gregory said. "Some kind of theater. He talked about it incessantly, but I never paid much attention."

CHAPTER 15

As I made my way to my car, I took out my phone and checked it for messages. There were two. First was a voice mail from Mark Baxter.

"Martin? It's Mark Baxter. I heard about what happened with Fielding. Give me a —"

I tapped over to the next message. This one was from Patricia Moore. Patty was an ER nurse at Denver Health Medical Center, and she occasionally called me about a patient.

When I got to my car, I plugged in my phone and played Patty's voice mail through the stereo speakers.

"Martin? It's Patty at the hospital. We have someone in the ER that you might want to meet. He's been treated, and he's about to be discharged. He's harmless, but he's, I don't know. You know. He's someone you might want to meet. I'm on until six, and he agreed to meet you if you can come down to the hospital by then. Come down, or let me know if you can't. See you then. Bye."

Crap. Not what I needed to deal with at this time. But Patty had never called me on something that wasn't interesting, and there was nothing else I could do for Fielding that couldn't wait an hour.

Traffic downtown was rough as the evening rush built up. By the time I got to the hospital, the sun had dipped below the foothills. I parked not far from the ER walk-in and went in to look for Patty. I found her at the intake desk checking paperwork, her short red hair flipping to the front of her head as she bent over a stack of clipboards.

"Hi, Patty, got your voice mail."

"Marty!" Patty looked up from her work and stood. "Glad you could make it. Good timing too — things have quieted down for now."

She gestured with her head to the exam rooms across the hallway from the desk. "Let's go where we can talk for a minute."

I followed Patty into a small exam room. She shut the door behind us. "Guy came in this afternoon. Arthur Keith. Cops brought him in. He got in a fight at the Home Depot."

"Yes, and?"

Patty closed her eyes for a second. "I don't believe this crap. But anyway — witnesses said he and this other guy in the store had words, and then the other guy started hitting the man I've got here."

"Sounds like a bad day all around. But I'm guessing there's more, since you called me?"

"Yes, " Patty said. "I heard the injured guy talking to the police, and he said that all he had done is tell the guy to get a tumor looked at. He says he was trying to help."

"Tumor?"

Patty sighed and rolled her eyes. "A tumor on one of the other guy's testicles."

"Um, okay," I said. "Still seems like a simple case of jackassery."

"Yeah, no, the best part is coming," Patty said. "All the while this guy's been in the ER, he's been looking at other patients. A little creepy, you know? And after looking at each one for a minute, he announces what's wrong with them."

"So he's a wannabe doctor. Announces that a guy clutching his crooked arm has a fracture."

"If that's all it was I wouldn't have called you. For every patient I heard him diagnose, he was absolutely one hundred percent correct. Including a subdural hematoma, a case of microbial dysentery, and a case of early-stage lung cancer."

"Cancer?"

"Patient came in for a cracked rib, and his X-ray showed something suspicious they decide to refer to Oncology. Not a formal diagnosis, but my friend in Radiology tells me the film shows a tiny tumor. An hour before we even took the X-ray, our creepy guy was telling the broken-rib guy how lung cancer is really hard to treat, even if it's caught early."

I wasn't sure what to say about that.

"I'd give pretty good odds," Patty added, "that the guy from Home Depot really does have a tumor on his … you know."

"Maybe this is someone I should talk to. Did you guys get a psych consultation?"

"No. No sign of mental illness. Not like —" Patty stopped and sighed again. "He doesn't seem crazy. He's a total arrogant prick, but he seems sane enough."

Now it was my turn to sigh. My long day was getting longer. "Okay, introduce me to the arrogant prick."

We left the exam room and returned to the waiting area. It was a little less crowded than it had been when I came in. I felt a slight headache, like a little dizzy tickle between my eyes.

"You okay?" said Patty. She put a hand on my arm as I leaned against the doorway.

"I'm fine," I said. "Just had a rough couple of days. Sorry."

I straightened up and the headache receded.

In the corner of one row of chairs was a pudgy man with curly hair, fidgeting and looking down at his hands. He held a paper cup of coffee, and had a bandage over the top right side of his head.

"Is that him?" I asked Patty, nodding toward the man.

"What? No. Not him. Over there." Patty gestured toward a man on the other side of the waiting area. He looked tall and painfully thin, his skin stretched out over his face and neck. He held his head up and glanced about at the murmuring ER crowd and scowled at no one in particular. His face was dotted with a few bandages, and he had a dark bruise under his left eye.

Patty led me over to him. "Mr. Keith?" she said. "This is Martin Rodak, the friend I told you about."

"Finally," said Keith. He spoke with a bored, flat Californian accent. "I hope this was worth waiting around for."

"I hope so to," I said. "Mind if I sit down?"

Keith sighed. "Sure, if you have to."

I sat down in the empty seat next to him. As I did so, I again noticed the pudgy guy across the room, still sipping his coffee. The tickle in my head was still there, so I was glad to sit down. "So, Mr. Keith, I understand you have had quite a day."

Keith snorted. "Yeah. Quite a day. Beaten up at a hardware store, sitting around in a hospital, and listening to your droll commentary."

"Well, I won't bother you for too long. But I may be able to offer you some help."

"I don't think I need any help. Do I look like I need help?"

"Most people could use some kind of help," I said.

"Well, I'd definitely say you could use some help. Borderline hypertension, and fifteen ... no, eighteen percent blockage in two of your coronary arteries." Keith snorted again, laughing with a sound like air coming out of a bicycle tire. "You must eat crap every single day."

"Too many days. Thanks for the tip — I'll make an appointment to see my doctor."

"Yeah, a doctor. Good luck with that. Useless club full of ignorant assholes."

"You don't like doctors? Must make a day at the hospital even worse than it is for most people."

"Yes, it must," Keith said. "Doctors. Fine if you need some basic plumbing work, like on that heart of yours, or some tape and spackle for a simple trauma. But for diagnosis? For actually knowing what the hell is going on? Idiots. Idiots who act like they're intellectuals."

Keith had been growing louder and more agitated as he went on. Now he turned to me and leaned in toward my face. "You know that's why they kicked me out of medical school, don't you? Because I was smarter than all of them. Every one of them."

"I understand," I said. "None of them could do what you do."

"Not one of them." Keith seemed to relax a little, and sat back in the plastic chair. "It was ridiculous."

"And if you don't mind me asking, how do you do it? How do you know things like that guy having lung cancer? Or my blood pressure, for that matter?"

"It's obvious," Keith said. "I mean, I just, well, you just had to look at the guy. Or you. Jesus, isn't it obvious?"

He folded his arms across his chest. "If you're too stupid to see it for yourself, there's no way I can explain it."

"Okay, well, I appreciate your trying," I said.

Something caught my eye across the room. The pudgy guy with the coffee was still there, staring out the window. I didn't know why he kept distracting me. Did I know him from somewhere?

Keith had followed my gaze. "I wonder who beats the crap out of that guy."

"Yeah, I wonder," I said, mostly to myself. Then I shook my head and turned back to Keith. "So, Mr. Keith, if you don't mind my asking, what kind of work do you do?"

"Landscaping," he said. "Mostly overnight and early-morning work so I don't have to deal with people like this." As he spoke he glanced around the waiting room, his nose wrinkled.

"Well, if you would be interested in some other work — more interesting work, I suspect — I'd like to talk to you some more."

"What kind of work?" Keith kept his arms folded and gave me an exaggerated sideways look.

"I'll know that when the time comes," I said. "If the time comes. But someday I may be in need of someone who can do what you do. Someone smarter than a doctor."

Keith snorted, but the corner of his mouth curled up and stayed there. "The nurse said you're not a doctor, as if that weren't obvious. What are you, a lawyer?"

"Not exactly," I said. "I used to be, but that's not what I do now. Here." I handed him my card.

"'Martin Rodak Investigations,'" he read. "So you're a detective?"

"Pretty much. If you're game, get in touch with me at that email address or phone number. Leave me your contact info, and I'll put you on my list of consultants. Then if a job comes up that requires your talents, I'll be in touch."

Keith looked at the card for a few seconds more. "All right. What the hell? I'll think about it." He put the card in his shirt pocket.

"Thanks. It was good talking to you," I said as I stood up.

"Yeah, yeah," Keith said. "Just ease up on that heart, for Christ's sake."

I walked back to the nurses' station, where Patty was starting to gather her things. It was just about six, and her shift was ending.

"So, what do you think of him?" Patty said.

"You were right on all counts," I said. "Arrogant prick, remarkable ability. Don't know if we can help each other out, but we'll see. Thanks for calling me."

"No worries," Patty said as she lifted her tote bag onto her shoulder.

"One other question," I said. "Who is that guy by the window?"

Patty looked over to where I had indicated with a nod of my head. The pudgy, nervous guy was still sitting there. "Oh, him." She sighed and gave a small shake of her head. "He's a sad case," she continued in a lowered voice. She never seemed to mind violating patient confidentiality where I was concerned, but I guessed she would still rather not get caught at it.

"I'd swear he's a victim of domestic abuse," she said. "He's been here four times in the past six months. No broken bones, thank God, but lots of nasty injuries. Burns, cuts, lots of bruises and contusions. Today was bad — he took a blow to the face. Scratched up his cheek, scratched his eye, bruised something awful. Must have been hit hard. Lucky he didn't fracture the eye socket."

"So, what's his story? Have the police looked into it?"

"Yeah, I think so. We had a counselor talk to him the third time he was in here. A cop spoke with him today. He just blows them off. I guess some people don't want help."

"Maybe." Or maybe he needed a different kind of help.

"Why are you so interested in this guy, anyway?" she said.

"I don't know," I said. "Just a feeling. You think it's okay if I talk to him?"

"I don't see why not. He shouldn't still be hanging around here, anyway. We discharged him early this afternoon. If we were more crowded we would have had to kick him out hours ago."

"Maybe he likes your vending machine coffee."

That got a laugh from Patty. "Right. To hell with Starbucks. Anyway, I gotta go."

As she exited through the automatic doors, I turned back inside and went to introduce myself to the guy by the window. "Hi. I'm Martin. Mind if I sit down?"

The man looked up. His eyes were wide, but then they narrowed to slits. "No, sit wherever you want."

"Thanks." I took a seat on the plastic bucket chair near him, leaving an empty seat between us. His coffee was sitting on a low table in front of him.

"Quite a day, right?" I said.

The nervous guy said nothing.

"Sorry for bringing this up," I said, "but it looks like you took a good crack to the head. You in a fight?"

The man gave a sad chuckle. "Not exactly a fight."

"Oh. I've done some boxing, and I've seen a fist do just about that same kind of work."

"I've never been in a fight," the man said.

"Do you mind my asking what happened?" I said.

He gave a long sigh, then said, "I got hit by a door. Seriously. It sounds stupid, it sounds lame, and it is, but it's true."

"Okay."

"I already told the other cop, and the doctors."

"I'm not a cop, or a doctor."

I think he heard me, but now that he was on a roll, he kept on talking. "I'm thirty-two years old. I live alone, and I don't have a girlfriend or a boyfriend who hits me. I'm just clumsy. I got bad luck."

"I'm sorry to hear that," I said. "This kind of thing happen a lot?"

The man stopped talking and took a breath. "Yeah, kinda. Not as bad as today, usually. But I have a lot of accidents."

"That really is too bad. You have my sympathies."

"Yeah. Thanks."

"So, why are you hanging around a hospital, anyway? Looks like they patched you up a while ago."

"No reason," he said. Then he looked down toward his scuffed suede shoes. "At least, no reason that's not stupid."

"Try me. What's the story?"

"I think my house is haunted. It's out to get me." He looked up at me, like he was waiting for a laugh or an insult.

I kept my face straight and tried to look calm and concerned. "Tell me more about that."

"Things attack me," he said. "Seriously I mean it. Like the door this morning. I swear, it moved by itself. I was late to take out the garbage, I reached to open the door, and before I even touched it, *bam*. It opened by itself, right into my face."

"Wow," I said. "And this kind of thing has happened before?"

"Damn right it has. Pots and pans. Books from my bookshelf. I swear that last week my toothbrush flew out of the holder and hit me in the eye."

"Ouch."

The man reached for the paper coffee cup on the table in front of him. As he did, he was still looking at me.

When his hand was still inches away, the cup began sliding toward him. Nothing was touching it. It moved across the table, picking up speed, until it crashed into his hand and spilled coffee over his wrist.

"Ow! Shit, shit, shit! Ouch, damn!"

I grabbed a small stack of napkins from the table and handed them to him. He mopped up the coffee from himself and from the table, and examined his wrist.

"You okay?" I asked. "You need some ice or something?"

"No," he said. "It wasn't that hot. Just wet. And surprising."

He rammed the napkins into the now-empty cup and smacked the cup back down onto the table. "Goddamn it. You see what I mean? Bad luck. And not just at home. Everywhere. It's not my house that's haunted, it's me."

"I don't think it's bad luck," I said. "And I don't think you're haunted. But I think I might be able to help you."

"What?" The man's wary look returned. "Why would you want to help me, and how? And why am I talking to you, anyway? Who are you?"

"Like I said, my name is Martin. Martin Rodak."

I took a business card out of my notebook and handed it to him. When our fingers were inches apart the card leapt from my hand, slid through the air, and landed neatly in his. He didn't seem to notice anything unusual.

"Martin Rodak Investigations," he read. "You sound familiar." He looked up at me. "Have I seen you on TV? Like with those ghost hunter guys?"

I chuckled. "Not exactly. Nothing that exotic. But I have a friend who would be happy to talk to you. Might be able to help figure out what's going on."

"Like, why my house is haunted?"

"Yeah, sort of," I said. "To be honest I don't really think your house is haunted. But clearly there's something going on, and maybe my friend and I can help."

"I can't pay much," he said.

"I won't ask you to pay anything. By the way, what's your name?"

"Hugo. Hugo Farmer." He reached out his hand, and I shook it.

"So, Hugo, like I said, if we can help you, there won't be any charge."

"So, why are you looking to help me?"

"I like helping people," I said. "And before you think this is a scam, or that I'm trying to recruit you into some cult, I'll admit that there's something in it for me."

"Aha," said Hugo. "So, what's that?"

"My work. I never know who I'll need to deal with on any given case, or what I'll need done. All strictly legal, of course. I just find my work goes more smoothly the more friends I have."

Hugo thought about that. "I don't know if that sounds suspicious, or just sappy. But you seem okay. I'll think about it."

"That sounds fair," I said. "Tell you what. I'm not going to ask you to give your phone number to a stranger you met in a hospital. So if you want, you can reach me at the phone number or email address on that card. Leave your contact info, and I'll have that friend I mentioned get in touch with you."

Hugo looked at the card again, then back at me. "Okay. Like I said, I'll think about it."

"Thanks."

I stood up and help out my hand. "It was good meeting you, Hugo."

"Same here."

I left Hugo in the waiting room and went back out to my car. I wondered how long he would stay in there before going home.

Once I was in the car, I plugged in my phone and pulled up the number for Toni Scalda. Another of my gifted associates, though she hadn't joined me on a case in a while. When the phone stopped ringing, there was a brief pause and a light thump before she spoke, as if someone had tossed the phone to her.

"Hello?"

"Hi, Toni," I said. "It's Martin."

"Martin. What have you been up to?"

"Oh, you know. Things have —"

"Yes, I *do* know," Toni said. "And I am not making small talk. *What have you been up to?* And exactly what is Fielding doing in jail?"

"He's not in jail. But he's undergoing a mental health evaluation. Court-ordered. Anyway, I can't — but wait a minute, how did you know about that?"

"Mark Baxter told me. Melissa told Cindy and Cindy told Mark and Mark called and told me."

"Great," I said.

"So don't change the subject," Toni said. "Why on earth is Fielding sitting locked up somewhere, and why the hell are you not getting him out?"

"I am working on that, Toni. I am. I can't go into details, but it all has to do with a case. And the best way to get Fielding out is for me to work the case and get proof that he wasn't involved."

"Wasn't involved in what?" The more emotional Toni got, the more her old mother's Italian accent crept into her voice.

"Toni, I told you I can't go into detail. But you know I wouldn't let Fielding down, don't you?"

There was silence for a long moment.

"I guess not," Toni said. "Listen, Martin, I know you do right by Fielding. But you've got to admit that you get people into pretty crazy stuff. Not everybody can take that. Especially Fielding. He needs more looking after than most people."

"I know, Toni. And I'm doing all I can to get him back home."

"The home the cops turned inside out last night?"

"Yeah, and — goddamn it, how did you know about that?"

"Cindy," Toni said. "She's been keeping an eye on a map of Fielding's neighborhood."

"Okay, I'm sorry," I said.

We were both quiet for a few seconds.

"So, anyway," I said. "That's not why I called. There's

someone else we might need to help out. Someone I met today. You and he have a lot in common."

Toni laughed. "Are you trying to set me up with a guy?"

"Not until I find one good enough for you."

"So, who's this guy?"

"I just met him. He's kind of shaky, but he seems okay. He's got a talent, and it's freaking him out a little. Makes him accident-prone."

"Let me guess."

"Yeah," I said, "his gift seems a lot like yours."

Toni is able to move things without touching them. That's pretty unusual, even in the company I keep. Most psychic talents have to do with information, learning things or communicating in strange ways. Only a few can affect the physical world, and I can't begin to understand the science that might explain how that works.

"So, what do you want me to do?" she asked.

"Just talk to him," I said. "If he calls me, which he probably won't do, though I hope he does. I won't tell him anything about you, of course, without your permission. But if he gets in touch with me, I'll send you his number, and you can call him if you want to."

"Okay ..."

"I just figured it would be good for someone with that kind of ability to talk to someone else who has it. Just to let him know he's not the only ..."

"The only freak?" Toni said, her voice hard.

"No, no, no. I never said anything like that."

"Yeah, okay."

"It would help him to know that he's not the only person dealing with it. It would convince him he's not haunted."

"Haunted?" Toni said, and laughed again.

"Yeah. That's what he thinks. That he's haunted or his house is out to get him."

"Wow. This guy is really in the dark. All right, if he does call you, give me his number."

"You're a princess, Toni."

"And you're a half-assed knight. Later."

I punched the screen to hang up the phone, then sat back and sighed.

These poor sons of bitches.

Most people don't think about psychic talents. Or when they do think about them, they assume that it would be cool. Who wouldn't want the ability to do what no one else can do? Know what no one else knows? Wouldn't that make life better?

In truth, for most of them it makes life more complicated. Makes them angry, paranoid, or alone. Toni could be paranoid, but she was reasonably well-adjusted now that her kleptomania was under control. But for every one like her, or Melissa, or Mark, there are dozens of people like Fielding, or Hugo Farmer, or Cindy. Sweet old Cindy, who hasn't been out of her apartment in seventeen years. Doesn't want to leave her maps. Doesn't want to miss anything.

CHAPTER 16

After the hospital I went home and pulled a pizza from the freezer while I did a little digging online. As the pizza was heating I thought about Arthur Keith and what he had said about my heart. Still, the pizza tasted damn good.

I found a website for the collectibles shop in Colorado Springs that Duds had mentioned. Then I sent a text to a friend who was still in the Denver DA's office working property crime cases. He confirmed that the shop was owned by a suspected fence and launderer named Johnny Tom.

I also Googled around until I found some information about a Native American community theater group, also in the Springs. The Second People Theater Company didn't have a website of their own, just a domain name that was parked at a cheap web company with a "coming soon" page. But I found a review from three months back about a performance by the group. The company was made up of young people of indigenous heritage, and the play had been written and directed by the group's organizer, Wilson Warner.

Looked like a trip to the Springs might be worthwhile. I'd

have a shot at getting a line on the Fenn sculpture, and possibly some more information about those Lacalma jars.

The story around the jars kept getting more sketchy. Andrew Gregory seemed all fired up to sell them, but he hadn't kept his story straight about how old they were. Maybe they weren't so historical or authentic after all?

I hoped Wilson Warner could help shed light on that. But first I needed to see Fielding. I still had not been able to give him his book, or anything else. I set my alarm for early in the morning and went to sleep.

AT 7:00 a.m. I crammed some coffee through my French press and dumped the results into an old mug. At 7:10 I called Liz Duncan's direct office line. She picked up, just as I knew she would.

"Thiz iz Liz," she said.

"Hi, Liz. Martin."

"Marty. If you'da gotten up this early when you were a prosecutor, you might have beat me."

"Yeah," I said. "Some lessons are learned too late. So, how is Fielding? What can you tell me?"

"I can tell you he's hanging tough through a bad situation," Liz said. Then she sighed into the phone. "He's still at Causeway House, and I made a deal for him to stay there for up to one month's treatment under voluntary commitment."

"Stay there?" I said. "For a month? Damn it, Liz, you're supposed to be trying to get him out."

"I know. And I'm working on that. But if I can't manage to get him freed before the psych hold period is up, he can either stay at Causeway or go back to jail. You tell me, what would be better for Fielding? Sleeping in the detention center downtown or in a five-year-old psychiatric facility built on what used to be a beet field?"

I didn't have to think about that for very long. "You're right, Liz. He's better off than he would be in jail. But we still need to get him out of there."

"I know. Like I said, I'm working on that. But, Martin, something else. Fielding caused a bit of a stir when they first admitted him to Causeway House. You can imagine. So now ..."

"What?"

"He's being medicated. Just to keep him calm. They're still trying to zero in on something specific to his condition."

"Goddamn it," I said, "that's not what he needs. He —"

"Well, don't blame me!" Liz interrupted. "It's not like I want him there. I'm just telling you how things are right now."

I took a deep breath. "You're right. I'm sorry."

"Besides," Liz said, speaking more gently, "are you sure that's not what he needs? I know this may not be the best way for him to receive care, but are you sure medication won't help?"

"I don't know. He went through a lot of that that when he was younger."

We were both silent for a moment.

"I don't think there's anything we can do about the medication at this point," Liz said. "But I think I can get you in to see him. Can you be at Causeway House at noon?"

"Absolutely," I said.

I hung up the phone and finished getting dressed. Then I made a few more phone calls. One call was to the University of Colorado, trying to get in touch with Karen Poole's old boyfriend Roger. I learned he was traveling out of the country, two weeks into a two-month leave.

Out of the country. And he had left around the same time as

the Vicar and Blake heist. I put a few extra lines under that in my notebook.

———————

ON THE WAY to Causeway House I thought more about Fielding.

I first met Fielding when I was in my third year of law school. I was working at a university legal clinic set up to help people with mental illness who found themselves caught up in the legal system. Fielding was in his fifties, and had already been caught up a hell of a lot.

When Fielding was twenty he was living with his grandmother in her house in the Harvey Park neighborhood. His parents had died years before. His grandmother was very protective, especially since he had been diagnosed with a mental disability — on the spectrum, as they called it later — from the time he was in elementary school. He was reasonably high functioning, but not very good with people.

Fielding's social worker had a very unpleasant surprise one afternoon when she stopped by to check on him. His grandmother had died nearly a week earlier. Fielding had not called anyone. In fact he didn't seem to understand when the social worker tried to explain to him that his grandmother was dead. He insisted that he been speaking with her just a few minutes earlier. He said that he knew his grandmother wasn't very happy, that something was bothering her, but it was ridiculous to say that she was dead or gone away somewhere. She was right here, he insisted. Why was everyone acting so strange?

Naturally Fielding was suspect. Not guilty, perhaps, by reason of mental incapacity, but the idea of a mentally ill young man staying in a house with his grandmother's dead body while denying that she was even dead painted a pretty clear picture.

Unfortunately for that theory, but fortunately for Fielding, the autopsy revealed that his grandmother had died of natural causes. As for his ongoing conversations with her, they were written off in light of his psychiatric history.

For the next few years Fielding was in and out of treatment, mostly with doctors eager to figure out just how much is wrong with someone who insists that he speaks with dead people. And he did continue to insist on that, especially in the hospitals they kept bringing him to.

Eventually the doctors decided they'd had enough of him. They declared him adequately functioning and not harmful, and turned him loose.

He tried to make it on his own for a number of years, getting into trouble from time to time as he tried to navigate the world in which half of the people he could talk to insisted that the other half were in his imagination. Finally a dispute with his landlord turned into a set of misdemeanor charges, and the potential for dropping him back into the criminal justice system. That's when he was put in touch with our legal clinic.

I remember meeting him for the first time. Something about him seemed different. Not just different in the way that most of the clinic's clients were "different." With Fielding there was something else, something that caught my attention. He was frustrating to work with at first, a guaranteed headache every session, but I was happy that the clinic was able to help him. The headaches eventually diminished, but the weird feeling that I got from Fielding never quite did.

We managed to help him avoid the criminal charges, and even straighten out the dispute with his landlord with the help of the school's housing-assistance clinic.

The next time I ran into Fielding was six years later, when Patty called from the hospital to tell me about a strange patient they had in the ER. He had been knocked down by a bicycle, but after they had patched him up he began talking about fatality cases that had come through the hospital years earlier. He knew some rather gruesome but remarkably accurate details. As soon as I got to the hospital, I recognized Fielding's short, graying hair and his lined, nervous face. And he recognized me as well. We chatted for a while, and when he was discharged I offered him a ride home.

As we drove he started asking me about the person following me. A young man whom Fielding said had been with me all day. He started describing the man, and it turned out he was describing the victim of a homicide for which I'd been helping develop a case. The same killing for which the police and my boss liked Harold Dudsen. But I wasn't convinced that a business-minded fence like Duds would be involved in the drugs-for-stolen-cars trade that had led to a murder in Wash Park.

Fielding backed me up on that. He said my invisible companion gave a good description of the man who had killed him. He was about fifteen years younger and eighty pounds heavier than Duds, and was a car thief and runner for an organization based in Albuquerque. That convinced me once and for all not to go after Duds for the murder, and eventually the big guy from Albuquerque was picked up and cut a plea deal by naming his bosses in the operation.

But by that time the damage to my job was done. Refusing to drop the hammer on Duds had pretty much sealed the fate of my never-promising career as a prosecutor. I was out less than a year later. But Fielding and I stayed in touch, and his knack for talking with dead people turned out to be awfully useful. Despite the headaches he always brought.

CAUSEWAY HOUSE WAS a cluster of buildings just off South Santa Fe Drive. It looked like an overgrown chain hotel, two broad three-story units with peaked roofs and homey architecture but a flat, spooky sameness.

The effect continued when I entered the lobby of Building 2, the unit with added security approved by the state courts. It was a like a Hampton Inn from a parallel world, with a guard booth of shatterproof glass next to the reception desk and heavy electronic locks on every door.

I got there around eleven forty-five. The guards thoroughly checked the book I'd brought for Fielding, and made a call to confirm that I had permission to give it to him. That took about five minutes. So I kicked around the lobby for another ten minutes, smiling at the polite staff members and reading a Jack Reacher novel on my phone. At precisely noon I heard a buzzer and a heavy door somewhere down the hall.

A young woman in a pink blazer left the reception desk and led me down the hallway to a small conference room with pale green walls and too much light. A second door at the back of the room led to some other passage deeper in the facility, and next to the door stood a beefy orderly in green and white scrubs. The orderly showed no sign that he intended to leave.

Seated at the small table in the middle of the room was Fielding. He wore a blue track suit with the Causeway House logo on the breast. On his thin left wrist was a plastic hospital ID bracelet. It took him a moment to notice me. He looked up slowly, and his mouth turned from a lazy frown to a straight line. If that was a smile, it was a small one even for him.

"Martin," he said. "You came to see me."

"As soon as I could," I said. I sat down in the plastic chair across the table from Fielding. "How you holding up?"

Fielding sighed. "It's not good, Martin." His eyes drifted

down to the table again "This isn't a good place for me. There are three of them here. Sad. A little angry."

So much for Liz's hope for no ghosts. I wondered if they were workers from the old beet farm, or recent Causeway patients.

"We're doing everything we can to get you out of here," I said.

"I know, Martin." Fielding stopped to cough, then continued. "They let me see Ms. Duncan yesterday. She said she's moving. She's ... no, she's making a motion. Filing a motion. With the court. To get me out."

Fielding slumped a little. The string of words seemed to have worn him out.

"Are they treating you okay?" I asked.

"I suppose. I don't like it here. There are doctors. I think they mean well. But they're so busy. And doctors never understand me."

"I'm sure they do mean well. But we'll get you back home."

"The first day was terrible. That was the worst. So sad and so angry. Once they knew I could hear them, they wouldn't stop talking to me. Yelling at me. All the time."

"I'm sorry," I said. My right hand hurt. I found that I'd been making my fist tighter and tighter as Fielding spoke. "And how is it now?"

"Better. Maybe. I don't know. I guess it's better."

He sighed again. "The doctors started giving me something. Some medicine. I can still hear them, the ..." Fielding glanced at the orderly, who seemed not to be listening. "The other ones," Fielding said more quietly. "I can still hear them, but they don't seem to notice me. They don't care about me anymore. So they leave me alone.

"But the thing is," he continued, "I don't notice me anymore either. I don't notice anything. I'm just tired all the time. And bored."

"Well, I brought you something. Maybe it will help." I put the book, yet another copy of *Robinson Crusoe*, on the table in front of Fielding.

"It's not one of yours," I said, "but I think you'll like it. I read this one in school." It had taken a half hour of rummaging in my basement to find it.

Fielding pulled the book across the table toward him, but never really looked at it. "Thank you, Martin." He thumbed lazily at the first couple of pages of the book, then slid it aside and yawned.

"So, Fielding," I said, "like I said, we're doing everything we can to get you out of here. Liz is working on the judge, and I'm working to find out what really happened at the auction house."

"I know," Fielding said. "Liz told me."

"Did she tell you about what the police found at your place?"

"Yes. She did. She —" Fielding suddenly sat up as if he had been shocked. "Martin! Liz told me that you'd been hurt! At my house! Are you okay? What happened?"

"I'm okay. Just a smack on the head. I'm sorry I wasn't able to stop the guys who broke in."

Fielding slumped back in his chair, just as suddenly as he had sat up. He looked exhausted. "That's all right," me mumbled. "I was just worried. Sorry I forgot to ask before."

"Never mind that," I said. "I just need to know — do you remember anything else about your conversation with Joseph? At the old Vicar basement?"

Fielding closed his eyes for a long moment. "No."

"Nothing about who killed him?"

"No," Fielding said again. "He said he didn't know who killed him."

"He was stabbed from the front," I said. "Were they masked?"

"He said it was dark, and they surprised him He couldn't see them. They stabbed him after he couldn't answer their questions."

"What questions? It had to have been the men he worked with to rob the auction house, right?"

"I don't know!" Fielding said. "He just said he didn't know who killed him."

"All right," I said. "And you're sure you never met Joseph before ... before you talked to him in that basement? Before we started this case?"

"I'm sure. I'd remember if I did. I guess. I never met him."

"All right. So, do you have any idea what those guys might have been looking for at your place?"

"The ... the thing, I guess. The jar. I guess? If they knew I had it?"

"I don't think they'd have known," I said. "Only you, me, Liz, and the cops know that."

"And Joseph," Fielding said.

"And Joseph," I agreed. "But I doubt they talked to him."

Fielding leaned forward across the table, suddenly enough that the orderly snapped his attention to him. Fielding coughed, then almost growled at me. "Those were not my papers. The ones Liz told me about. The ones the police found. They were not mine! I never saw them. Never knew those people."

"I know. They were in the new book I gave you just this week."

"I wouldn't stuff things into a book."

"So ...," I said. "Maybe they weren't there to find anything. Or if they were, they wanted to frame you as well. To plant those letters, set you up for the burglary at the auction house."

"If you say so," Fielding said as he slumped back in his seat.

"That means that someone involved in the robbery is still keeping track of all this, and is still involved enough to want to set you up."

"I see." Fielding yawned again.

"So I've got to go," I said. "This means I'm on the right track. If I find out who robbed Vicar and Blake, I find out who set you up, and who killed Joseph Vargas."

I stood up and nodded to the guard, then looked back at Fielding. He looked almost asleep.

"I'll come back to see you as soon as I can," I said.

CHAPTER 17

The orderly got Fielding to his feet and led him back through the door on his side of the table, into an antiseptic hallway. The woman from the front desk returned to usher me out the way I had come in.

I drove out of the parking lot and wheeled my way south on Santa Fe. Near Castle Rock I picked up I-25. The midday traffic was light, and the miles ticked by. Soon I was past Castle Rock, then halfway to Colorado Springs.

I could try to blame it on having been pushed down Fielding's front steps, but how could I have not thought before about the letters and the book at his place? Those letters were weeks old, and were supposedly hidden. So they had no business being in a book that I had given to Fielding just a few days ago.

It was enough to convince me of Fielding's innocence — not that I'd had any doubts — but it would not be enough for Carson. And even if Fielding was not charged with the Vicar heist, or with Vargas's murder, if we didn't get him out of custody and away from those well-meaning doctors soon, it might not matter.

Someone who had just met Fielding recently might not recognize how he had changed in just two days of jail and "treatment." I did recognize Fielding that morning. But it was a Fielding from a low time that I'd hoped he'd been able to leave behind him.

It was closing in on three o'clock when I reached Colorado Springs. Driving into the Springs always seemed to me like driving into an airport. Some might think that's the influence of the Air Force Academy. But really it was because the past fifteen years of highway upgrades had turned that stretch of I-25 into a long series of wide, sweeping ramps and curves, the kind of roadway that ought to lead to big parking lots and modern concrete terminal buildings. Usually the highway was about all I saw of the Springs as I drove straight through on my way to Santa Fe or Albuquerque. Today, though, I took an exit a little way past the city line and started listening to my GPS as it guided me toward Johnny Tom's shop.

I found it on a corner in an old part of town, next to a trendy-looking restaurant that used to be a bank. The shop was fancier than I had expected. It looked more like a mid-range jeweler's than a typical hangout for the cards-and-comics crowd.

I checked my look in the mirror. Straightened my hair and snugged my tie to my collar. Then I left the Clubman and went into the shop.

The place smelled like paper, tobacco, and a hint of orange oil furniture polish. I wished my house had a study just like it. It was divided into three roughly equal sections: one for comics, one for trading cards, and one for other collectibles. The store's only customer besides me was in that last section, peering through the glass front of a display case to inspect a set of *Planet of the Apes* statuettes. Behind the counter at the front were a portly kid with close-cropped red hair and an older, taller Asian man wearing a red turtleneck under a sharp blue cardigan.

I ambled back to the trading card section, wanting to watch and listen for a little while before I approached anyone. The store had a surprisingly extensive stock of hockey cards, including some of my favorite Philadelphia Flyers players. I got so engrossed in the selection that I nearly missed it when the guys behind the counter started talking.

"I didn't take a lunch yesterday, Johnny," the younger one said.

"Isn't that something?" said the older man. There was a bit of East Texas in his accent.

"So you're gonna pay me for the extra half hour, right?" the kid said.

"Seems peculiar that you forget to take your lunch, so I have to pay you more money." Johnny spoke slowly, as if he'd be more interested in a nap than in having this conversation.

"C'mon, Johnny. I worked all that extra time instead of going out to eat my lunch. Fair is fair."

"Yeah, fair is fair. That doesn't mean that I'm fair." Johnny paused for a second, then gave the kid a lopsided smile. "We'll see about it on payday, awright?"

The kid smiled. "Thanks, Johnny."

As they finished their conversation I made my way toward the front of the store.

"Anything I can help you with?" Johnny asked.

"As a matter of fact, there is," I said. "You've got a graded Bobby Clarke MVP card back in the hockey section. I'd be interested in a closer look. And a price, if I like the looks of it."

Johnny gave me a nod and a thin smile. He took a key with a paper tag from a drawer full of little cubbies and handed it to the kid. "Stan, go get the card for this gentleman," he said. "Please."

Stan took the key and shuffled out from behind the counter toward the display case.

"You've got a nice shop here," I said to Johnny. "I don't make it to the Springs too often, but I made the trip thanks to a suggestion from a friend of mine in Boulder."

"I'm pleased to hear that," Johnny said. "Must be a good customer of mine."

"Oh, I suspect he is," I said. I knew Duds was never a customer here, and I wasn't about to give Duds's name anyway, but seeing how precious the shop looked, I guessed Johnny Tom had at least a few regular customers from Boulder.

"I understand you sometimes deal in artwork a little more ... substantial, than comics and trading cards," I said.

Johnny's eyes narrowed a couple of millimeters, but his smile remained friendly. "Is that right? Well, as you can see we also have an extensive stock of collectibles. Figures, posters. Replica movie props. A fine selection of items, some of them quite hard to come by."

"Oh, it does look like a nice collection. But I'm really asking for my employer. He's a baseball fan. Interested in mint rookie cards."

That was the code Duds had given me. "Mint rookie cards" meant an interest in buying art, no questions asked. "Signed lobby cards" meant an interest in selling.

"Here." I took out my notebook, tore a perforated page from the back, and wrote down the number of my burner, a prepaid flip phone I keep in my car's glove box. "You can reach me at this number." I handed the paper to Johnny.

Stan suddenly appeared at Johnny's side. He must have been hanging back, waiting for a lull in our conversation. "Here's that card, sir," he said, placing on the counter a small lucite case containing a Topps hockey card from 1975.

I picked it up carefully and examined it, front and back. "Not bad." I looked up at Johnny Tom and smiled. "My employer may be one for fine art, but this is more my style. How much?"

"Well," Johnny said, "the card is not an out-and-out rarity, but the signature and the condition raise the value. I could part with that for ninety."

I pretended to consider for another moment. "That seems reasonable."

I took some cash out of my pocket and peeled six fifties. I tried to keep from wincing as I did it, and hoped it would be enough to get Tom's attention.

"I appreciate the conversation," I said as I passed him the bills. "Are you sure there's nothing else for us to talk about?"

Johnny Tom looked at the bills, and the curved smirk on his face straightened out a bit. He looked me up and down as if seeing me for the first time. When his gaze reached my eyes he stared into them for a moment. I held his gaze and raised one eyebrow.

He sighed and nodded slightly. "Stan, watch the front for a few minutes. I need to talk to this customer in the back."

Stan straightened up and stepped toward the counter. "You got it, Johnny."

Tom came out from behind the counter and led me through the collectibles section, past a glass case full of nickel-plated spaceship models, to a wooden door bearing a neat framed sign that said "Staff Only, Please." He opened the door and gestured to invite me through.

The door led to a narrow paneled hallway. Off to the left was an office with its door ajar, and at the end of the hallway I could see daylight.

"Through there, up ahead," Tom said.

I didn't feel great about walking down a dim corridor with a reputed criminal right behind me. I'd have liked my odds in a straight-up fight, but my fifty-pound advantage wouldn't mean much against a weapon at my back in close quarters. But Johnny Tom was a fence, not a killer or a strong-arm artist, and I hadn't given him any reason to overreact, so I went along.

I did get a surprise when I got to the end of the hallway. I found a heavy door with narrow diamond-shaped panes of frosted glass near the top, and when I opened it I found myself in a small square garden.

It was surrounded by tall, solid wooden fences that screened it from the back lots of the surrounding shops, and green hedges that hid most of the fencing up to a height of five or six feet. The rest of the space was a meandering web of river rock, mossy patches, ornamental plants, and pale stone pavers, leading to an octagonal patio made up of more paving stones. A small painted wrought-iron table and chairs sat at one end of the patio.

Johnny Tom stepped around me and gestured toward the table. "Please, have a seat." His expression suggested a hint of pride at this little oasis behind his hobby shop.

I went to the table and took a seat in one of the narrow metal chairs. From somewhere I could hear the gurgling of a small fountain.

Johnny Tom took another chair near the table, and as he sat down he pulled from his pocket a thin black electronic cigarette. He clicked a tiny button, and a little blue light flicked on at its tip. The device made a faint whistling noise when he took a drag.

"So who sent you to me?" he said.

It seemed the code words Duds provided had put me on the right track with Johnny Tom.

"I promised our common associate that I would be discreet," I said. "But I was told you're a good man to do business with."

"That's not an answer."

I sighed and glanced around at the hedges, a little nervous about the enclosed space even though we were outdoors. Then I shrugged. "Lou Franz. Like I said, he had good things to say about you. Said if anyone needed to move art in or out of Colorado, you'd know about it."

"I suppose you telling me who you work for is out of the question," Tom said.

I smiled and gave a slight nod. "Lou said you were discreet, but I still can't tell you that. I represent a collector who appreciates art, but who prefers to let me handle the acquisitions. And who doesn't want too much information about the process."

Tom nodded again and took another pull on his plastic cigarette. It gave off a faint smell like warm oil and spices, but the odor was quickly lost in the fragrance of the shrubs around us. "Well, if this employer of yours is interested in paintings, I have a line on something currently available in Las Vegas that I can tell you about."

"Actually my employer is more interested in sculpture," I said. "Twentieth-century American West, specifically."

Tom rolled his eyes. "What, he wants a goddamn Remington?"

"No, he wants a goddamn Fenn."

Tom stared at me for a moment, and then chuckled and shook his head. "So your employer reads the papers. That's rich. A piece of art gets stolen and Lou sends you to me while the stuff is still warm. Sounds like Lou."

Tom sucked on his electric cigarette again, then took it out of his mouth and looked at it with a sneer of displeasure. He clicked the switch, dousing the blue light, and slipped it away into his pocket. Then he leaned over the table toward me. "Sorry to disappoint, but I don't have anything to do with that Fenn that got stolen."

"Oh, I'm not suggesting you did," I said. "It's just I was told that if such a piece were being handled somewhere in Colorado, or being moved in or out of the state, you'd know about it."

Tom smiled again and sat upright, then swept his hands

outward and gave a little bow of false humility. "What can I say? Our friend Lou is right. I would know about it. It's bad for business if I don't."

My play on Tom's obvious vanity was well placed, but I still wasn't getting any information.

"So, what do you hear?" I asked.

"Nothing," Tom said. "Not a word."

"Sounds pretty odd to me."

Tom frowned. "It is odd. In the two weeks since the piece was grabbed, there's been no sign of it on the market. Now, if someone has a discreet buyer all lined up beforehand, maybe they can keep things down low enough that even I won't hear about it. Maybe. But that job was sloppy. Done by lucky amateurs. Not anyone professional enough to have a buyer lined up before going in. And not anyone professional enough to sit on a piece like that while it cools off."

"If they were amateurs, maybe they didn't have the right contacts to move the piece?" I suggested.

Tom shrugged. "Maybe. Lots of things are possible. All I know is that someone stole a Michael Fenn, and so far they're not trying to sell it."

BACK IN THE car I put my expensive hockey card in the glove box next to my burner phone, then checked my notebook for the address of the Second People Theater Company. The GPS app on my phone told me it was on the south side of town.

A while later I pulled onto the correct block on Fountain Boulevard and found a squat whitewashed building between a trophy company and a wholesaler of Asian foods. It had a twelve-car parking lot in front, where a tall stepladder took up two spaces between a Toyota Corolla and a well-worn Chevy truck. At the top of the stepladder was a lean man with a gray-white ponytail, wrestling with the bulb in a giant lamp mounted high on the structure. He wore faded, loose-fitting blue jeans and a bright red shirt.

I pulled into one of the remaining spots at the far end of the small lot, then got out and walked over toward the ladder. I didn't say anything, as I didn't want to distract the man as he wobbled at the top. He finished unscrewing the large bulb from the lamp and deftly removed a fresh one from the big cardboard box balanced next to him. When he swapped the burned-out bulb into the box, a few white packing peanuts escaped and flew off on the breeze.

As he packed away the old bulb, he glanced down and noticed me watching him from the parking lot.

"What do you want?" he called down.

"I'm looking for a Wilson Warner," I said, raising my voice to reach him on his perch near the roof.

"What do you want with Wilson Warner?" he said.

"I just want to ask him a few questions."

The man sighed. "All right. He'll talk to you as soon as he gets down from this fucking ladder."

The man turned back to his work. He screwed the new bulb into the lamp, gripped the box under his right arm, and came down the ladder in a nimble two-footed, one-handed scramble.

At the bottom he shifted the box to his left arm and shook the hand that I offered.

"I take it you're Warner?" I said.

"Right. And who are you? No, wait a minute. Let me get this away. Here."

He handed me the box with the dead softball-sized light-bulb, then turned to the stepladder. He lowered the center extension, folded the ladder, and swung it up to balance on his shoulder. With the ladder out of the way, I noticed the mural that would be illuminated by the new lightbulb after sunset. It was a pastel landscape incorporating stylized petroglyph images and the words "Second People."

"Here, this way." Warner led me around a corner from the little parking lot and through glass double doors into the front of his little theater. The lobby was about the size of a large elevator. The walls were covered in thin rec-room paneling, on which hung posters for two plays: one that had run a few months ago, and the one that was scheduled to open in two weeks. A counter that looked more like a tiny bar completed the 1974-finished-basement look.

I followed Warner around the corner, past small doors labeled "Men" and "Ladies," to a utility closet at the end of the narrow hall. He managed the long ladder with ease, raising and lowering one end or another to navigate the small space and tight corners while keeping the thing balanced lightly on his shoulder. I dodged the ladder when he backed up to pull the closet door open. He slid the ladder into a perfectly sized space behind one long shelf unit, then took the cardboard box from me and tucked it onto a shelf labeled "Recycling."

Finally he turned back to me. "So, Mr. ..."

"Rodak," I said.

"Rodak," Warner repeated. "So, what are these questions you want to ask me? You're not a reporter here to give some publicity to our play, are you?"

"No, I'm not," I said. "I want to ask you about —"

I stopped because Warner suddenly picked his head up and looked away, as if he had heard something, or remembered something. "Wait a second," he said.

He walked away, and I followed him back to the tiny lobby and through another set of double doors into the auditorium.

The space was hardly big enough to call an auditorium. The room was a plain black box, with about a hundred seats arranged on risers, looking toward a square stage of black-painted plywood. A small empty area separated the front row of seats from the stage. There were no curtains, except for the heavy black drape that we pushed through as we came in from the lobby.

Up on the stage were four young people in jeans and T-shirts. One girl wore a Rockies cap. On the house floor in front of the stage was another young man, a little rounder than the kids on the stage, holding a clipboard.

"Don't bother lying to me," said the girl in the cap. She turned her back to the rest of the group and moved a few steps across the stage. "I know that you won't be coming back. You tell me you will, but that's to make yourself feel better. It's not for me." She lowered her head and rubbed at a corner of her eye with one palm.

"That's good, Ronnie," the boy with the clipboard said. "But you need to move farther stage left, more toward the corner. That way when Bob follows you the two of you will be more separated from the others."

The girl opened her eyes and looked at the stage floor around her. "Oh. Okay," she said.

"Okay my ass," said Warner, stalking up to the front of the stage. He glared at the kid with the clipboard. "What do you mean, 'Good?' Never mind where she's standing. It's about the scene." Then he turned back to the girl. "Ronnie, you're only getting part of this scene. Maria High Bird is both sad and pissed off. You've got the sad part down, but not the pissed-off part. Just think about what Sam is doing to Maria here! How he's treating her! Wouldn't you be pissed off?"

The girl took that in, then nodded. "I think I know what you mean, Wilson."

"Good. And you," Warner continued, turning back toward the clipboard kid, "stop focusing only on the small stuff."

"I will, Wilson," the kid said.

Warner softened his expression a little. "Remember, Taylor, if you want to direct, your job is to think about the big picture. The play, the whole thing, as it will get to the audience. Their job" — he pointed toward the four actors — "is to make their characters real. Your job is to make sure all those characters and all that realness come together to build something bigger. But if they don't have the realness, you need to help them find it."

Warner clapped his hands once. It was a surprisingly big sound, and it echoed in the small space. "Okay, you kids keep at it," he said. "Two weeks to go. Make them count."

Warner led me out of the auditorium and back into the lobby, then through a door behind the counter to a small office. It contained a short, dented filing cabinet and a card table where a desk might have been. The table was flanked by two folding chairs. An oscillating fan hummed on top of the filing cabinet, and the table and parts of the floor were covered with stacks of paper, each topped with a stone or a piece of brick to defend against the fan's breeze. Warner sat down in one of the folding chairs and nodded me toward the other one.

"So, Mr. ..."

"Rodak," I told him again. "Martin Rodak."

I took a business card from my notebook and handed it to him. He studied it for a minute, then looked up at me.

"'Investigations,'" he read. "So you're some kind of detective?"

"Yes," I said. "Mainly I help people find things."

"I see. So, what do you need me for? I don't think I've lost anything lately. Except a few nights' sleep wondering if this play is ever going to come together."

"I'm looking into the theft of some objects that I think you have an interest in, and I'm hoping that you might be able to give me some information about them."

"Theft of some objects …" Warner trailed off in thought for a moment, then looked up sharply. "You're talking about the peace jars."

"That's right. Three jars consigned for sale by your tribe were among several items stolen from the Vicar and Blake Auction House in Denver. I'm looking for information on all of the stolen items. I'm hoping to learn something that might tell me who would be interested in them. Which might lead me to the people who stole them."

Warner sat back, rocking his folding chair onto its hind legs. "So you work for the insurance company. Trying to save white men the money they'd have to pay for losing and ruining a piece of our history."

"I was hired to look into the theft, that's right," I said. "But my greatest hope is to find the stolen items, including the Lacalma jars — peace jars, you called them? — intact and in good condition. In which case the tribe could have them back, or choose to go ahead with the sale, whatever your council decides."

Warner leaned forward, bringing the front legs of his chair down with a tinny thud. He planted an elbow on the card table and jabbed a finger in my direction as he spoke. "I didn't decide to sell those jars. I wouldn't even say the council decided anything. A few ambitious men had a big idea for themselves and rammed it through the council process. Not a council decision. Just a lot of power politics."

"So you were not happy with the decision to sell," I said.

Warner gave a short laugh. "I think it was one of the worst damn decisions ever made for the nation. And was on that council for a long time. Saw some pretty bad decisions."

"So you think the jars should be back with the Lacalma."

"You want suspects? You want somebody who would have wanted those jars back?" Warner held his arms out in front of him, wrists crossed. "Then I'm your guy. Take me in, book me. I sure as hell didn't want them sold."

For once there was no humor in Warner's voice or manner, but I couldn't help but chuckle.

"I'm not a cop, Mr. Warner," I said, "and I'm not taking anyone in anywhere. I'm not even suggesting that you stole the jars."

Warner put his arms down. "And why not?" He sat up straighter in his chair, his chin raised. "Are you saying I wouldn't make a dramatic gesture for the sake of my people?"

"I'm sure you are very capable of dramatic gestures," I said. "But you seem pretty busy with the kids and the theater here. And I bet that probably provides you with an alibi for a crime committed in Denver."

"People like me here," Warner said. "They might lie to protect me."

I thought about that for a few seconds. "I suppose they might. But I don't think you'd steal a heavy cowboy sculpture and a bunch of camera equipment if you were just interested in getting back those jars."

"Maybe I stole them to just to muddy the waters, throw the police off the scent."

I smiled again at that. "Maybe you did. You seem smart enough to have planned this all out. You know, I have friends at the Denver DA's office. I could put in a word, try to get them to charge you for the robbery. You seem pretty eager to prove that you did it."

Warner sat back and laughed. "Fuck that. I'm not going to prison for those things. Truth is, I didn't do it. And I do have an alibi if you want one, mister not-a-cop."

He fell silent for a moment, looking down at the table. "I can't say I was sorry to hear that that auction house isn't going to be able to sell those jars. But trying to get them back wouldn't make any sense."

"Why not?"

"Because they're not our jars anymore. Once they got into the white man's system of buying and selling, they were no longer special. They no longer had their power."

"They lost their magic?"

"Maybe. Probably not. But magic, power, whatever you want to call it, that's not the point. Bottom line is, they weren't ours anymore. They were yours."

"What was special about them?" I asked. "What kind of ... of magic did they have?"

"Nothing I can explain to you," Warner said. "Nothing I really understand myself. And don't get me wrong, I'm not talking about some miracle show. I'm talking about the way in which they were special to my people. The way they had been special for hundreds of years."

Warner turned and rummaged through a stack of papers on top of the file cabinet behind him until he produced a red soft-cover notebook with his name written on the front. He thumbed through the book and then turned it over to show me a sketch, a drawing of the three jars. The way he had drawn them, they looked almost alive, like a family clustered together for a portrait. They seemed to glow faintly from the way he had depicted the light around them.

"They were called peace jars," he said. "Peace as in quiet. Long ago, our stories say, our shamans could use them to communicate. They used them to bring wisdom to our people, and peace to those who were troubled."

He took the notebook back and examined the drawing himself as he continued speaking. "More than five hundred years ago, the peace jars were taken from us by a rival nation. Some say they were stolen, others that they were destroyed.

Either way, our people were without peace jars for the first time in generations."

"And what happened then?" I said. "In the stories?"

"It was a terrible time," Warner said. "Our wisest men and women could not do their work anymore. Some ran off and left the tribe. Others went mad. The few that remained spent three years, using medicine that had nearly been forgotten, to craft new peace jars. And slowly, over time, peace returned to the Lacalma people."

Warner closed the notebook and tossed it onto the table. "And those very jars are the ones that were to be sold to some college or museum."

"Andrew Twofires Gregory seems to think there is a lot of good that could come to your people as a result of that sale."

"So you talked to that jackass, have you?"

"I did," I said. "He seemed to have pretty big plans for helping people with that money. And a bunch of his own. Education, computers —"

"What a bunch of horseshit," Warner said. "Education we have, and need more, but not at the cost of giving up our past, giving up who we are. And the internet. Big deal. Maybe our kids can get on Netflix, see Johnny fucking Depp play Tonto."

I wasn't sure what to say about that, so I said nothing and waited for Warner to fill the gap.

"I know Andrew," he said. "I grew up with him. Never agreed with him on anything, and don't expect I'll start anytime soon. He had this great speech he gave in the council, to convince us to back the sale. Talked about wanting the Lacalma to be a people of the twenty-first century."

"Yep," I said. "I heard that one too."

"Andrew's problem is that he takes for granted that *you* get to decide what the twenty-first century has to be."

"Me?"

"You," Warner said. "The white man. No offense."

"Not at all," I said.

There was a knock at the door and one of the girls from the stage poked her head into the room. "Wilson? It's after seven o'clock. We're going to be heading home."

"Okay," said Warner. "Thanks, Gracie. Leave the ghost light on the stage. I want to clean up a bit in there before I go."

The girl disappeared back into the lobby. The closing door muffled her voice as she started talking to the others.

"Good kids," said Warner. "They're up here in the Springs going to school. Pike's Peak College, like most of the kids I get here at the theater. I spend about half my time up here at the theater, and half teaching on the reservation. Like I said, we know education is important. These kids can go to school and still work on the rez with their people for part of the year. They go to college, and they also learn right here at the theater. Writing, performing. Organizing people. We do a mix of modern plays, student pieces, and traditional native forms."

This was all pretty impressive. I could definitely understand why Warner would not have wanted to sell the jars. And I understood less why anyone would have considered it a good idea.

"We can be a people of the modern world, without having to be a people of a world designed by others," Warner said. "We can make our own future."

"All alone?" I said. "Apart from everyone else?"

"Not all alone," he said. "But it would be nice to be equals."

Warner was something of a hypnotic speaker, even more so than Gregory. But we were getting far away from the topic I'd come to talk about.

"So, about the jars themselves," I said. "You're not interested in returning them to the tribe."

"Like I said, they're not our jars anymore. We'll work to make new ones, like we did centuries ago, but it won't be easy."

"Can you think of anyone who might be interested in getting their hands on them?"

"Try one of those museums the auction people said were so interested in them."

"I'm thinking maybe someone who might be interested in the jars, but not interested in buying them aboveboard at an auction."

"Ha! 'Aboveboard.' If you say that place is aboveboard. But no, I'll be damned if I know who would want to steal them. Nobody from the reservation, leastways no one I know. And nobody else I can think of."

"Okay," I said. "Thanks for your time, Mr. Warner." I stood up. "You've provided valuable information. If you think of anything else that might help track down those jars and whoever took them, I hope you'll give me a call."

"I suppose I will," Warner said. "As much as I hate that auction house, I hate the idea of some mystery man having those jars for the wrong reason."

CHAPTER 18

I t was dark by the time I got out to the Clubman. The only car left in the lot besides mine was the dusty white pickup that must have been Warner's. Inside the car I checked my phone — no messages, no email. I put the car in gear and headed back toward the highway. Traffic was light, just one car behind me on Nevada Avenue pulling onto I-25.

I liked Wilson Warner, though I wasn't sure why. At least I felt like he was telling me the truth. I probably should have told him about Joseph Vargas's death, but that wouldn't have helped Warner any and I didn't think it would have persuaded him to be any more helpful with my investigation.

Just north of Colorado Springs proper, I realized I hadn't had anything to eat since breakfast. Always doing that to myself. I saw a sign for Five Guys and decided to stop for a burger, maybe a shake.

As I pulled off the highway, I noticed a dark sedan a few car lengths behind me. Looked like the same one I'd seen back on Nevada Avenue. A new-looking Ford, no front plate. It was either a coincidence or a pretty sloppy tail.

I decided this was worth an experiment. The burger place was in the middle of the block, between a hardware store and a nail salon. It had one set of exits and entrances onto North Academy Boulevard. I pulled into the parking lot for the burger place, and parked behind the building so my car could not be seen from the street.

I went in and ordered my cheeseburger and shake. While I waited I glanced out the big front window. Across the street, partly lit from the light washing over from a car dealership, was the dark sedan. It was hard to tell from this distance, but I thought I could see just one man, in the driver's seat.

When I got my burger I went out through the door on the far side of the shop and walked to my car. I left my bag of food on the passenger seat, then went to the trunk and got the flask of whiskey I keep in my emergency supply kit. I locked the car and crossed to the side of the parking lot.

A walking path joined the lot to that of the hardware store. I followed it past that, past the guitar store on the other side, and out to the side street. From there I walked back up to North Academy and crossed the road, careful to keep away from street-lights as much as possible.

On the other side of the road I stepped carefully up toward the dark car. As I got closer I saw that I'd been right, that the driver was the only one in there, and he was intently watching the exit from the Five Guys' parking lot.

And I was pretty sure I recognized the car. This was one of the guys who had tossed Fielding's place.

I went the last half block in a low crouch, trying to stay out of view of the driver. It wasn't very hard, as he was staring out the other side of the car, through his closed window.

When I reached the car, I practically crawled around to the driver's side, and carefully adopted a catcher's squat with my back to the driver's door. I scraped up a few pebbles from the ground and tossed them up and behind me so that they clattered against the back-door window.

I heard some muffled words from inside the car. I repeated the trick with the pebbles.

I heard the door unlock behind me, and felt the driver try to open it. I braced my feet against the ground and leaned my weight into the door, holding it closed.

Now I heard some cursing from inside the car, and the driver's window rolled down. A slim head with short blond hair emerged, looking to see what was blocking the door.

My punch came from a lousy angle, but I got lucky and caught him squarely on the chin. His head lurched upward from the blow and bounced off the top of the window frame. By that time I had grabbed the collar of his green polo shirt. I held on to it as I stood up and turned to face him, twisting his collar tight as I did so.

His eyes bugged wide in shock, and he went slack for a second. Then he started struggling. Surprisingly he didn't try to hit me. But he reached into his jacket pocket.

I twisted his collar a little tighter. "If you've got a gun in that pocket, I bet I can crush your windpipe quicker than you can get the safety off."

He froze, then pulled his empty hand from his pocket. I reached in with my free hand and found a cell phone. I put that in my own pocket, then gave him a shake to get his attention back.

Now that I got a good look at the guy, I was surprised. He was young, and he was skinny. Too young to have been hired for his surveillance experience, and much slighter than anybody I'd ever encountered as hired muscle.

"You're going to tell me why you're following me, and who hired you to do it," I said.

"Dnno wtchtr tlknggg bot," the kid managed to choke out.

I loosened the twisted collar a little bit. "I think you know pretty well what I'm talking bot. You've been following me since the theater, which probably means you've been following me since I left Denver this afternoon."

"Immmm jusssss drvvr."

"If you're just a driver, who were you driving? Looks like it it's just you."

Even as I finished speaking, a cold feeling crept up my spine.

I looked over the kid's shoulder into the car. Two coffee cups sat in the cup holders.

I quickly looked behind me and around the car, still holding on to the kid's collar, half dragging him out of the window as I swiveled my head back and forth. I saw no one but a group of kids going into the burger place. I turned back to my stalker and gave his collar a shake.

"There were two of you," I said. "Where's your partner?"

He didn't answer, so I pulled him a little farther out the window and twisted his collar a little tighter. Lucky for me the kid wasn't a fighter; the collar trick was working better than it should have.

"Want to try that again?" My face an inch away from his. "I know there were two of you. Where is the other guy?"

"Juss me. I came up heeerrrrr to kkp an eye on yu."

Just he came up. Up? From the Springs? From the theater?

If they'd been following me from Denver, they would have seen me go in to talk to Johnny Tom. Then they would have seen

...

"Wilson Warner? The old man? Is your partner with him?"

The kid said nothing, but he turned his eyes away.

Damn it. The other guy must have gone after Warner. And I led them right to him. And if this not-too-strong, not-too-bright kid was the driver, the other guy must be the brains. Or the muscle.

"Sorry, kid. Can't have you following me." I pulled his collar sideways, clocking his head against the window frame. It didn't knock him out, but it stunned him pretty good. Then I gave him a shove so he collapsed onto the driver's seat. I patted his pockets until I found his key fob. Finally I got out the flask of whiskey I'd taken from my car. I opened it and poured it out on him, soaking his jacket with the smell of Heaven Hill bourbon.

Then I bolted across the street back to the parking lot at the burger place and around to my own car. As I got in, I tossed the kid's keys on the ground. I didn't want them on me, I just wanted to be sure he'd stay put.

I jammed my phone into its cradle and cranked up the engine. As I pulled out of the lot, heading back toward I-25, I punched the voice dial button on the phone.

"Call Colorado Springs Police," I shouted.

"Calling Colorado Steam Cleaners," the phone said.

Shit.

I hit the End button and tried again.

"*Call. Colorado. Springs. Pee. Dee.*" I remembered that's how it appears in my address book.

"Calling Colorado Springs Police Department," the phone said.

I was back on the highway and a quarter mile farther south when a dispatcher picked up.

"Colorado Springs Police."

"Hello, Police Department? I'd like to report a possible drunk driver. He's on the north side of North Academy Boulevard. He was driving erratically, then stopped across from the Five Guys just east of Twenty-Five. He had some kind of bottle, and was shouting something out the window."

"Okay. We'll have Patrol check it out. Thank you. Can you give me your name for the report?"

"My name is Michael Gr —"

Halfway through my made-up name, I hit the End button. With luck she'd just think my call was dropped, and I was sure they'd check out the report anyway. They should at least keep the kid off my tail, and there's only so much he'd be willing to tell the police.

I shifted through the gears as I picked up speed back toward Colorado Springs, and when my hand was free I hit the Redial button.

"Colorado Springs Police," came the answer. Fortunately it was a different dispatcher.

"Please send a unit to the Second People Theater on Fountain. I believe a Mr. Wilson Warner may be in danger there."

"Who am I speaking with?"

"My name is Martin Rodak. I'm a private investigator. I'm on my way there myself and I'll talk to your officer when I arrive."

"Okay, Mr. Rodak, can you tell me why you think Mr. Warner is in danger?"

"Can't talk now. Like I said, I'll talk to your officers there. Just get someone there."

"We will, Mr. Rodak. But if the situation is potentially dangerous, you should stay aw —"

I hit the End button. I was almost at the exit to Nevada Avenue. When I reached it I pulled off the highway and raced through the turns and side streets until I flew into the parking lot of the Second People Theater. No sign of a CSPD patrol unit, just Warner's white pickup.

When I got to the glass front doors I could hear nothing from inside. I tried to open the doors, but they only budged an inch. A broomstick was shoved through the handles on the inside. It looked loose, so I pulled hard with my right hand. I managed to open a gap big enough to put my left hand in and slide the broomstick out of the way and get the door open. The stick clattered to the floor with a noise that echoed through the small, empty lobby.

I pulled the door open and went inside.

"Warner!" I shouted. No point trading speed for quiet now that I'd made a racket getting the door open.

I heard muffled voices from Warner's office across the lobby. I'd taken two running steps in that direction when a man emerged through the office doorway. Not Wilson Warner. He also wasn't either of the men Melissa had drawn from the pictures of the Vicar and Blake basement, which I suddenly realized I had been expecting. This was a tall, square-headed man in black jeans and a brown bomber jacket. He also had a nine-millimeter handgun, which he pointed at my chest.

"Who are you?" he said.

"Just a friend of Warner's. You?"

"Turn around," he answered.

I didn't like the idea of turning my back to a man with a gun pointed at me. But I also didn't like the idea of disobeying a man with a gun pointed at me. I turned around.

"I really don't have to stay," I said. "I really didn't see anything. You've obviously got business with Warner, so if I'm interrupting I'll just —"

"Shut up." I heard him take a step toward me. Then I heard the ripping sound of duct tape being pulled from a roll. That meant he must have put the gun in his pocket. So maybe I could —

The next thing I heard was a loud clanging thump, followed by a heavy thud.

I risked turning around. The tall man was laid out on the floor, his tape rolling away from his slack left hand. In the office doorway stood Wilson Warner. His wrists were bound by duct tape, but he was using his hands as a claw to grasp the fire extinguisher with which he'd just brained the thug. There was a large ugly bruise across one whole side of Warner's face, and his left eye was starting to swell up.

He spat a red glob into the wastebasket next to the counter. "Any more nasty white guys you plan to bring around?"

CHAPTER 19

I took out my handkerchief and used it to pick up the tall guy's gun, which I put up on the counter. Then I got a chair for Warner and sat him down. He was pretty well out of it. Taking down the thug had used up whatever he had left in the tank. I checked his wounds. He'd had a few bad whacks on the side of his face, but not with any hard objects. Probably the thug's fist wrapped in a cloth. Some really bad bruising, and probably a couple of loose teeth, but no bones broken.

Next I took my multitool from my pocket and used the knife blade to cut away the duct tape binding Warner's wrists. That was a bit of a trick, as Warner refused to let go of the fire extinguisher he'd used to put out the big guy's lights. He stood it up on the floor and held on to the top of it between his knees.

Finally I took the roll of duct tape and wrapped short strips of it around the thug's wrists and feet. I was finishing that up when I saw the flashing lights of a patrol car snap in through the glass doors from the parking lot.

A moment later a young face over a blue uniform peered through the doors. I waved him in. "Thanks for coming, Officer.

I thought I was going to have to start giving manicures to kill time until somebody got here."

The cop stood at the open door with his hand hovering over the butt of his gun. He took in the scene — the bound guy on the floor, the battered Warner on his gray folding chair fondling his fire extinguisher, and me, a guy in a suit being careful to keep his hands in plain view. Then the gun on the counter.

When he saw the gun on the counter he drew his weapon and held it in a ready grip — two hands, barrel in my direction but aimed slightly downward. He stepped into the room carefully, making space for his partner to follow him.

"What's going on?" he said.

"My name is Martin Rodak," I said. "This" — I nodded toward Warner — "is Mr. Wilson Warner. This is his theater."

"And who is he?" The cop pointed at the tall guy on the floor.

"I really don't know," I said. "He was giving Mr. Warner here a beating until I interrupted them."

"So, what happened to him?"

"He pulled that gun on me. Then Mr. Warner tapped him on the back of the head with that fire extinguisher. Saved my life."

"Bullshit," Warner said. "Just returning the favor for you saving mine."

The cops seemed to buy our story, at least well enough to start dealing with the scene in front of them. First, they radioed for an emergency medical unit. Then one of them checked the thug's pulse and replaced the duct tape around his wrists with a pair of handcuffs. Meanwhile the other cop spent some time with Warner, checking his eyes and asking him "what's your name" and "where are you" kinds of questions. Warner handled the questions just fine, if you don't deduct points for swearing.

About nine minutes later the EMTs rolled in and started giving Warner and the thug proper first aid. When they put an ice pack on the thug's head, he woke up with a start and a grumbled curse.

The EMTs insisted on transporting both the thug and Warner in their ambulance. Apparently being beaten about the head or being cracked with a fire extinguisher carries a risk of concussion.

I was taken to the police station in the back of a patrol car. At the station a detective who smelled like snuff tobacco and Dr Pepper took my statement. I sat on an uncomfortable chair alongside his desk and answered a few questions, then waited while he typed my name into his computer. His eyebrows went up a fraction of an inch, and then he left me sitting there while he went to take some pages off the printer and have quick, quiet conversations with a few other people in the station, which included plenty of glances in my direction. Eventually he came back to the desk.

"Martin Rodak," he said.

"That's right."

"So you're the psychic detective."

"I'm not any kind of psychic," I said.

"You're not any kind of detective either," he said. He pretended to keep it under his breath while making sure I could hear him.

"You're the professional," I said. "Anything else I can tell you about what happened tonight at the theater?"

"Yeah. A hell of a lot."

For the next fifty minutes I answered his questions. I tried not to dwell on Fielding's predicament or the fact that I'd been fired from the Vicar case by Pioneer West Insurance, but I didn't bother to hide them. I knew this guy would be checking out my story in detail.

Eventually I was free to go. I wanted to check on Warner, but all I could find out was that he was in the hospital. I was also curious about the guy who had attacked him, but I guessed he was in the hospital too. A patrol officer gave me a drive back to my car, still parked outside the theater.

It was late and I was tired and I probably shouldn't have been driving. But I drove anyway, up I-25 that was mostly deserted except for long-haul truckers, a few state police, and other lonely drivers.

I hadn't been able to tell the Colorado Springs police anything about Warner's attacker, and I hadn't even mentioned the driver who had tailed me after my visit to the theater. But now I had some time to think it through.

I was sure these were the guys who had broken into Fielding's house. Had they followed me all the way from Denver? Or were they mixed up with Johnny Tom in some way, and he had sent them after me?

As I approached Denver, dawn was starting to threaten the horizon across the eastern plains and early-morning commuter traffic was gathering on the highway. I have no idea what time it was when I finally pulled the car into my driveway, stumbled inside, and crashed on the sofa to sleep.

I DO KNOW that it felt way too early when I woke to a fast, loud banging on my front door. I rolled off the couch, got to my feet, and stumbled to answer it. The clock in the corner said it was ten thirty.

I opened the door to see Toni Scalda. Her short, shiny black hair looked like a helmet, and her expression was ready for battle. Behind Toni I could see Mark Baxter and Alison Goldsmith.

Alison had been one of the first consultants I'd worked with. She is able to draw detailed plans for any building after touching an outside wall for a few minutes. I'd nicknamed her "The Architect," until I decided that sounded stupid and ditched the idea of nicknames.

"Hey." I rubbed the back of my neck and tried to wake up some more. "What are you doing here?"

Toni scowled. "What are *you* doing here?"

"Um. I live here?"

Toni's scowl deepened. I'd had a gun pointed at my chest a few hours earlier, but that look from Toni might have been scarier.

"All right, come in."

They did. Toni stared me in the eye as she passed on her way into the house. Alison kept her blond head bowed, and Mark's brown eyes gave me a look I could not quite decipher.

"Have a seat," I said. I picked up yesterday's suit jacket from the floor and went to toss it on the back of a dining room chair. On the way I realized one reason why I was feeling so awful: I never did get to eat that burger last night, and it was now a cold, hard lump sitting somewhere on the floor of my car. I went into the kitchen to quickly start some coffee, and took the jar of granola bars down from the top of the fridge.

"Anyone else?" I said, gesturing with the big glass jar as I walked back through the dining room.

"No," Toni said. The other two just shook their heads.

I shrugged, put the jar on the dining table, and took out a bar for myself.

"Fielding is still in jail," Toni said.

"No," I said. "He's at a medical facility, undergoing a court-ordered mental health evaluation."

I unwrapped my granola bar and sat down.

"The point is, he's locked up," Toni said. "Whatever you want to call it. Are you really okay with that?"

"No," I said. "And I'm working to get him out."

"He's there because the police think he's a murderer," Toni said.

"No, he's there because he caused a violent disturbance in the middle of a courtroom in front of a judge. And in doing so he screwed up a pretty sweet deal his lawyer, my friend, had negotiated with the DA's office."

Toni sat back to think about that. I munched on my granola bar.

"But the police think he's a murderer," Mark said.

"Some, maybe," I said. "But mainly they think he knows more about the murder in question than he's told them so far."

"And does he?" Toni asked.

"I don't know." I stuffed my empty granola wrapper into my shirt pocket. "I do know that he lied to me, so I'm not sure what he might know."

"So you're going to let him sit there, locked up, because he hurt your feelings?"

"I am working this case." I leaned toward Toni and spoke slowly, tapping the coffee table to emphasize each word. "His lawyer, the lawyer *I got him*, has arranged to keep him under medical care beyond the psych eval, if necessary, because he's better off there than in jail. But the DA could still try to charge him in connection with robbery or murder."

"Will they do that?" Alison asked.

"Maybe. So the best thing I can do for Fielding is give the DA another suspect. If I can find out who actually committed these crimes, I think they'll go easy on him for the rest of it and let him go."

"Burglary," said Mark. His voice was soft and he raised one finger hesitantly.

"What?"

"You said 'robbery.' Technically robbery is theft from someone's person. So the job at the auction house was burglary. Or just theft. Larceny."

"I know what it's called," I said. "I've been dealing in this stuff for a while. It's my job, you know?"

"Oh, I know," said Toni. "It's your job. Find the stuff, get paid. You're doing the same job that dragged Fielding into this mess in the first place."

"Hey," I said, "just so you know, that insurance company fired me. But Fielding will get his paycheck for that job, and he'll still get his bonus if we find the stolen goods. Same terms you all get. I haven't heard any of you people complaining until now. And if you're planning to start, save it. I have work to do."

"'You people,'" said Alison.

I looked away from Toni's scowl and into Alison's frown.

"You said 'You people,'" Alison repeated. Her head was tipped down, but she looked up at me from under the bangs of her sandy hair. "That's how it is, isn't it? There's you, and then there's 'us people.' Weirdoes you can call on whenever we're useful."

"That's how it's always been," Toni added. "There's you, and then there's us. Like that guy you called me about. Just somebody you took an interest in because he's 'one of us'?"

This was too much.

"You want to know why there's me on this side of the line, and you on the other side?" I picked up my notebook from the table and fished around in its back pocket for a business card.

"This is why." I slammed the card down on the table, hard enough to make a mug jump and spill some cold coffee. I thumped the front of the card with my finger. "You see what it says there? Martin Rodak Investigations. Not Martin Rodak and Friends. Not Goldsmith, or Scalda, or Baxter. Or Fielding. I'm the guy who's out of business if the state pulls my license. I'm the guy who had a gun pointed at his chest last night. So don't come into my house and tell me I'm not doing enough to set this all right."

My voice was rising in volume. Alison had withdrawn deeper into the sofa, and when I stopped speaking I could hear Toni breathing fast and shallow, her gaze grown cold.

I sat back in my chair and stared right back at her. "I don't much care what you think of me, but are you going to deny that I've helped you? God knows why I end up tripping over so many of you people —"

"There it is again!" Toni threw up her hands and looked at Alison and Mark.

"— but when I do, I do everything I can to help," I finished. "Everything I can."

"And you always find a way for us to help you," Toni said.

"Is it a two-way street? Absolutely." I leaned in to pick up the business card and used it to point at each of them. "This business gives you a way to use those talents of yours. And it pays you pretty well when you do."

"When you decide to let us," Mark said.

"Right," I said. "When I decide it's called for."

"Well, I want to help Fielding," Mark said. "Now."

I closed my eyes for a second and massaged my aching forehead. "Look, Mark, I know you want to help, but at this stage the ability to talk with animals is not going to —"

"I am not just the guy who talks to animals," he said. Now his voice was raised, and he leaned forward on the sofa. Mark was always easygoing, and this was an attitude I'd never seen from him.

"That's not what I am," he went on. "That's not who I am. That's not my 'thing.'"

"Look, I know, I didn't mean —"

"I have a master's degree in art history. Did you know that? Plus a bachelor's in business administration. Do you think there might be *something* I can contribute to investigating *a theft from an art auction*?"

That shut me up for a good few seconds.

"You're right, Mark," I said then. "I'm sorry, I didn't know —"

"Of course not," he said. "It's only come up half a dozen times. This is why I've been trying to call you on the phone for the past two days."

He stood up and turned to face me squarely. "You just let me know when you decide I can be useful." Mark stalked heavily to the door and out of the house.

Toni, Alison, and I looked at each other for a moment. Then they shared a glance between them, rose, and followed Mark out.

After the door closed behind them, I stared at it for a good five minutes as the conversation replayed in my head. I wasn't sure if I'd lost them, or how I might get them back.

In my hand I still held my business card. I read it again. "Martin Rodak Investigations."

I crumpled the card and threw it back onto the table as I got up to pour some fresh coffee for the agency's sole proprietor.

Once the coffee was ready I spent the next hour adding to my notes and going over the facts, including the ones I'd gained the night before.

I didn't think Warner had been involved with the heist. The idea just didn't feel right based on the short time I'd known him, and his speech about the jars losing their meaning after they were put up for sale seemed sincere.

But someone had followed me to him, and tried to beat something out of him. It seemed likely that they were interested in the Lacalma jars, and that they were not the people in possession. If they had the jars, why go after Warner? Unless they had two of them, needed all of them, and didn't know the third was in a police evidence locker?

Then there was the theft of the Fenn sculpture and the camera. Why would they grab those heavy, unwieldy extras if they were really after the jars?

I was about to start looking through the files again when the phone rang. The call was coming from Jeff Lang's private cell phone.

"Jeff? What's up? Is Fielding okay?"

"What? No, yeah, Fielding is fine. At least he was last I heard."

When Lang paused I could hear a lot of background chatter, and what sounded like the squawk of police radios.

Lang continued. "I'm calling because we found the lawyer."

"What?"

"McKelvie. The guy who was selling the sculpture. We found him in Longmont."

"Longmont? I thought his office said he was out of the country."

"Yeah, that's what they said."

"So, what was he doing in Longmont? How did you find him?"

"Well, that's a hell of a thing," Lang said. "He's been holed up here for two weeks, it seems. Living in a motel off of Route 119. Paid cash for a month ahead of time. The only reason we found him is that he was clipped by a car crossing the highway, on his way to a storage unit that he's been renting for about the same time. The motel guy thinks that's the only place he ever went other than his motel room."

"Can I talk to him?" It was a long shot, but couldn't hurt to ask.

"No way, Marty."

I wasn't surprised, but I still let out a sigh of disappointment. I had a lot of questions for that lawyer.

I heard some shuffling noises as if Lang were moving the

phone around on his end, and then he spoke in a quieter voice. "It's bad enough that I'm calling you. I'm at the Longmont Police Headquarters. They took him in, but they gave Carson call as a courtesy when they recognized him from our BOLO."

"So, what else can you tell me?" I said. "What was in the storage locker?"

"Well, that's the fun part." I could practically hear Lang's smile come through the phone. "Nothing in the storage locker except a wooden chair and the stolen camera."

Lang waited patiently while I took a few seconds to process that.

"Seriously? He has the camera stolen from Vicar and Blake?"

"No. It's my grandma's Polaroid. Of course I'm talking about the stolen camera."

"What was he doing with that?"

"Near as I can tell, he was worshipping it."

I took another few seconds to think that through, but this time it didn't help. "What?"

"Worshipping it," Lang repeated. "That's what my friend Gabe here at the Longmont PD says, anyway. Hey, you might know him. Gabe Casco? Worked for the Denver Sheriff's Department for a year or two?"

"No, don't recognize the name. Now, what is this about worshipping the camera?"

"Gabe says that the motel owner told him McKelvie would leave the motel to go across the highway every day at about five o'clock, and come back a little after sunset. McKelvie himself says that he was spending his time sitting with the camera. 'Letting it see into him,' 'gaining its wisdom,' stuff like that. Apparently he's been doing this all day, every day. Eating a little something every day or two."

"Doesn't sound to me as if he was gaining a lot of wisdom." I reached across the table to grab my black notebook and flipped back a few pages. "But the behavior does sound similar to something I heard from the camera's previous owner. She said her boyfriend became obsessed with it."

"Well, obsessed sounds like the right word for whatever this guy's got."

"Did he say anything about where he got the camera?"

"Apparently he's the guy who stole it."

I thought for another few seconds. At this rate I ought to get good at it one of these days. "Are you telling me this lawyer who is now off his rocker was behind the heist from the Vicar and Blake?"

"Sounds like," Lang said. "Carson spoke with him and says that in among the crazy talk the guy let go some telling details about the heist. He seems like our guy."

"But not alone, right?"

"Probably not. But we can't get much more out of him right now. Longmont has a shrink talking with him now."

"So this lawyer puts a statue up for sale with Vicar and Blake," I said, "then breaks in to steal a camera that has nothing to do with him."

"I don't think that was his plan," Lang said. "The guy keeps saying the camera wanted him to take it. Says he did what the camera asked him to do."

"That sounds both crazy and probably true," I said. "So, what did he break in for in the first place?"

"He's not saying. But the first thing to look at is his own property, the statue."

I thought about that, and sighed. "You're right. And I think I have someone who can help us look into that."

I hung up the phone after getting Lang's promise to fill me in if they should get any more information from McKelvie.

Then I made a difficult phone call. When Mark Baxter answered, his voice was cold. "What is it?"

"First, I'm sorry. You're right, I should have answered your calls. And I should have taken more seriously your offers to help."

Mark grunted what might have been a "yes."

"So, what else?" he said.

"I need your help."

"Do you?"

"I do," I said. "Fielding does. I have some new information, and it seems like the stolen sculpture is important. I need to you to help me look into it."

Mark was silent for almost a full minute.

"Okay," he said finally. "I'll be there in twenty minutes."

Fifteen minutes later he was at my front door again. His expression hadn't softened from the time he'd marched out, but he was ready to work.

I filled him in on the new information, that the prior owner of the sculpture had been involved in the theft.

"We need to know why," I said. "Was it some paranormal thing, like the camera seems to be? Or some scheme about the money involved?"

"Just give me all the information you have about the sculpture," Mark said.

"It's all there in the file on the dining room table. What else do you need?"

"Some peace and quiet. And some tea."

I left Mark with the file and went to the kitchen. I filled the kettle and set it on the range, and while it heated I hunted in the back of my cupboards until I found some tea bags.

When I got back to the dining room table and set down a mug for Mark, he was poring over the paperwork for the Michael Fenn sculpture.

"Weird thing is," I said, "the sculpture is not even on the

underground market. If that was the target, why steal it and then not try to sell it?"

Mark ignored me. He flipped back and forth between pages in the file, and ran his fingers through his thick hair while he stared at them. From time to time he would focus on some detail, making odd chirping noises through tight lips, until he began flipping pages again. Then he pulled out his phone and squinted at some photographs on web pages.

Finally he startled me by slapping both palms down hard against the oak tabletop. "I don't know what this means, but it's pretty important."

"What is it?"

"The Fenn is a forgery."

It took me a moment to process that, and even then I had trouble understanding. "What?"

"The stolen Michael Fenn sculpture," Mark said. "It's a forgery. It's fake. It's not a real Michael Fenn original."

"What are you talking about?"

"Here. Look at this." Mark spread out some pictures from the case file. They were close-up details of the Fenn sculpture. "Look here, at the signature stamp." He pointed to a picture, and I squinted at it. It was a close-up of the letters *Mchl Fenn* engraved on the horse's rump.

"Okay," I said, "I see a signature."

"But it's the wrong signature," Mark said. "Up until 1911, Michael Fenn engraved his signature into his sculptures by hand. On equestrian sculptures he put it on the horse's butt, like a brand. Then in 1911 he started using a custom die — a kind of sharp stamp that he'd use to strike his signature into the bronze."

Mark pulled up a picture on his phone and handed it to me. "I thought there was something weird about the signature in the photos of the stolen piece, so I checked out some pictures."

He pointed at a signature in the picture on his phone. "Here's a picture of a piece from after 1911, so you can see what the stamped signature looks like. Look especially at the last *N* in the name."

In the picture on Mark's phone the signature looked exactly like the one on the stolen piece in the case file. The final *N* was large and stylized, about as large as the initial *M* and with a long final stroke that swept back under the whole name.

"Looks the same as the one in the file," I said.

"Okay," Mark said, "but look at the surface around the signature. See what the stamp does to it?"

I looked more closely at the picture. The whole surface of the sculpture had a bright polish, but a fine brushed texture. Then, in a tiny rectangle around the signature, the pattern of the brushed metal was flattened, and pinched just a bit inward toward the lettering.

"I think I see," I said. "The surface texture looks distorted around the stamp."

"Now go back one picture. It shows a pre-1911 signature."

I swept a finger backward on the phone's screen and looked at the other picture. The signature still said "Mchl Fenn," but it was in much simpler lettering, with the final *N* small and nondescript like the one before it. Also, there was none of the distortion around the signature; the letters cut neatly across the grain of the brushed-and-polished surface.

"Now look again at the picture from your case file," Mark said.

I picked up the case file and looked at the photo of the signature on the stolen sculpture. It had the same big, stylized final *N* as the die-stamped signature Mark had shown me on a post-1911 sculpture. But it was cut neatly into the bronze, with no distortion of the brushed surface, just like the older one. No way was that signature struck with a die.

"I'll be damned," I said. "You're right. At least I think you're right."

"Well, I wouldn't swear that this is a forgery," Mark said, "without doing more research and seeing the piece itself. But there is definitely something weird going on with the stolen sculpture. Looks like someone took care to recreate Fenn's later style of signature, but made the mistake of using his older technique."

"How did you happen to notice this?" I asked.

"I worked as TA to a professor who was writing a book about Fenn, while I was going for my master's," Mark said. "The second one."

He gave a sideways grin and looked down at the table as if he were embarrassed. "I mainly liked the horses. And when I heard a Fenn had been stolen, I thought I might be able to help."

I put down the file and thought.

Instead of narrowing down the important facts, I kept running into new ones. All three items seemed weird in some way. Poole's boyfriend Roger behaving strangely after buying the antique camera. The Fenn sculpture apparently being a fake. And whatever it was about those Indian jars that made Fielding, and maybe the dead Joseph Vargas, go crazy.

"Okay. You're the art-business guy," I said to Mark. "We have two possibilities: the last owner of the sculpture, this lawyer from Fort Logan, either knew about the forgery or he didn't. What are the odds he didn't know?"

"Hard to say," Mark said. "According to the history listed in the file, he bought it at a gallery in Cheyenne. Probably an honest place, but that kind of gallery might not be too diligent about confirming the work's authenticity. Apparently they relied on a certificate that goes back several owners, to people who are now probably dead."

"And how about Vicar and Blake?" I asked. "They authenticated it, right?"

"Yes. They would normally be a lot more careful," Mark said. "An auction house has a reputation to keep up with both with buyers and sellers. So they have independent experts on call to check things out."

I sat down at the table and thought for a moment, drumming on the edge of my coffee mug. "So, what are the chances that a house like Vicar and Blake would miss this? That they would go ahead and sell a fake Michael Fenn without knowing it?"

"Pretty damn low, I would think," Mark said. "Maybe I'm a freak, but I found this from reading your case file and poking around on Google for fifteen minutes. Any auction house whose experts couldn't notice this wouldn't be in business very long."

I drummed on the coffee mug some more. "So, let's assume Vicar and Blake knew the Fenn was a fake. If they sold it, it would be discovered pretty quickly and discredited. What would they do?"

"They wouldn't sell it. They'd throw it back at the seller," Mark said. "If Vicar gets a consignment, checks it out, finds out that it's a fake, and refuses to sell it, they've done nothing wrong. Hell, if word gets out that their experts have exposed a fake, their reputation goes up."

"So, if they do know it's a fake, why might they keep it a secret?"

"They want to make the sale anyway," Mark said.

"But they can't make the sale," I said. "So the only way they could get paid ..."

"Is from an insurance company."

"Right. As a payout if the piece were stolen." I pushed the coffee mug away from me to stop myself from drumming on it. If I smacked it any harder with my fingertips, it would break. "So we have a motive. Arrange a theft of the fake Fenn, report it stolen, get a payout. Split it with the consigner, probably."

Mark nodded. "Ordinarily the insurance payout for a presale loss like this would go entirely to the seller. In this case, if the house and the seller were in cahoots, they might arrange a split in exchange for the auction house setting up the 'theft' and then keeping things quiet."

I nodded. I could feel more thoughts creeping into my tired head, but nothing that seemed clear. I started to reach for the coffee mug again, then decided to stand up and start pacing instead.

"That gets us partway there," I said. "But there's an important rule: companies never do anything. A building does not do anything. A corporation can't do anything. An institution. An auction house. Nothing."

I reached the end of the dining room for the third time since I'd started pacing and turned around to face Mark again. "Only a person can do something."

"So," Mark said, "who at the auction house was responsible for setting up this scam?"

"It sure wasn't Joseph Vargas," I said. "This was not the work of a disgruntled former box hauler. This had to be someone still inside, well positioned. Maybe high enough to deal directly with the insurance company and smooth over any potential problems."

"So, who is that at V and B?"

"I've got one idea." I pulled out my phone and told it to dial John Harris.

CHAPTER 20

An hour later Mark and I were sitting across a wobbly table from John Harris at his favorite coffee shop in the Bonnie Brae neighborhood, not far from my house. Down the block a short line of people fidgeted in the cool air, waiting for a post-lunch cone from the ice cream place. I do like their ice cream, but Harris is more of a coffee-and-cookies guy, so we sat in the cafe across the street and I drank an espresso while Mark laid out his ideas.

He tapped a finger on one of the photos from the case file that lay spread out on the table along with printouts from his internet research.

"It seems clear to me," Mark told Harris. "The sculpture in these photos is a fake. A good forgery, probably an old forgery, but with one sloppy detail."

Harris stared at the pictures and took a long sip of his mocha. "So you figure the Fenn was the real target." Someone wanted it stolen not because it was valuable, but to hide the fact that it wasn't."

"That's our bet," I said. "So now the question is, who was behind it?"

Harris shrugged and wiped some foam off his mustache. "The lawyer from Fort Collins? Pioneer West's payout for a consigned but unsold piece would go to him."

I drank the last of my espresso and stared at the dregs in my cup for a moment. "I thought about that. But it doesn't add up. If the seller knew it was fake, offering it for sale by Vicar should have exposed it, and he'd be out of luck."

"Should have happened," said Mark. "If they'd had a decent expert."

Harris nodded. "So, even if the seller was in on it, it wasn't all his idea. There had to be someone involved at the auction house."

"Exactly," Mark said. "So, who do we have there?"

"How about we start at the top?" I said. "What's the deal with this Mrs. Lansing who suddenly seems to like me so much?"

"I don't know," Harris said. "She's got plenty of money, and the house's reputation ought to be worth a lot to her. She had every reason to handle things by the book and expose the fake."

"Exactly," Mark said.

"Okay," I said. "I get the point. Mrs. Lansing is not a likely suspect. So, who else have we got?"

Harris didn't answer, so I scanned the employee list again. "What about William Tucci?"

Harris wasn't listening. He had flagged down a girl from behind the counter so he could order another oatmeal cookie.

"You know they don't really have table service, right?" I said as the girl walked back to the pastry cases.

"Yeah, but they know me here," Harris said. "Anyway, what were you saying?"

"Tucci. William Tucci."

"Tucci," Harris said. "Oh, Tucci! That jerk. Yeah, we should take a close look at him."

"So, what's his story?" I said. "Besides being V and B's operations manager, and having a stick up his ass."

"He pretty much runs the show as far as day-to-day business is concerned," Harris said. "Everything except the finances. Schedules, auction and event planning, hiring and firing —"

"Hiring and firing? And dealing with employees who quit?"

"Yeah," said Harris. "And cutting off their access, which he insists he did."

"Let's check on that," I said. "I think there was a key card on the table in that V and B basement. Let's see if we can find out who that belonged to."

"Won't the police have that in evidence by now? Probably they'd check that out, but they won't tell you."

"Damn. You're right." Sometimes I forgot that the Denver PD wasn't actually in my corner like when I was a prosecutor. Lang might share some info with me, but there were limits.

"Tucci says he did deactivate Vargas's key card," said Harris. "His logbook shows that he did."

"Of course he says that," I said. "And of course his own logbook backs him up. But I'd like to check for any use of Vargas's card after he supposedly quit, or at odd hours just before he quit."

"The key card wasn't used for the actual theft?" Mark asked.

"No," I said. "That was done at night by forcibly breaking several locks. Probably to throw off suspicion of an inside job. But it was done in a way that shows really good knowledge of the security systems and guard schedules."

"Which Tucci also has," said Mark.

Harris took a long slurping slug from his mocha. He smiled and nodded, but didn't pause his drinking, when the blond girl from behind the counter brought him his cookie. Fueled up for more thinking, he set the nearly empty cup down on the table with a soft smack.

"So, what's Tucci's motive?" he asked.

"Money?" Mark asked.

"Maybe," I said. "He made a good salary from the auction house, but half the insured value of the Fenn would be a nice piece of change. Nothing he could retire on, but still."

"How about spite?" Harris said. "Or revenge for something?"

"We'd need to know more. Did he have anything against Vicar and Blake? Any beef with Mrs. Lansing?"

"I don't think so. He always spoke of her in very respectful terms, and he's been with the company a long time." Harris broke off a piece of his cookie and popped it into his mouth. "But really, who can say? We don't know much about her. She used to be seen out a few times a year, charity events and such. But since a few years ago she hasn't seen a lot of people. I mean, seriously, she's been a hermit. I'm surprised the *Biz Journal* didn't do a story on the fact that she actually picked up a phone to complain about Pioneer West firing you."

"If Tucci felt she was ignoring him, that might get under his skin," I said. "But this heist was careful, even if it was amateur. Not something done out of anger."

"And he runs the place, so the theft makes him look bad," Mark said. "It doesn't really hurt Lansing much."

"True," I said. "The crime hinges on security and personnel, and they're both his responsibility."

"So we're left with three so-so suspects, McKelvie, Lansing, and Tucci, and no great motives."

"Did Tucci hire the authentication experts?" Mark asked.

"Yeah," Harris said.

"So, who'd he get to look at the Fenn?" I asked

"Max Wells," Mark said. He shuffled through the file looking for something. "He's worth taking a look at. If anyone should have seen through the fake, it's him. So if anyone was in a position to set up a scam, it was him."

I glanced over the online profile of Wells that Mark had printed out. "Freelance, not a V and B employee. You think he could have planned all this himself?"

"Depends on what kind of guy he is," Mark said. "But he didn't have to, if he worked with Vargas and McKelvie."

"And his motive?" I asked.

"Money," Harris said.

"Not just money," Mark said. "Reputation. What if he authenticated the piece, and only later realized he had made a mistake?"

"Stealing it would be a pretty drastic method of cover-up," Harris said.

"Who knows how many strikes he already had against him?" Mark said. "Besides, reputation is everything in that field. Even one big mistake like this could have ruined him."

"Hmm," Harris murmured around the last of his cookie. He followed it with the last of his mocha.

"So we'll check him out," I said.

"Okay," he said, "I think you've done a solid day's work. You're also kicking a big-ass hole in some careers back at Pioneer West, among the guys who were ready to approve the payout on this claim."

"Glad to be spreading sunshine," I said.

"Well, keep spreading it," Harris said. "As of now you're back on the case for Pioneer West, if you want to be. I'll get it straightened out with my bosses."

"That sounds good," I said. "Thanks. But I'm really staying on this for Fielding."

"I know," Harris said. "How's he doing?"

"Okay. We hope to be getting him home soon."

Harris stood up. "I can take these copies?" He gathered up the printouts from Mark's research.

"Yes," Mark said. "I made extras for the file."

"Did the new investigators get anywhere?" I asked Harris. "Did anyone at V and B recognize Melissa's sketches?"

"I don't think they ever showed them around," Harris said. "Did you send the original file back to me?"

"Yeah, and I included copies of the sketches." I took our copy from Mark's hands and flipped through it to find Melissa's artwork. I handed the three pages to Harris. "Any of these look familiar?"

He looked carefully at the first page for a few seconds and then shook his head and handed it back to me. When he saw the second page his eyes widened. "This is Max Wells!"

"Seriously?" I stepped forward to look at the page. It was the stocky man with the worried smile.

"Yes, that's him," Harris said. "I just met him once, about a year ago when I was at a meeting at Vicar and Blake and he happened to be in the office. But that's him."

"That means we have all three men," I said. "Vargas, McKelvie, and Wells. McKelvie was out of the picture right after the robbery, holed up in a motel with the camera stashed nearby. Then Vargas was killed about a week later. That leaves Wells. If someone turned on Vargas, it must have been Wells."

Harris looked at the picture again. "He doesn't look all that dangerous."

"Doesn't take much to change a person. Maybe it was money. Maybe Vargas threatened to expose him."

"Hmm." Harris stroked his mustache and looked at the sketch some more. "What are you going to do now?"

"Check on Max Wells."

"Even though he might be a killer?"

"I'm just going to check on him, not confront him. See if he's still around or if he took off. Then I'll figure out if we have enough to let the Denver PD get a warrant to search his place."

"I suppose he could have the phony sculpture, and maybe the remaining jars," Harris said.

"Right. And if we can wrap up who pulled off the heist, and prove that Wells killed Vargas, that should clear Fielding."

"All right," Harris said, "I'll leave you to it." He extended a hand to Mark. "It was good meeting you, Mark. Every time I meet one of Martin's associates, I'm impressed, but I had no idea he had an art expert in the bull pen."

Mark shook the hand, but he gave a steely sideways glance at me.

"Glad to meet you too," Mark told Harris, "and glad to help."

With a nod, a wave, and a stop at the counter to pay for his extra cookie, Harris was out the door and driving away.

A minute later Mark and I had followed him outside. A pair of sparrows hopped out of our way on the walk, pausing in their fight over a large bread crust to look up at us with sharp black eyes and give a synchronized chirp.

"Well, Mark," I said, "looks like we have a few people to talk to."

"Who asked you?" Mark demanded.

I turned to him. "What the hell?"

"Sorry," Mark said, gesturing down the path. "I was talking to the birds."

CHAPTER 21

Back at the car I found Max Wells's number in the file and tried calling. No answer, and his voice mail was full. So I plugged his office address into my phone and found that it was about twenty minutes east, near Parker Road. Must have been a home office, as the little red pin on the map was in the middle of a residential block.

"Want to take a ride?" I asked Mark. "Talk to Wells?"

"Sure," he said.

I pulled out into the easy afternoon traffic and pointed the Clubman toward I-25. We drove in silence for ten minutes.

"One thing I don't get," Mark said.

"Who beat up the old Indian?" I said.

"Exactly. If the theft was all about the Fenn sculpture, why did someone follow you to Colorado Springs? And what did they want with Mr. Warner?"

"His only connection to the robbery has to do with those jars."

I thought in silence for a minute. "They must have followed me and seen me go in to talk to Johnny Tom. A known fence.

Saw me go right from Tom's to Wilson and decided to watch us both, figuring one of us would lead them to the Fenn."

"Did more than watch. Pistol-whipped an old man."

"Some guys run out of patience faster than others," I said.

"But if the reason for the theft was to make some fake artwork disappear, who would follow you?" Mark said. "Who would want it back?"

"No idea. Maybe someone wanted it back, or maybe someone was afraid I'd find it. Wanted to make sure it stays hidden."

"Seems like a lot of trouble and violence over not all that much money."

I thought about some of the cases I'd seen as a prosecutor. It no longer surprised me, how much trouble and violence some people will go to over how little money. "The guys who followed me. I think they are the same guys who broke into Fielding's house."

"Makes sense."

That means they knew I was working on the case from the start. I started thinking through a list: Harris and some others at Pioneer West. Tucci and probably a few more people connected to Vicar and Blake. Liz Duncan and maybe some people at her firm. And the Denver PD. Some of my own people, of course, not that that mattered. The list was longer than I'd expected.

I put that aside when we got to our exit off the highway, and soon we were driving through twisting side streets, following my phone's purple GPS line to Wells's place. It was a neighborhood of small, neat houses. Blocks and blocks of three or four repeating styles, their sameness thinly disguised by different shades of paint and decades of small changes. Wells's house was in the middle of the block, a white-sided box set back by a tiny brown yard of grass struggling to rebound from a dry spring and a dryer winter. A red Acura was parked in the driveway. Pooled about its back tires was a small heap of plastic-wrapped *Denver Posts*.

I gestured at the newspapers. "Seems like Wells decided to take an unplanned vacation. Didn't put a hold on the paper."

Mark nodded. He wasn't listening to me. He was staring out the window toward the house with an uneasy look on his face. I gave him a tap on the shoulder and undid my seat belt.

"Come on," I said. "We're here, we might as well look around. Maybe talk to some of the neighbors."

Mark, still in his cargo shorts, pet-store polo shirt, and boots, wasn't really dressed for interviews. But over the years I'd brought stranger people to more normal places, and I didn't want to leave him alone. I could tell something was wrong.

We both got out of the car and went to the foot of the driveway. I picked through the newspapers with the toe of my shoe, counting and trying to read the dates through the orange plastic bags. There were a dozen papers, the oldest from nearly two weeks past.

I looked up at the house. The shades were down, and the porch light was on. "Looks like he left at night. In a hurry."

I glanced around. No one else on the block. I went to the front walk and up to the door. Mark followed slowly, a couple of steps behind.

"Martin ...," he said.

I turned. "What's up?"

Mark looked around with jerky moves of his head, then back to me. "Never mind. I don't know."

I nodded, then went up the three steps to the porch. Mark followed me as far as the bottom step. I was sure Max Wells had flown, but I knocked on the door anyway.

I was surprised to hear sound from inside. A scurrying. A soft thud. More scurrying. Then a loud meow just inside the door.

"Martin," Mark said, "he has a cat."

"I can hear that," I said.

"But something is wrong ..."

"Why? Is it, um, saying something?"

"I ... I can't tell. It sounds upset."

"Of course it's upset. He left the poor thing locked up and alone for more than a week. What's it saying?"

"I can't hear it from here," Mark said. "But I can tell something's not right."

"Then get the hell up here," I said. "What's it saying?"

Slowly Mark came up the steps to stand next to me at the door. He bent slightly and turned his ear to the door. For a moment he appeared to concentrate; then his jaw dropped and his face went pale. "Oh God, Martin. He's in there. He didn't leave. He's still there. He was ... He's been ... The cats have been ... Oh God —"

Mark ran down to the bushes alongside the steps, where he started to vomit.

I could see that our panic and vomiting requirements were taken care of, so I stepped over to one of the large windows that looked out on the porch. I picked up a flower pot, pulled my suit jacket up to protect my face, and smashed through the glass.

The windowpane had two layers, but it was wide enough that with a little more damage to the decorative vinyl I was able to pull myself up and inside. I stepped on a cushioned window seat and almost slid off onto the floor before I could safely step down.

The first thing I noticed was how cold the air was. The AC must have been cranked to its maximum. The next thing I noticed was the smell — an awful, unforgettable smell of death.

I called back out the window, "Mark? You okay?"

He made a loud but stable-sounding grunt in reply. Seemed okay enough.

"Call 911, then stay outside and wait for the police. Tell them we're responding to an emergency. Give them my name as well as yours, and wait for them outside."

Mark made another grunt to let me know he understood.

I looked around. I was in a small, square living room, with a tiny fireplace, nice-looking modern furniture, and a bookcase filled mostly with large art books.

A hefty gray cat stepped into the room from the right, from near the front door. It hugged the wall but otherwise seemed remarkably calm, maybe just annoyed it had taken me so long to show up. It looked clean and well fed.

Another, smaller cat came in from a wide, open archway that led into the kitchen. Looking past the cat, I saw a dark pool gathered against the bottom of the kitchen island, staining the legs of two wooden barstools. When I looked again at the small cat, I noticed that it left on the carpet a trail of red-brown paw prints, and it was cleaning some red and yellowish scraps from its damp snout.

I moved toward the kitchen, taking care to avoid the little cat and its trail of gore. There were several old, dried trails leading from the kitchen, big paws and small, showing the patterns where the two cats had been coming and going for days.

When I reached the kitchen archway I craned my neck to look inside, trying to avoid stepping into the heart of a crime scene. Slumped on the floor, in a pool of fluid between the island and the burgundy-enameled refrigerator, I saw what was left of art expert Max Wells. His midsection was bloated, well beyond the potbelly that had shown in his website photo, and the skin that I could see was a dark yellowish brown. He had bled out from a deep gash across his neck.

I realized then what had upset Mark so much. The cats had been locked in here, but they hadn't gone hungry.

Then I glanced around the kitchen. In a far corner of the

room, away from the dead body, a bag of dry cat food was lying on its side, little brown nuggets scattered across the clean tiles. Some dark paw prints clustered around the pile of food. The cats had investigated the body, but they'd been eating only Purina One.

Police arrived within five minutes. "It was an emergency situation," Mark was telling the two Aurora PD patrol officers. "We heard something inside, and we thought, well, we thought someone was in trouble."

The cops were startled when I climbed out of the window. They turned sharply, and one of the cops' hands moved toward his gun. The other cop was more calm, but she eyed me carefully.

"Step over here with us, sir," she said. "And make sure we can see your hands."

I held up my hands, as casually as possible, and walked over to the little party.

"He's who I was telling you about," Mark said. "This is Martin Rodak. He's a detective."

"Just a private investigator," I said.

"And that lets you break into people's houses?" said the jittery cop.

The other officer turned to give him a stern look, then turned back to me. I spoke up before the conversation could get off track.

"Max Wells is dead," I said. "He's in the house. Stabbed, it looks like."

Suddenly things changed. The jittery copy drew his weapon, but fortunately kept it pointed low and away as he started moving toward the smashed window. Mark went back to the edge of the porch and vomited again. The senior cop smacked the radio handset clipped to her shoulder strap.

"Unit one-one-three, possible four-nineteen in thirty-two-hundred block of South Evanston. Request additional units, notify detective on call and CSU on standby." She looked up from her radio and eyed me again. "You have any ID, Mr. Rodak?"

I took out my wallet and handed her my driver's license, my PI license, and a business card.

"Martin Rodak, Investigations," she read. "Sounds familiar. Any relatives on the job?"

"No," I said. "I used to be a prosecutor, probably before your time."

She eyed me again, sizing me up. Apparently decided I was trustworthy enough. She handed back my paperwork. "Stay here," she said to me. She glanced at Mark, then looked back to me. "Stay put, both of you."

She and her partner, now both with guns drawn, made their way into the house through my broken window.

"Careful of the cushion on that window seat," I said. A second later there came a muffled thud and a curse.

Marked looked up at me. "How bad was it?"

"Pretty bad," I said. "He's been dead for a while."

"And the cats ..." He paused and closed his eyes. "Were they ..."

"They knocked over a bag of cat food. Don't know what they've been drinking, probably out of the toilet, but they seem fine."

Mark's eyes opened wide. "Cat food? They've been eating cat food?"

"Looks like."

"But they said ..."

"Who said? The cats?"

"Yeah. When I heard them through the door, they said they'd been ... they said it was him ... they said they've been eating ..."

"Do cats ever lie?" I said. "Because I think they were messing with you."

Mark just stared for a moment, then turned toward the house and shouted, "You think that's funny?"

A small feline face appeared at the corner of a window and then disappeared.

"I hate cats," Mark muttered. "I love animals, but sometimes I hate cats."

As I struggled to stifle a laugh, I strolled over to sit on the teak bench under the unsmashed window at the opposite side of the front door. Mark stayed near the edge of the porch overlooking the shrubbery bed, no doubt in case his stomach turned over again. A siren sounded in the distance, growing louder. I took a deep breath, trying to get the smell of death out of my nose, and took out my phone. I didn't have Detective Carson's cell number, so I texted Lang.

> Db in aurora. 3208 south evanston.

> Possible link to vargas and VB theft. Vic worked for VB.

> On scene now with APD.

> Tell carson.

By the time I hit Send on the last message, a second Aurora PD patrol car had pulled up, lights flashing, and parked across the street. Another soon followed. I slowly rose from the bench and walked toward the porch steps as the first reinforcements came up the walk.

"Officers," I said. "Officer Keel and her partner are inside. My name is Martin Rodak. This is my associate Mark Baxter. I found the body inside. I suspect it's the homeowner, Max Wells."

"And what were you doing here?" one of the cops asked.

"I'm a private investigator, and was here to interview Mr. Wells in connection with an insurance claim. We heard noises, and went inside because it seemed like an emergency situation. Turned out we just heard the cats. Looks to me like Wells has been dead for at least a week, maybe two."

At the mention of the cats, Mark gurgled and put a hand up to his mouth. The other policeman looked at me closely. "Rodak. Are you that psychic detective? From that missing-person thing a couple years ago? And that train derailment case?"

I tried not to grind my teeth. "I'm not a psychic detective. Just a working PI."

"Oh, right," the cop said. "I remember now from that magazine. But you've got those friends, right? Magic powers and stuff?" He looked at Mark. "I guess you're the talent on this case?"

Mark managed a brief glare at me and at the cops before he went to the railing and heaved again.

"Yeah," I said. "He's the talent."

Behind them the once-calm suburban street was getting crowded. A crime-scene van rolled up, followed by another patrol unit. The CSU guys went to the back of their truck to gather boxes of equipment. The patrol officers blocked the street with their unit, lights flashing, and began unspooling a perimeter of yellow tape. They paused and withdrew the tape long enough to let a gold Ford sedan drive through and park in front of the van. Homicide detectives. The patrol car had its radio turned up, and the squawk echoed off the houses across the street.

The cop I'd been talking with grabbed my attention again.

"Mr. Rodak," he said, "I'm going to ask you to come down here off the porch and wait for our detectives. They're going to want a statement from you and Mr. Baxter."

Mark joined us and we went down and across the lawn to

the sidewalk. The detectives hadn't gotten out of their Ford yet. They were talking to one another and fiddling with clipboards. One of them rolled down his window and said something to one of the crime-scene investigators, who waved and shook his head before returning to his own kit.

Eventually the two detectives got out of their car and crossed the street to where Mark and I stood with the uniformed cops. Their suits were dark, and as style-free as their car. Both detectives seemed cut from the same block. Their square shoulders and square haircuts, one dark and one white-blond, made them look like rooks from opposite sides of the same chess set.

The cop I'd been speaking with gave them my name and Mark's.

"I'm Detective James," said the white-haired one, "and this is Detective Gleason." He took a leather-covered notebook from an inside pocket. "Martin Rodak? I've heard of you."

"I haven't," said Gleason.

"Sure," said James. "That psychic detective. In the paper a while ago."

"From that missing-person case," said the uniformed cop I'd been talking with. "Those two boys."

"Right," said James, pointing his pen at the uniform.

"Sorry," said Gleason, continuing his stare at my face. "Still not ringing a bell."

"No reason it should," I said. "And you can forget the psychic stuff. I'm not one of — I'm just an insurance investigator."

Gleason broke his stare long enough to roll his eyes. The move made him look like a fourteen-year-old, and didn't do much for his would-be tough-guy image.

James had begun writing in his notebook. "You know, Mr. Rodak, we don't often get private detectives showing up first on scene at a homicide."

"We don't like people contaminating crime scenes," Gleason said.

"Nothing was contaminated, as I explained to your officers," I said. "And I'll give you all the details in my statement."

"Okay, okay," James said as he made more notes.

"Do you carry a weapon, Mr. Rodak?" he said.

"No," I said. "Now, if you'd like me and my associate to give you our statements, we would —"

I stopped, as I was distracted by another unmarked car. A green Chevy Lumina had rolled onto the crowded block. This one also had police lights behind its glass, but they weren't flashing, and it parked just outside the police tape line.

The massive driver got out, stretched his back, looked around at the growing bustle of the crime scene, then ducked under the yellow tape and came toward us up the sidewalk.

"You lost, Detective?" Gleason called out.

"Right where I need to be," the newcomer said. It was Detective Fred Carson.

"I'm sure you're here to help," James said, "but you might have noticed the sign you passed on the way from Denver. This is Aurora. Aurora crime scene. Aurora body."

"Just here to observe, for now," Carson said. "I have reason to believe that your DB is connected to a homicide we're investigating in Denver. And a burglary. And maybe more."

"Sounds like you have a lot of work to do back in Denver," said Detective James. "Sure you want to spend your time here?"

"Like I said, I have reason to believe that there's a connection. Right now my boss is on the phone with your boss. I'm just here to observe, and offer whatever help you might require."

James sighed. "You can start by telling me about this 'reason to believe' there's a connection."

"A trusted informant indicated there may be a link between our cases and your victim," Carson said. He couldn't help himself from glancing at me as he said it. Probably the shock of using the word *trusted* with reference to Martin Rodak.

James and Gleason noticed the look.

"Goddamn private eyes," Gleason mumbled.

"You wait here, Detective," James said. "We need to look at the crime scene."

"We'll let you know if we need any help," Gleason added.

Carson watched their backs as they went up the walk toward the house. Then he turned to me. "If this pans out, I just might owe you one." Surprisingly generous coming from Carson, but he did emphasize the "if."

As Carson and I waited on the sidewalk, yet another official vehicle pulled up to the tape line. It was a long white SUV with a wire cage visible through its back windows. County Animal Control.

"Must have heard about the cats," I said.

"Cats?" said Carson.

"You'll find out soon enough.,"

Two animal control officers with thick gloves and heavy plastic pet carriers marched past us to the front door, which had been unlocked and was manned by a uniformed officer. As the officer opened the door for the animal cops, Gleason pushed around them to call to us from the doorway.

"Detective Carson! Detective, get up here. Sounds like your boss and ours want us to play nice."

Carson started up the walk. I followed close behind.

"What the hell are you doing?" he asked.

"Being a trusted informant," I said. "Come on, Detective, I got you out here. Maybe I can be of help."

Carson signed. "Okay. But keep your mouth shut. And he stays here." He pointed at Mark, still wobbling at the edge of the porch. Mark waved us off and nodded agreement as vigorously as his churning stomach would allow.

I wondered just how closely Mark could communicate with animals. I never really asked him about the details, though he had mentioned that it's not exactly like talking with a person. Maybe it's like telepathy. But the cats had still managed to lie to him.

As we went in I pulled a pair of blue nitrile gloves from my jacket pocket and snapped them on. Carson did the same with a pale latex pair that he pulled from his own pocket.

Gleason glared at me but didn't raise a fuss about my presence. He just warned us not to touch anything, gloves or no gloves.

"No sign of forced entry," I said, looking back at the intact lock and doorframe. "Any sign in the back?"

"No, back door and windows are intact," James said.

"That suggests the victim knew whoever did him," Carson said.

"Either that or a push-in," Gleason said. "No chain on the door, and no peephole."

"Not likely to have a push-in and not knock that over," I said, pointing out the narrow table by the door holding a slender glass vase with three dead yellow roses. "And there's a lot of valuable stuff in this room. Carson's right, he probably knew whoever it was."

Gleason grunted. He and James led the way across the living room toward the kitchen. The CSIs had set up a line far to the left side of the wide archway, keeping the police personnel as far as possible from the body and far away from the most direct path into the kitchen.

I went to the right and crouched near the transition from living room carpet to kitchen tile, right in the high-traffic strip. I stayed up on my toes, touching as little of the carpet as possible, while craning my head to the side to get a low angle on the surface.

"Any prints off the carpet? I asked.

"CSU barely started on the body," James said. "So you get the hell away from there!"

"If your pet private eye can't stay quiet, he can wait outside with his sideshow act," Gleason said.

"Hey," Carson said, "I'm here because your boss said so. And Rodak is here because I said so. So let's look at the body."

Before following James and Gleason on the long route into the kitchen, Carson turned to me where I couched and poked a finger at my forehead. "Don't fuck this up, Rodak. What's the matter with you?"

I shrugged and made to follow Carson into the kitchen. As I stood I reached down to steady myself, and as my hand touched the floor I tightened my fist so that a few yarns from the carpet pile were gripped between my knuckles. After I stood I quietly removed the glove, turned it inside out, and buried it in my pocket.

Max Wells was still where I'd left him. And the smell was still awful. The medical examiner was testing rigidity of the neck and abdomen, but I knew there was little he could tell on scene from a body that was this old. Three others from the crime-scene unit were taking samples of the blood caked on the floor, and were photographing and shining UV light on the scene in a pattern that spiraled away from the corpse.

I didn't get much else of interest from crashing the crime scene. No doubt the Aurora PD would process the place thoroughly, and Carson would get to see the file in exchange for giving the Aurora cops a look at the file on Vargas and maybe the Vicar and Blake theft. But I was betting Carson and his superiors would try to downplay any connection to the theft, because seeing it become a multi-county thing could give the feds fresh incentive to leverage the Indian angle and take over the investigation.

My car was still parked right in front of Max Wells's house, in the middle of the maelstrom of emergency vehicles, cops, and near-cops. A uniformed officer was standing between me and the car, but he stepped aside as I rounded the Clubman's stubby nose and got in behind the wheel.

Mark was already in the passenger seat, looking more calm than he'd been on the porch.

"You feeling better, Mark?"

"Yeah, a bit. Thanks. That was just ... Ick."

I suspected he'd been doing better ever since animal control took away Wells's cats. "I'll drop you at home if you like."

"No, really, I'm feeling better —"

"I know," I said. "But there's not much left to do today."

"Nothing from the house that you want to follow up on?"

"Well, yeah. I got something I want to show to Melissa."

CHAPTER 22

It was dark by the time I got to Melissa's place. I parked in a visitor's spot near her apartment and jogged up the walk to her door.

"Just a minute, Martin," I heard her say, just before my finger hit the bell.

True to her word, a minute later Melissa opened the door. She wore slim blue jeans and a top with a pale flower print. Her hair was in a bun, and there was a streak of black ink on her left cheek, just below the frames of her huge dark glasses. Immediately I felt better, just seeing her. As I always do. Even on a day like this one. I felt a familiar lightness behind my brows that turned into a tingle across the top of my head and a warmth in my chest.

"Hi, Melissa," I said. "This an okay time?"

"If it has to do with poor Fielding, it's a perfect time." Her brows angled down over the tops of her glasses. "And it had better have to do with helping Fielding."

"It does, it does," I said. "Can I come in? I have something I want you to check out."

Melissa led me into her living room. "I hope you brought me something better to work with than photographs."

"Um, maybe. Something you can hold, at least. If you're careful and don't blow it away."

Melissa sat down at her worktable as I fished in my pocket for the glove I'd removed at the crime scene. Carefully I turned the glove right side out and held it up to the light. A few beige wisps of carpet fiber clung to the blue synthetic rubber in between the first and second fingers. I harvested the fibers and held them out toward Melissa.

"Hold out your hand," I said.

Melissa stretched her left hand toward me, and I laid the fibers on her small ink-stained palm. "There you go."

"What?" Melissa said. "I don't feel anything. No, wait. What is it you gave me?"

"They're carpet fibers."

"Carpet — God, Martin, how do you expect me to get anything from something as flimsy as carpet fibers? I'm not a crime lab. I can't —"

Melissa had started shaking her palm as she spoke, as if she were sifting the fibers she held cupped there. Now she stopped, her hand and her head both motionless. "Wait."

I waited.

"Cats?" she said

Uh-oh.

"Forget the cats," I said. "What else? Any people? Maybe two weeks ago?"

She curled her hand to touch the fibers gently with her thumb. "Yes. Wait ..."

I held my breath as I watched her. A few seconds later she fumbled around on the table before her and grabbed a stick of charcoal, which she waved frantically over the table. "Paper. Paper, paper, paper, paper —"

I shoved the other materials aside and tore a page from a large spiral-bound sketchbook. I spread the sheet out in front of her. "Here."

Immediately Melissa brought the charcoal down on the paper and began drawing madly. Her head was fixed straight ahead, and in her left hand her thumb continued to caress the nearly invisible carpet fibers. It was a weirdly gentle gesture compared to the violent activity of her right hand as it flew about and crashed into the paper. I held the edge of the sheet so that it would stay in place as Melissa drew. I felt feverish just watching her, and my perspiration dotted the edges of the paper where I held it.

In about thirty seconds she had filled the page with black and gray streaks.

"More," she said. "Another. More."

I tore off another sheet as quickly as I could and replaced the finished page in front of her. Instantly she began drawing again.

We repeated the process six times over the course of ten minutes. All the while her head never moved, and her left hand remained raised level with her shoulder as her thumb stroked the fibers. Her right hand slowed during the last three sheets, as if she were drawing more carefully. Still, she filled every sheet.

Melissa slumped back in her chair with an explosive sigh. Perspiration shone on her forehead. I went into the kitchen to get her a glass of water. Once she had that in her hand and was sipping it, I bent down to gather the pile of drawings she had produced. I had tossed them to the floor during her trance as I rushed to keep her supplied with paper.

The first two were of Max Wells. I recognized him from the photo on his website more than from the state I had found him in that afternoon. One drawing was like a portrait, similar to the drawing Melissa had made a few days earlier. Maybe it showed the way Wells would have seen himself in a mirror. The other was a candid sketch of Wells in a big, tattered sweater watching TV, a wine glass on the table next to him and a magazine perched on his knee.

The third drawing was an action scene. Wells stood in his living room, surrounded by three people. Wells looked frightened. The other three were in shadow, and seemed to loom over him. Probably an image of how he had felt at the time.

Next was a picture of the four people in the kitchen. Wells had turned to confront the others. A large kitchen knife was in his hand. I suspected that the Aurora crime-scene unit would find that knife missing from Wells's kitchen knife block.

The next page skipped right to the end. The knife Wells had been holding now protruded from his neck. Blood showed on the drawing as thick black pools of charcoal. Wells's eyes were wide.

Something else in the drawing surprised me. One of the attackers was a woman. She bent toward Wells, shaking a finger, her face contorted into a sneer or a shout. It looked like she wanted to make sure Wells heard all of her anger before he died. The hand she held up was dark with blood.

Finally I got to what I'd hoped for. The last three pages were clear portraits, like the work of an unusually expressive courtroom artist.

Two of the men I recognized right away. The tail I had made and then shaken down near Colorado Springs, and the thug who had beaten Wilson Warner and might have shot me.

The woman from the murder picture was one I didn't recognize. Late middle age but expensively maintained, in a sharp-collared suit and a few stylish streaks of gray in her dark, well-coiffed hair.

"So," I said out loud. "Who is this lady?"

"Don't ask me," Melissa said. "I might have drawn a roller-skating pig for all I know."

I stared at the portrait some more, then at the two men. Something nagged me. Something I'd seen before.

No, something I hadn't seen before.

"I'll be right back," I said. I went out to my car and grabbed my copy of the Pioneer West case file. When I returned I opened it on the table and sifted through the contents until I found the drawings Melissa had made from my photos of the old Vicar and Blake basement.

The old sketches showed Vargas and two other men. One of the men was Wells, of course, and I knew the other two had to be Vargas and McKelvie. And neither of them matched Melissa's new drawings. The Tail and the Thug I'd been dealing with, the ones I now knew were involved in Wells's death, had not been in that basement, planning the heist with Joseph Vargas.

I should have known, as soon as I found Wells dead, that my original theory was shot. And the drawings confirmed it. Wells and McKelvie, the other two thieves, were accounted for. So Vargas's murderer wasn't an accomplice who had turned on him.

"It was a different crew," I said.

"What? Who?"

"The theft," I said. "And Wells's murder. They were different sets of people. I've been assuming that Vargas was killed because the Vicar job went wrong, or there was a disagreement about splitting the take. Killed by his own crew. The sketches you made from the basement pictures showed Vargas and two others, since that's where they had planned the robbery."

"That's why Cindy sent you there," Melissa said.

"Right," I said. "But the drawings you made today are not the same people. A different set of people killed Wells."

"Different than the ones who killed Vargas."

"Not necessarily," I said. "My experience is that killers are rare. If you've got one set of killers in a case, odds are that they did all the killing. These sketches you just did tonight make it clear that these three people — this woman and these two men — killed Wells. That tells me they're probably the ones who killed Vargas."

"And that's why Vargas couldn't tell Fielding who had killed him," Melissa said. "He had never seen them before."

I looked again at Melissa's drawing of the murder scene. Three people standing over Wells as he bled out. One man was now in custody down in Colorado Springs, and the other man either in custody or at least, I hoped, positively ID'd thanks to the DWI I'd set him up for.

So, who was the woman? And where was she now?

Whoever she was, she appeared to be unleashing volcanic anger at Wells even as he died. Hard to imagine anyone getting that worked up over the Fenn statue, real or fake. But there were two murders to prove me wrong on that point.

On top of that, she had known just how to track down the thieves. Wells to his home, Vargas to a secret midnight meeting. The third thief, McKelvie, had probably saved his own life by holing up to worship his stolen camera.

"So, what did they have in common?" I said out loud.

"Who?" Melissa said.

"The three people. Not the ones you drew tonight. By the way, you did draw a fine picture of Max Wells's murder. But I mean Wells, Vargas, and McKelvie. The three people who had carried out the theft. What did they have in common, besides the theft itself?"

"The auction house."

"No, besides the theft. How did they meet?"

Melissa gave an impatient sigh. "I know. That's what I mean. The auction house. You said one was a client, one was an ex-employee, and one was a consultant."

Oh.

"Right!" I said. "That's one thing, probably the only thing that they all had in common. The auction house."

I paced to the front door and back, quickly. Just long enough for another brain cell to start firing. "So a person with the information to suspect them and then to track all three of them down, and quickly, would also be someone connected with the auction house."

"That's right," Melissa said. "So, you have profiles of the employees? Any female suspects?"

"No, we looked again at the employee roster as soon as Mark discovered that the sculpture was a fake."

I thought for a minute as I shuffled through the file some more. "Someone connected with an employee?" I mused. "Wait. Maybe ..." I searched through the file and found the page I wanted.

"Can I use your computer?" I said as I moved across the room to Melissa's iMac.

"Sure, but —"

I tapped the keyboard to bring the machine to life. It was a lot like my old Mac, except for the bigger keyboard and the braille display running along the bottom below the space bar. Melissa didn't always like to use her talent for "seeing" things. I heard the computer's disk start spinning, and only then did I notice the huge crack running diagonally across the right side of the screen.

"Screen's broken," Melissa said. "Got it cheap, and makes no difference to me."

I growled a little as I fished in my pocket for my phone. I woke up the phone, opened a web browser, and typed in a search.

It took a couple of minutes of digging before I found what I was looking for: a photograph of Frieda Lansing. The photo was ten years old, taken in bad light at some charity event organized by Vicar and Blake. But as I squinted at the phone's tiny screen, it became clear to me that it was the same woman as in Melissa's drawing.

"It's her," I said.

"Who?"

"The woman in your picture is Frieda Lansing, head of Vicar and Blake. Lansing killed Max Wells. And was probably behind the death of Joseph Vargas."

For the hell of it I thumbed James McKelvie's name, and "Fort Logan," into a web search. This time it was easier to find a picture. As expected, the man smiling at me from a photo in the bar association newsletter looked just like the third man in Melissa's earlier set of sketches. I told Melissa.

"So Wells, Vargas, and McKelvie worked together on the burglary at the auction house," I said. "They stole back the Fenn sculpture, and a few other things — maybe to hide their tracks, maybe to pay off Vargas, who knows? Then Lansing and her two heavies hunted them down. Killed at least two of them."

"A pretty extreme measure to recover a stolen sculpture," Melissa said.

"That is true," I said. "Like John Harris would say, that's why you buy insurance."

CHAPTER 23

I said good night to Melissa and drove home. Now I faced the tough part of the job. I knew who was behind the murders, and who was behind the theft, but I had no proof.

Oh, I had plenty of proof for my own confidence. Melissa's drawings are better than eyewitness testimony as far as I'm concerned. But I needed proof that would stand in court. I needed evidence that would convince a judge to issue a warrant, and a jury to hand down a conviction. And above all, I needed proof that would convince the cops and the DA to let Fielding go.

I also hadn't recovered all of the stolen property yet, which is why I'd been hired in the first place.

Once I got to the house I dropped my jacket on the sofa, went straight to the back room, and turned on the computer. While it started up, I went to the kitchen to take a potpie from the freezer. I left it spinning in the microwave and went back to check the computer.

I pulled up a web browser and repeated the search for Lansing that I had run on my phone from Melissa's house. I selected the same charity event photo I'd seen on my phone and studied it again on my computer's bigger screen. No doubt at all, the woman killing Wells in Melissa's drawing was Frieda Lansing.

I looked more closely at the crowd of people surrounding Lansing in the photograph. Several society women of about Lansing's age, smiling and holding glasses of wine. A few men of about that age or older. And one younger man near the edge of the photo. I dragged the mouse to zoom in on that edge of the picture.

Zooming in made the picture blurry, but still I recognized the man. Younger than when I'd seen him in the flesh. And not holding a gun. But it was definitely the same man who had beaten Wilson Warner at his theater. In the photo he was standing near Lansing, but not too near. Bodyguard distance.

I sent a copy of that photo to my printer and went back to searching the web for information about Frieda Lansing. Found lots of references to her role at Vicar and Blake. A two-year-old feature about the auction house from the *Denver Business Journal*. A *Denver Post* obituary from the death of her husband twelve years ago, and a business section piece from a month later about how his death left her in control of Colorado's premier auction house. A six-year-old piece from the Lifestyle section about an auction of Beat Generation memorabilia for which Vicar and Blake was donating its commissions to a University of Denver literacy program.

I looked more carefully at the photos that ran with the story. There, in a photo taken during the gala that followed the auction, was a photo of Frieda Lansing's two children, Eleanor and Kyle.

Eleanor was about twenty at the time the photo was taken, but it was hard to tell her age from the picture. She had a very high forehead and large eyes, which gave her a distinctly child-like look. But she also had a tired, haggard expression that aged her. She was smiling for the photographer, probably as well as she could, but seemed pained or nervous about her surroundings.

Standing next to her with his hand on her arm was her brother, Kyle. Him I recognized right away. I'd clocked him in the chin and doused him with whiskey outside a Five Guys before calling the cops on him. Lansing's son was the guy I'd found tailing me.

So Lansing's son and a man who was probably her body-guard had followed me to Colorado Springs. The bodyguard attacked Wilson Warner at gunpoint.

And helped Lansing kill Wells. And probably Vargas. And broke into Fielding's place and knocked me out during their exit.

The medical examiner would have to confirm it, but it looked to me like Wells had been killed at least a few days before Vargas. So in sequence these guys had gone from Wells to Vargas. And then from Vargas to Fielding? No. I still didn't believe Fielding was involved, not at the time Vargas was killed, so Vargas must have been a dead end.

So they followed some other link to me. The insurance company, probably. Then from me they went to Fielding for some reason, and also followed me to Wilson Warner and Johnny Tom.

That timeline pointed to Lansing wanting me to lead her to something. One of the stolen items. Maybe the fake Michael Fenn sculpture, as that's the only item Wells had authenticated. But this was a pretty extreme reaction to the theft of some fake artwork. And why frame Fielding?

As I thought about that I began running Google searches for Lansing's bodyguard. Didn't come up with much. I sent an email to my friend Oscar Hanks, a private security consultant and ex-CBI agent, to ask if he'd heard anything about Lansing's thug. I included a link to the photo of the guy hovering near Lansing at the party.

Next I searched for information about Kyle Lansing. He was a bit less of a mystery. Good prep schools, college in California, now thirty years old but not a standout achiever. Held some vague-sounding "coordinator" job at Vicar and Blake. His public profile had diminished in recent years as he got older.

Then I searched for the daughter, Eleanor. She was four years younger than her brother. There was much less information available about her, but what there was seemed interesting. Good schools, like her brother, and some time in college back east, but judging by the dates, she returned to Colorado before she finished a degree. Then more social activities, but these ended abruptly. I couldn't find any reports of her being out in public in the past three years.

One Colorado gossip site had a short piece about Eleanor Lansing being admitted for treatment at a private residential medical facility. The blogger made some catty remarks about it being typical rich-girl rehab, but I was not so sure. There were other hints that Eleanor had been "away for treatment" several times during her youth, starting when she was about fourteen.

I checked the clock on the corner of the computer screen. Twelve forty-five. I went into the kitchen and ate a few bites of my now-cold potpie, and cleaned up the mess in the microwave. Then I warmed a mug of milk and went to bed.

MY PHONE WOKE ME EARLY. I grabbed it off the nightstand and fumbled with it for a minute before I realized there was no incoming call, just an alarm I forgot I'd set. I rubbed my eyes, but that didn't make them feel any better.

I walked barefoot into the kitchen and put on a pot of coffee. While it brewed I ate an apple and flipped through email.

Oscar Hanks had already replied to my message from the night before. I was surprised by that, given how early it was, but he mentioned that he was in Atlanta on a consulting gig. Time zones were working in my favor.

Hanks offered to dig up more information if I needed it, but he was able to tell me that Lansing's bodyguard was named Steven Sacks.

With that information I was able to find more, mostly in the professional tracing databases I subscribed to as a P.I. Sacks had spent some time as an army MP, gotten some more experience in uniform as a cop for Denver and in Douglas County, and then put on a suit for private security jobs. He went to work as personal security for Lansing and her family shortly after her husband died, and served in that role for over ten years. Then six months ago he was let go, for unspecified reasons. Hanks had no word on what Sacks had been doing since then.

Six months. Based on the information we'd found in the old Vicar and Blake building, that was quite a while before Wells, McKelvie, and Vargas started planning their heist about a month and a half ago. But Sacks, like Mrs. Lansing and her son, apparently had no involvement with that theft. At least, they weren't in Melissa's sketches.

I sat down at the dining room table with a coffee mug and my notebook to lay out some ideas for approaching Lansing. Harris had said that Lansing pushed to keep me on the case. Which seemed a little odd to me, if she had been involved in at least one murder. But it seemed to support the idea that she wanted me to lead her to something. Maybe that was why she'd had her guys plant evidence to implicate Fielding — to give me another reason to keep digging. Maybe that would give me a hook for getting to see her.

I had finished my coffee and was about to make a call to Lansing's office when my phone rang. I answered it and pushed my mug aside, but I didn't even have time to say hello.

"You goddamn lying shithead son of a bitch."

It was not a voice I recognized, or a greeting I was accustomed to. "I love you too, whoever you are."

"This is Wilson Warner, you bastard."

"Warner. You're out of the hospital?"

"Yes, goddamn it. Got out last night. Now I'm on my way to Denver. Just be glad I've got more important things to do than to come over to wherever the hell you are and kick your ass."

"Hey, hey, I'm sorry. I didn't know I was being followed. I never meant to lead anyone to your place, let alone what they were going to do."

"Forget that," he said.

"Then what?"

"You talked to me for half the goddamn day and never told me that the case you were investigating was my own nephew's murder."

This time I was too confused to say anything. Then the light dawned.

Joseph Wilson Vargas.

"My nephew, Joseph Vargas. Didn't bother to tell me that, did you? Didn't think I'd care about that detail? Or maybe you thought I might not spend time answering your questions if I knew?"

"Look, I had no idea. I mean, maybe I should have told you there was a murder involved, but I had no idea that Joseph was related to you."

"Hell you didn't. Why else did you come to me?"

"I told you, I got your name from Andrew Gregory. I was just tracking down the jars."

Now Warner was silent for a moment.

"Joseph had been dead for more than a week by the time I came to see you. How come you hadn't heard yet?"

"Joey didn't have any family up there in Denver. Not much family at all. I was the closest he had, and that was not very close. Hadn't spoken to him in a year."

"I'm sorry to hear that," I said.

"Yeah, me too."

I got up and went into the kitchen to pour some more coffee. "So, how did you hear the news about your nephew?"

"Denver police finally tracked me down," Warner said. "While I was in the hospital."

"Well, again, I'm sorry. Really, I didn't know."

Warner went on talking as if he hadn't heard me. "And as soon as I got back to my place, I found a letter from him. From Joseph. Told me about his job at that damn auction house, and he sent me a key."

"A key? Wait, did you say you were on your way to Denver?"

"Right," Warner said. "Joey sent me a key to a mailbox up there in Denver. Why, who the hell knows."

"Where?" I said. "I'd like to meet you. I think there might —"

"You can kiss my ass," Warner said. "I got no more time for you. I just called to let you know what I think of someone who can meet up with a man and act all friendly and not let him know about the death of his own flesh and blood."

I heard Warner take a deep breath and hold it, then let out a rumbling sigh.

"I didn't know," I said.

He paused again. "Maybe you didn't. I still think you're an asshole."

"Many do."

Warner let out another noise, possibly a laugh, and hung up.

I put down the phone and drank more coffee while I looked at the notes I'd scribbled during my conversation with Warner. Then I flipped back through my notebook to look up an address.

Joseph Vargas had given someone a key before. The key that led Fielding to a mailbox that had contained one of the missing jars. I had an idea about what the second key would reveal.

CHAPTER 24

Thirty minutes later I was in the Clubman, in a strip mall parking lot, keeping an eye on the entrance from Colorado Boulevard and on the front door to the Mile High Mail Store between a pink and yellow frozen yogurt place and yet another nail salon.

I'd tried calling Warner back to get him to agree to meet me, but he didn't pick up. I was willing to bet that if Joseph Vargas had left him a key to a mailbox, it was probably another box at the same place he'd sent Fielding.

Whatever was in that box, it must be evidence related to the Vicar and Blake burglary, and probably Vargas's murder. If Warner had been out of touch with his nephew, then the timing of the letter, right between the V and B job and Vargas's death, couldn't have been a coincidence.

The box probably contained one of the other Lacalma jars. Or Maybe Vargas had used a mailbox to hide information about where the Fenn sculpture was stashed. The piece itself would not fit into a rented mailbox.

Of course, the box could just contain money, Vargas's take from the job. Not that there was any evidence they'd sold anything. Money would be the least useful thing for me and Fielding.

After almost an hour I started to wonder if I wasn't wasting my time sitting in a half-empty parking lot on a Sunday morning, waiting for someone who didn't want to see me.

Sunday. Four days today since Fielding went in for his evaluation.

I poked at my phone to call Liz Duncan. I got her voice mail, so I left her a quick update on my last day and a half and asked if she had any news.

Twenty minutes later I suspected I'd missed Warner entirely. Or maybe I'd been wrong about where Vargas's mailbox was. Then I saw a dusty white pickup pull into the lot and clamber over the speed bumps. It parked near the mailbox store, and Wilson Warner got out of the truck to go inside.

I waited and watched for him to come out, and used the last of my coffee to wash down some ibuprofen. I'd started getting a headache around the time Warner arrived.

Ten minutes later Warner emerged, carrying a square brown box under his arm. I got out of my car to approach him.

Just as Warner arrived at his truck, another vehicle pulled into the spot next to his. A dark green minivan, caked with mud from recent rains up in the hills. I could just barely see Warner as he unlocked the door to his truck and hefted the package to put it inside.

Before he could put the box in the truck, the side door of the minivan flew open. A man in a dark jacket reached for the package and tried to grab it from Warner's large, age-spotted hands.

I am glad Wilson Warner and I hadn't gotten into a fight. He was one tough old man. He held on to the box, and still managed to strike his attacker with an elbow across the cheekbone. The man reeled back, then reached farther out of the car toward Warner. Warner tried to back out of the small space between the cars, but was hemmed in by his own truck's big side-view mirror.

I ran across the lot to where the men fought. Before I got there, the man from the van landed a vicious punch across the side of Warner's face. Right where he'd been bruised before by Lansing's bodyguard. It dazed Warner long enough for the attacker to deliver two more powerful blows.

Warner staggered and slumped, but did not crumple. Still, he offered little resistance when the other man grabbed him by his shirt and his belt and pulled him into the van. The square package was still in Warner's grasp. As he disappeared into the vehicle, I saw two hands dart out and take the box from him, saving it from damage and bringing it into the van before Warner fell inside.

The minivan's tires smoked as it blasted out of the spot and out of the parking lot. It made a quick right onto Colorado Boulevard, in the direction of I-25.

I hadn't been able to reach Warner to help him, but I was able to get a plate number from the van. A partial number, at least, as the middle of the rear plate was obscured by mud.

I sprinted back to the Clubman and pounded the Start button. It seemed to take a long time to get into gear and moving. I made my own quick right turn out of the lot, trying to follow the van.

Less than three blocks south, I still had not caught sight of the van, and I was coming up on the entrance ramp to the interstate. Had the van taken the highway, or kept going south on Colorado?

On a Sunday morning, traffic on 25 was light. Still, if I were trying to flee the scene of a crime, I would avoid it at all costs. Tie-ups seem to happen randomly on that stretch the interstate, and a fugitive could easily be trapped in a cage of trucks and delivery vans.

I kept going south, still trying to spot the green minivan. Between gearshifts I punched my phone's voice dial and shouted slowly. "Call. Jeff. Lang. Mobile."

"Calling Jeffrey Lang, mobile."

For once, the voice thing worked. I listened impatiently through a few rings until Lang picked up.

"Detective Jeffrey Lang," he said.

"Jeff, listen," I said.

"Rodak? What's going on?"

"No time. I just witnessed a kidnapping. Shopping center parking lot, northwest corner of Colorado and, uh, Florida Avenue. Suspect turned south on Colorado. Probably heading south on Colorado or north on I-25. Maybe south on 25 or a different turn."

Lang was silent for a moment; I could hear him fumbling with a pen. I kept searching for the green minivan, with no success.

"Kidnapping?" Lang said. "Like a kid? What's the description? I'll get out an AMBER."

"No, not a kid. Man, late sixties, about six-one, Native American, long gray hair in a ponytail. Wearing jeans and a tan jacket. Attacker was about the same size, dressed in black. Driving a green minivan, partial plate starts with *R*, ends with 746."

"Okay, I'll get this out to units in the area. You come over to the district station right now so you can —"

"No, I'm heading south on Colorado, trying to find these bastards. Oh yeah, there are at least two people in the van that grabbed Warner. That's the victim's name. Wilson Warner. Lives in Colorado Springs and on the Lacalma Reservation down south."

Still no sign of the van, as I left the busy area around the interstate and traveled deeper into the suburbs, past churches, hardware stores, and family restaurants.

"Crap," Lang said. "This have to do with Carson's case?"

"Yes. And I think Frieda Lansing is involved. In the murders, and probably this kidnapping."

"Okay, I need you to come down to —"

"I'll talk to you later," I said, and punched End Call.

I kept looking for the van, driving south on Colorado Boulevard until it ended at Quincy Avenue. I was surrounded by parks, golf courses, and gated communities. The Lansings had owned a home here once, before they traded up. I was reaching for my file to look up where their house had been when my phone rang.

"Martin? It's Jeff. A patrol unit found the minivan, parked and empty in a school parking lot off Dartmouth. They must have changed cars. We've updated the BOLO, and officers are picking up the search. Why don't you —"

"Thanks, Jeff," I said, and hung up.

I turned around and went back north on Colorado Boulevard, and made a left onto Dartmouth. I knew the school Lang mentioned. It was a little ways west on Dartmouth, near University, not too far from my own house.

I slowed when I neared the school. From the street I could see that toward the back of the lot two Denver police patrol units were parked near the green van, their lights flashing. It looked like the van door was open.

A crime-scene unit would be there soon. Not soon enough to do any good, I thought. If only I had a way to track Warner. If only I had —

Wait. Of course I did.

I poked at my phone again and pulled up Cindy's number. It

seemed to ring for a long time before her kind, creaky voice came on the line.

"Hello?"

"Hello, Cindy. It's Martin."

"Martin? Well, this is a surprise." Pause. "And what are you doing sitting there on a Sunday morning? With those police nearby?"

"It's about the case, Cindy. The case you helped on last week, the one that got Fielding into trouble. I'm trying to fix that. I need your help."

"Well, of course, Martin. What can I do?"

"Someone has been kidnapped."

"Oh dear," Cindy said. "That's terrible."

"Yes, it is. But it just happened, so I have a chance to find the person, and find the people who did it. I need to find out where they went. Can you help?"

"Well, I can try," Cindy said. "I must be honest I haven't been feeling very well lately, what with the terrible news about Mr. Fielding and —"

"That's why I need you to try, Cindy. Can you try finding them for me?"

"Yes, Martin." Cindy sighed. "What do you need?"

"I need you to find a man for me. His name is Wilson Warner. He's the man who was kidnapped. Just think about that, Cindy. He's been kidnapped, and he may be struggling. The last place I know where he was is right near where I am now, where the police are investigating."

"Okay, hold on just a moment while I get my things." I heard a loud clack as Cindy put the phone down, then the rustling of paper and the clink of a glass jar.

"Okay, Martin, I have the right map and a glass bead. This might take a little time. You know, it's not easy to do this while I'm handling the phone."

"Can you put me on speaker?"

"I don't know how to do that, Martin. Does my phone have that? I —"

"Never mind, Cindy, just do your best."

The line went silent except for Cindy's light breathing. The breathing turned to a gentle tuneless hum. The hum stopped abruptly.

"I'm sorry, Martin, I'm getting so much. There are so many people in the area, and I don't know what I'm supposed to find. You know I can't find just a person. I need an event."

"Isn't a kidnapping a pretty big event, the kind of thing you can see?"

"Maybe if he were still struggling, I would be able to pick something up," she said.

I tried not to think about what it might mean if Warner was not struggling.

"He's probably swearing a lot," I said. "Gagged, maybe, but swearing."

Cindy was quiet for a moment. "Yes, I think that will help. Let me try again."

I heard Cindy fumbling with her things again. She started murmuring. Then the murmur turned into a hum. The hum grew stronger and more melodic as the seconds ticked by.

"I think I have him, Martin," Cindy said at last. "He's in another car."

"What kind of car?" I asked.

"I can't tell that, Martin. I just know that your Mr. Warner is in a car with two other people. They are not driving very fast, though."

No surprise there. They would stick to the speed limit to avoid any police attention.

"Where are they, Cindy? That's the important thing. I'm sitting here and they're getting away."

"All right, Martin, all right. They are on 285 heading west."

I put the Clubman in gear and muscled it through a tight turn so I could head back on Dartmouth. A few blocks west I made a left onto University, and then went south to reach Hampden Avenue, which was the name of US 285 as it claws its way across the south side of Denver.

Hampden was filled with traffic. Predictable for a late Sunday morning, or practically any other time. But that was okay. As I drove, I devised a plan.

"Okay, Cindy, here's what we are going to do. You're going to be my GPS tracker."

"GPS? That's those electric maps for cars, right? I read about those. I don't like them."

"Neither do I," I lied. "That's why I have you. You still have Warner's location?"

"Yes, they're right here. Still going west on 285, just coming up to Broadway."

"And you know where I am?"

"Of course, Martin. You just turned onto 285 yourself. I must say, if you're trying to catch them you'll have to do better. You're falling behind."

"I know," I said. "But I don't have to catch them. Not yet. For now it's better if I don't. For one thing there's too much traffic. For another I don't know what kind of car they're driving, so I couldn't catch them if I wanted to with this many other cars on the road."

"So, what do you want me to — Oh! You just need me to keep track of them?"

"Right," I said. "I need you to keep track of where they are, and where I am. I need to stay close enough to keep on their tail, and far enough away that they don't see me and get suspicious."

"Okay. I can do that. This is exciting!"

Yes, very exciting. Not too exciting for Warner, I hoped.

I was counting on two things. One, that they were taking Warner somewhere away from the city. And two, that they would not risk doing anything serious to him until they got somewhere secluded. I figured they really wanted what was in the box, and that they grabbed him only because he had put up more resistance than expected.

I thought about calling Lang with more information, but I didn't want to risk confusing Cindy or hanging up on her.

"Still going west, Martin," Cindy said. "They are almost to Santa Fe."

Santa Fe was the last major north-south road before 285 crosses the South Platte River. There the road begins transitioning into the freeway that carries it out of Denver and through the western suburbs. My speed would pick up then, but so would theirs.

A few minutes later I crossed Santa Fe myself, then the river. "How are we doing, Cindy?"

"You're doing fine," she said. "They're about a mile and a quarter ahead of you. Keeping right up to the speed limit. I don't think they plan to get off 285 anytime soon."

I stayed in the middle lane and kept to the speed limit myself. The road snaked through a construction area and then stretched out again with two lanes in each direction.

"Still okay," Cindy said. "They got slowed down more than you did in that construction, so they are a little less than a mile in front."

There was still enough traffic that I wouldn't have been able to pick them out even if I got closer. And I didn't want to get any closer.

When you are tailing another vehicle, the biggest risk is when your subject changes course — makes a turn, takes an exit, suddenly changes lanes or speed. If you don't react quickly enough, you risk losing sight of your target, and when that happens there's no guarantee you'll ever get it back. React too quickly to match the target's action, and you risk being spotted. If that happens, then the tail turns into a chase, or worse.

A tracking device helps by letting you stay farther away from the subject, and it can give you more time to follow along with their twists and turns. But trackers are expensive, not very reliable, and of questionable legality when planted on someone else's vehicle. They can even lead to felony stalking charges. And a tracker can be found by your target, which lets him dispose of it or send you on a snipe hunt by sticking it onto a bus or a stray dog.

But an accurate, remote, undetectable tracker like Cindy was proving to be a real winner. And the law doesn't even recognize the existence of her talent, so it's never been ruled illegal.

Ten minutes later I was crossing Colorado Highway 470 and cutting through the hogback that marks the beginning of the foothills in that part of Jefferson County. The road continued to the southwest, and after a long straightaway it grew twistier as it climbed through the hills and into the small mountain communities, the places tucked in among the forests in between the Denver metroplex and the pricier high country.

"Think they're headed toward Conifer," I said to Cindy.

"You may be right," she said. "Don't worry, I'll keep you on their tail. You're still doing fine."

The farther we got from Denver, the more I worried. Worried about what they might have done to Warner, or what they might plan to do. Worried about how far we would be from help once we got wherever they were taking us.

"Yep, they're getting to Conifer right about now ...," said Cindy. "And now they've passed right through it. Still on 285, heading southwest."

Less than a minute later I passed Conifer's little main drag myself. I was driving faster. I tried to ease up, as I didn't want to attract the attention of the driver I was following. Or of a state trooper who might be inclined to stop a speeding MINI in the mountains.

Something else was making me nervous too. Not how long we'd been driving, but where. At this point any twist in the road might bring me into a cellular dead spot, and drop my call with Cindy.

"Cindy," I said, "listen, I want to tell you something important. If we get disconnected, I want you to call the Denver police. Ask for Detective Lang or Detective Carson. Tell them you work with me. Tell them exactly where I am, and where the other car is, and what is going on. Talk to Lang if you can, but talk to Carson if you have to."

"All right, Martin. I will. This is so much more exciting than the work we usually do together. I do hope that poor man is okay."

I remembered the scene of that poor man denting the back of a gunman's head with a fire extinguisher. I hoped he'd been able to take care of himself as well this time around.

We drove for another fifteen minutes. The highway wandered south toward the town of Bailey, then curved again to the west.

"Oh, Martin! Martin! They just turned! On Route 64. They're going south."

With a turn between me and them, and no sign of cops, I dropped my foot to pick up some speed and close the distance. Leaving the main road meant they were probably getting close to their destination, and I didn't want to lose them when we were almost there. Wherever there was.

I turned onto Highway 64. It was a county road, a narrow two-lane highway closed in by trees and walls of rock. Cindy guided me through some turns to stay on the right course. There weren't too many places they could go, unless they turned into one of those driveways poking down toward the road, leading up to private grounds and homes. That seemed more and more likely the longer we drove.

"They went left at Payne Gulch Road," Cindy said. "You're coming to the turn now."

I made the turn, heading south and deeper into the Pike National Forest.

"They're going west again," she said a little while later. "Right turn on Greene Valley Road."

Two minutes later I was heading west on Greene Valley. "They still ahead of me?"

"Yes, Martin. They're — Oh! They're turning! They turned left! Must be into a private driveway! They're just up —"

I didn't hear anything more from Cindy. Just two long, low beeps from my phone to let me know that the call had been dropped. I checked the indicator in the corner of the screen. "No Service."

I hoped that Cindy would follow my instructions and contact Jeff Lang, but I couldn't wait to find out. I kept going.

I continued down the road until I got to a private drive on the left. I stopped as near as I dared and examined the driveway. A wide gate of steel tubes stretched across the entrance. At the base of the gate there was a wash of leaves and debris. Clearly the gate had not been opened recently.

A mile down the road was another driveway. The gate was newer and more handsome than the first. I could see fresh tracks in the mud that lay across the opening. I could also see a line of cars parked along the side of the drive as it wound its way through the trees. I couldn't see a house from the road, but through my car's open window I could hear music and chatter drifting down the hill. I doubted that anyone was bringing Wilson and his package to a party, so I moved on.

A half mile farther on I found another driveway with a gate

in much the same condition as the first. No one had been there recently.

I was starting to get farther away than seemed right, given what Cindy had said. I was about to turn around when I came upon a fourth gate. It was bigger than the others, and led to what was more like a private country road than a driveway, flanked by tall, old trees. When I examined the gate and the surrounding ground, I saw that the gate had been opened very recently. There were fresh tracks through the mud where a car had pulled through, and a deep arc-shaped track where the gate had swung open and then shut.

I peered up the drive, trying to see through the trees beyond where it curved to the right. I thought I could make out a house or a cabin up the hill. There was no name or other signage except an address on the mailbox that sat in the top of a square brick pylon.

It seemed clear that this was the place. They couldn't have been farther ahead than this when Cindy told me they had turned.

I pulled my car a few yards farther up Greene Valley Road to put it out of sight, then got out and walked back to the driveway. I stayed low as I approached, and took a closer look at the gate. There was no visible lock, but from the style of gate and the way the hinges were installed, I concluded that there was an electric opener and an electric lock.

That might also mean electronic security, but I had to take that chance. And if I was caught, they'd probably take me to wherever they'd taken Wilson.

It occurred to me that now that they had reached their destination, Wilson might no longer be alive. But my point was still valid — if they caught me I'd probably end up in the same place.

The gate was not very high. Its main purpose was to keep out motorists who might mistake the drive for a public road. I got a foothold on the ironwork and lifted myself up and over, trying to stay safely between the decorative spikes at the top. Decorative, but still pointy.

One of the spikes caught a pocket of my suit pants and tore out a seam, but otherwise I made it to the other side with no damage. I stayed still for a moment, crouched low, and listened for alarms or commotion. Nothing. Either there was no security system to alert anyone to my presence, or the security system was designed to play things cool.

One edge of the driveway was protected by shadows from the early-afternoon sun, so I kept to that side as I moved slowly up toward the house. The drive stretched a good quarter mile through the trees, curving and climbing until it reached a cabin. It was actually a log home in that large spread-out style popular in the nineteen nineties, and calling it a "cabin" would be a little ridiculous. The place was three times the size of my house, and worth probably ten times as much.

The curving drive spread out into a large oval of raked gravel that washed up along the front porch like a frozen lake. Parked on the gravel were a late-model Hummer, a Jaguar in a dark silver-gray, and an old Honda minivan. I was willing to bet the Honda was the car they'd used to haul Warner and his box up to this place.

I was starting to get a headache again as I approached the house. I should have gotten more coffee after all, I thought, or maybe some food. Too late for that now. I crept right up to the dressed logs that made up the exterior wall and pressed myself against it, crouching to stay below the window line. It seemed the place with the most cover from being spotted from inside the house.

I took my phone out of my jacket pocket and risked a look. Still no service. I wondered how long it would take Lang to get the local sheriff's department, or somebody, out here.

I could hear voices and movement from the room behind me, but could not make out any words through the thick panes of energy-friendly glass. I took another risk and raised an eye just a little bit, trying to get a look inside.

The window looked in on a great room. The space had a high ceiling laced with wooden beams, starting at the front entrance and stretching to fill nearly half the first floor. A large, squarely built man paced near the front door. He was dressed in black, and I suspected he was the man who'd punched out Wilson Warner and pulled him into the van. Replacement thug for Steven Sacks.

Warner himself was across the room, sitting in one of the tastefully rough-hewn chairs surrounding a huge dining table. I could not see any ropes from my position, but from the way his hands rested stiffly on the arms of the chair, I figured he was bound. His face was a little bloodied, but I was relieved to see that he didn't seem hurt otherwise.

As I watched, Frieda Lansing entered the room from a door at the back of the house. Probably the kitchen. She was carrying the package Warner had taken from the mailbox store. She put the box on the table, then started talking to Warner, who looked up at her from his chair. I still couldn't hear them through the thick windows.

After a few moments Warner must have said something she didn't like, or refused to answer her questions, because her expression grew dark. She stared at Warner for several long seconds, then looked up and said something to the thug near the front door. He nodded and started up the stairs to the second floor.

Lansing disappeared into the kitchen again, and emerged a minute later carrying a bottle of oil. She put the oil next to Warner's box and resumed talking to him.

With Lansing's muscle out of the room, I decided to risk

getting closer. I crept toward the back of the house and around the corner. There I found a large patio with a set of French doors on one end and a solid door on the other.

I looked through the French doors and saw a game room with a pool table and overstuffed sofas. I passed that by and went to the other door. When I tried the handle I was surprised to find it unlocked.

Inside was the kitchen, decked out in expensive stainless appliances. A narrow hallway led off to the left, and across the room were the big swinging doors I'd seen Lansing use earlier from the other room. I moved quietly to the doorway and peered through the crack.

Lansing had her back to me. I could now hear her, speaking in a clipped accent that gave away her wealthy Chicagoland upbringing.

"I know there's more you can tell me, Mr. Warner," she said, "and now that you're here you might as well. I have the jar. I just want to know how it works."

Lansing paused, but Warner said nothing.

"I know step one is filling it with oil. I've done that. And I've warmed it in my hands. I learned this much from that idiot Gregory when I convinced him to let me sell them. But it still doesn't work."

Lansing sat down on one of the high-backed dining chairs, across the corner of the table from Warner. She continued in a low, soothing voice. "I know you can tell me more, because I know you care about these jars. They are important to you. And you know what else? You're right. They are important. That's why I wanted them. I never intended to steal them. I wanted to pay money for them. Money to help the children on your reservation. I had someone set up to bid for me at the auction, and I was ready to pay more than anyone else. All to help your kids. It was all set up, and it was good for everyone, until that horrible, incompetent Wells stole them."

Lansing leaned over the table toward Warner.

"And I still will pay," she continued. "I will still donate that money to the Lacalma education fund. So, won't you help me? Won't you help me help my daughter?"

Warner managed a dismissive laugh, but his voice quavered when he spoke.

"Your daughter," he said. "What about my nephew? Joey died because you wanted those jars, and now I'm supposed to help you?"

Lansing stood up and took a few paced away from the table. Her voice rose again.

"That was not my fault," she snapped. "Joseph died because Max Wells roped him into a plan to steal from me, to cover up his own mistake. All I planned was to purchase those jars for a price more than fair. It had to be secret, but it was going to be fair. It was Wells who convinced your nephew to help rob my business. Wells and that lawyer had to cover up the fake sculpture, and they promised Joseph that he could claim the jars if he helped them. Wells told me all of that. Eventually."

Sure, I thought. *Had Wells not interfered, you wouldn't have had to kill him or Joseph Vargas.* Small comfort for anyone.

"So tell me about the jars," Lansing said. "How do I use them?"

Then she said nothing. She just stared at Warner. She stood stock-still, but her eyes looked like she was trying to pull him into her head.

Then she looked away, and pounded a fist on the table. "Why can't I read you, goddamn you? All I can hear from inside your head is that awful mocking laugh."

"Because I'm trained," Warner said. "Like a hundred generations before me. I've learned things that you can't imagine. Your little tricks are a joke."

Lansing whirled to face him again, and her voice cracked with fury. *"Tricks?"* she shouted. "Tricks? You think it's a joke? Hearing the thoughts of everyone around you, unable to stop it?"

She took a step closer to Warner. "Not everyone can control it like I can. This curse killed my mother. She went mad before I was ten. Killed herself in the next room while I slept. Now my daughter has it, and it's killing her. Driving her away from the world."

She sat down again, lowering her voice and wringing her hands. "Please. I've done the research. I know what these jars do. I know that your medicine men used them to quiet the voices."

"They did," Warner said. It was clear that he was afraid, but he somehow managed to sound both smug and solemn. "Voices of the sky, voices of the earth. Voices of the dead. Voices of other spirits. The jars could make them quiet. When the voices were quiet, a shaman could share with the rest of the people what the voices had told him."

"So tell me how to use them," Lansing said. "I never meant to take you, but as long as you are here, you may as well tell me. There are only two jars left, and I don't want to harm them."

"But why would I tell you?" Warner said. "You're a cheat, a thief, and a killer, not a shaman."

Lansing reached across the table and slapped him. "I'm a mother trying to care for her child," she growled. "And don't you dare forget that there's nothing I won't do for her."

As I listened I fit together the pieces of the story Lansing was telling, along with what I'd learned already.

Frieda Lansing had a talent. A gift, the same gift as her daughter and her late mother had: telepathy.

Frieda seemed to have some control of it, but not her daughter. I could see how that would drive someone crazy. Hearing the thoughts of everyone around you, all the time.

According to Lansing, and as Warner seemed to confirm, the jars could block that ability. Judging by Fielding and the way he used the one Vargas had led him to, maybe they could block all psychic talents.

Lansing wanted those jars. She convinced Gregory, probably with the help of her powers, to get the tribe to sell them. Then she planned to have a false bidder buy them for herself. Or she'd have been willing to steal them from her own auction house, I guessed, if necessary.

Then Max Wells and James McKelvie had stepped in and ruined her plan. They broke in to steal the fake Fenn sculpture before it could be discovered. And they got Joseph Vargas to help, by promising that he could take back the jars for his people as part of the heist. The jars were gone, and Lansing wanted them back.

So she went to her insurance company. Got them to put an investigator on the job to get the jars back. When it looked like Pioneer West might take me off the case, she framed Fielding to make sure I was properly motivated to keep digging. And to distract the police. She'd read about my psychic colleagues, so that may have convinced her that I was right for the job.

As I thought about Lansing, it occurred to me: why was she not hearing my thoughts? If she had the same telepathic gift, or curse, as her mother and daughter had, why was I still hiding safely in the kitchen not ten feet away from her?

Before I could think too much about that, I saw Lansing's new muscle coming down the staircase.

He was not alone. His hand held the arm of a young woman, and he was guiding her down the stairs as gently as he could manage. Which was not very gently, as he clearly had more training in hitting people than in caring for them. But they made it down the stairs okay, stopping at the bottom to look across the room at Frieda Lansing and Warner.

The young woman I recognized as Eleanor Lansing. She was several years older than the last picture I'd seen of her, but she hadn't changed much. Age, or just the effect of seeing her in person, seemed only to enhance the strange air that surrounded her. She looked distracted, pained, and a bit otherworldly. I shook my head to clear it, but that just made my headache worse.

"Thank you, Robert," Frieda Lansing said to the muscle. Then she turned toward her daughter. "Ellie, my darling, I have wonderful news. This man here," — she gestured to Warner — "has a way to help us. To help you. We're going to do what the doctors couldn't."

Eleanor did not reply. She stared at her mother for a few long seconds. Then, slowly, she turned her head. Toward me. She stared straight into my eye, through the crack between the doors I had been using to watch her mother and Warner. I could feel her gaze stabbing into my head.

Her mother gave a backhanded wave in my direction. "Oh yes dear, I know he's there. I've been listening to him listen to us since he came in. Don't be concerned. Marco is dealing with it."

Marco?

I straightened up and turned around just in time to see a kid, maybe nineteen, with dark, curly hair clipped short. He was staring at me with a crooked smile, and in his right hand was a short-barreled .22 semiautomatic. A small gun, but big enough.

"Hi, Marco," I said as I raised my hands.

Marco ushered me into the great room. Eleanor took a half step backward as we entered, as if the huge space was getting crowded with just six of us in there.

I glanced over at Warner. He sat stiff and upright in the big wooden chair, his wrists bound to the arms with duct tape. He did not acknowledge me at all, but kept staring at Lansing.

"Mr. Rodak. I should have expected you to join us, but I really was not counting on it. You had a simple job, to find out where the stolen pieces were. If you had just done that and reported it to the insurance company, this would all have been so much simpler."

"Your son and his pal made it less simple, the way they dropped in on Warner here right after I did."

Lansing sighed. "Yes, they were too enthusiastic. They were just supposed to follow you, make sure you stayed on the case, and report to me once you'd found something. I've already sent Kyle away, and I'll have a word with Mr. Sacks as soon as he's out of jail."

Marco gestured to a seat at the table near Warner. I sat.

"Don't bother with the tape, Marco," said Lansing. "The Indian is a challenge, but I can handle Mr. Rodak."

Marco took a step back, his gun leveled casually in my general direction.

Lansing turned to stare at me. Not a long stare, but it seemed to bore deep into me.

My head was pounding, and something had happened to my arms and legs. I tried to move. I wanted to move. But somehow that wanting could not make it out of my head to the rest of my body.

"I really was not prepared to have to deal with you two," Lansing said. "I just wanted the jars. But Mr. Warner simply had to be difficult, and you had to follow him. For now, I'm going to do for my daughter what I'd planned all along. Having one more mind in here might make this a more useful test. There will be plenty of time for Robert and Marco to dispose of you when we're done."

She turned to Warner and narrowed her eyes. She was trying

one last time to read his mind. Warner just returned her stare, unflinching, but the pain in my head increased and soon I had spots swimming in my vision.

After a few more seconds Lansing broke off her gaze. "You know," she said, "I couldn't read Joseph's thoughts either, when we confronted him about the jars. He wouldn't tell me what had happened to them, and I couldn't pull the information out of him."

Warner showed a thin, grim smile. "I taught him well," he said. "Joey could have grown to be a great man if you hadn't killed him."

"Yes," Lansing said. "You taught him very well. But you know what I've learned? I've learned that at the moment of death, defenses like yours tend to weaken. When we killed Joseph, I learned from him that the jars were still in Colorado, and that he'd hidden them safely. I didn't have time to learn where, and I didn't learn anything about you, but I learned enough to know that someone like Mr. Rodak could probably find them."

Lansing leaned in to place her face a few inches from Warner's. "Maybe if your defenses drop I'll learn more from you."

Warner just shrugged, as best he could with his wrists taped to the chair.

Lansing straightened up, then closed her eyes and sighed. "I'm beginning to think that you don't know any more than I do about how to use these jars. No matter. Maybe I know enough."

She turned toward to the table. Laid out in front of her were the cardboard parcel from Warner's nephew, a bottle of corn oil, and a small porcelain dish containing wine corks in a variety of sizes. She reached into the cardboard box and gently removed a small item concealed by layers of bubble wrap. She undid the wrapping and unwound it to reveal one of the stolen Lacalma jars.

She placed the naked jar on the table and carefully withdrew her hands. It was the middle-sized of the three jars, about three inches across and a little more in height, with a short neck that curved outward. It was textured with smooth swirls that encircled its wide middle, and its plain earthen colors seemed at home amid the rough natural wood of the table, the walls, and the ceiling beams.

"There it is!" said Lansing.

She took a moment to clasp her hands in front of her and beam at the artifact. Then she picked up the bottle of corn oil and unscrewed the cap.

Suddenly she stopped, and looked back at Warner. "Does it matter what kind of oil I use?"

He just stared at her, his face as stony as the jar's dry clay. Lansing rolled her eyes and made a delicate snort as she turned back to her work.

She lifted the jar in her left hand and with her right she slowly, gently poured some of the oil into the jar. She kept a careful eye on the jar, easing up on the pouring as it began to fill up. All of us in the room watched her. I held my breath, and I don't think I was the only one.

She put down the oil bottle, and picked through the tray of corks until she found one of the right size. She seated the cork in the jar and gently screwed it down.

Then she took the jar in both hands and lifted it in front of her. She held it lovingly, surrounding it with both her palms, as if she were warming a sick bird.

She turned toward her daughter, her face lit by a bright, craggy smile. "Come here, darling."

Eleanor walked across the room with short, halting steps, drawing closer to her mother and the jar. She seemed to flinch away from where Marco and I were, as if she expected one of us to throw something at her.

Her pained expression didn't change even when she stood four feet away from her mother. She looked away, looked down, shook her head.

"Do you feel any better, dear?" Frieda said.

Eleanor just shook her head again.

Frieda Lansing's eyes widened and her brows knit in confusion. She lowered the jar.

Not working? I thought at her.

"Shut up!" Lansing snapped.

"Goddamn it," Warner said finally. "Okay, okay. If you're going to use that, then use it right. I don't want to watch you make an insult of it."

Lansing gazed at him. "What do I do?"

"Lift it up again, like you did before," Warner said. His voice sounded tight and sad. "Almost up to your chin."

Lansing held up the jar in her hands like an offering.

"Now blow on it," Warner said.

Lansing's eyes widened at the new information. She puckered her lips and blew gently on the top of the jar. Her breath evoked a low whistling sound from the shape of the jar's neck.

Eleanor suddenly looked up at her mother, then at me, and at Marco. She looked back to her mother, and began to nod.

"It's working!" Lansing said.

As I watched the women's reaction, my headache lifted. I hadn't realized how oppressive it had been until then. My limbs also felt free of whatever Lansing had done to them, though I was careful not to give that away by moving them.

With a newly clear head I watched as Eleanor took a half step toward her mother and the group of us at the table. I could almost see a smile creeping into the corners of her mouth.

"Now put it down on the table," Warner said. "It's supposed to be on a ceremonial stone, but the table will do."

Lansing followed his direction. Solemnly she placed the

little round jar on the table and lifted her hands away from its sides. Then she turned back toward her daughter.

I glanced at Warner. He caught my eye, and with a small movement of his lips he gestured toward the jar.

"Ellie?" said Lansing.

"Mom?" Eleanor's voice was barely above a whisper. "It's quiet, Mom. I can't hear them. I can't hear any of them. It's so quiet."

"You feel better?" Lansing said.

"I think so," Eleanor said. She glanced at Warner and Marco and me, then looked back to her mother. "It's a little scary. But it's good."

"Oh, my little lamb!" Lansing said as she rushed toward her daughter.

As Marco and Robert watched the two ladies, I brought up both my legs and kicked at the table. My feet made a solid connection on the table's edge, and I knocked myself and my chair backward to the floor. In front of me, the table's giant wooden slab tipped far enough that it almost flipped over. It came back down on its legs with a heavy thud.

The jar was on its side, rolling toward the opposite edge of the table.

"*No!*" Lansing shouted.

The jar reached the edge and plunged to the floor. The impact smashed it to bits, spreading shards of clay and runnels of oil across the boards.

Suddenly I felt as if a spike had been driven into my head, right next to my left eye. I felt dizzy and nauseated. I heard shrieking, and thought it was me. It wasn't. It was Lansing and her daughter, Eleanor, both crumpling to the floor and clutching at their heads.

I blinked and swallowed a few times, and the pain in my

skull abated slightly, though it still felt like I had lump of something magnetic stuck in my brain.

Warner remained bound to his chair. He was glaring at the two women, and though his mouth was closed his jaw muscles worked as though he were speaking. Considering the usual vocabulary of that old shaman, I could only imagine what kind of weapons-grade thoughts he was throwing at the Lansings' unshielded minds.

Young Marco was still standing next to me, but the kid was staring open-mouthed at the Lansings as they writhed and cried out. His gun wavered at his side, forgotten in his panic. I quickly grabbed his wrist and held the gun out away from us. As I stood up I pulled him down toward me and snapped my other elbow into the side of his head. He went down hard, and I pulled the gun from his slack grasp as he fell.

I turned just in time to see Robert charging from the other side of the room. He had been heading in to help Lansing and Eleanor, but when he saw me turn he slowed and reached into his jacket.

"Don't," I said, and leveled the .22 at his head. I took a step back so I could keep both Robert and the unconscious Marco in my line of sight, but kept the gun trained on Robert.

Robert paused. Then he made as if to dodge to his right, reaching for his gun at the same time.

I fired, aiming outside and a little high. The sharp sound echoed in the big room, and a chip of wood flew off a beam somewhere behind Robert.

A small gun, but big enough. Robert got the idea. He stopped reaching for his holster and raised his hands over his head.

The Lansings' shrieks had diminished into soft sobs. Over that sound I could hear police sirens closing in.

"Nice," said Warner. "Finally we get some fucking cavalry."

CHAPTER 25

"So, Lang and Carson seem happy enough," I said to Melissa.

We were sitting together on the sofa in her bright little living room, next to her disconnected television. Across the room stood her drafting table, which she'd abandoned along with her latest card design to sit with me and drink tea while I told her all the details of what had happened since she drew those latest sketches for me.

After I had gotten Lansing's man Robert under control, deputies from the Park County Sheriff's Department arrived. Cindy had called Lang, and Lang had called the sheriff's office. Cindy gave them my precise location.

I called out to let the deputies know where we all were, and to identify myself. I also told them that I was holding a gun, and why, so they wouldn't shoot me before I had a chance to turn the weapon over to them.

I'll admit that I didn't really look like the good guy when the deputies came in. I was standing in the Lansings' home, holding a gun on their personal security staff while the women cowered on the floor. If I'd been in their place, I might have shot me on sight.

Instead the four deputies were models of professional law enforcement. They kept all of us covered while they relieved Robert and me of our guns. One of them radioed for an EMT unit and more backup. They put me and Robert in zip-tie cuffs and sat us on opposite sides of the room. Then two of them knelt to attend to the Lansings, who were now calmer and quieter. Probably succumbing to shock. Another deputy cut the tape holding Warner to the chair and sat him up at the table. His commentary throughout that process assured them that the old man would be okay to sit on his own while waiting for the medics to arrive. The fourth deputy went to check on Marco, who joined us in the zip-tie club after he took a swing at the helpful officer who roused him.

Soon I heard more sirens, then more vehicles crunching across the gravel drive and up to the house. EMTs came in, checked on the Lansings, and prepared to transport them to the hospital. I recommended a law enforcement escort, which was reluctantly assigned after Warner seconded my suggestion.

Another medic attended briefly to Warner's fresh bruises, until he told her to get away from him and she attended instead to the swollen knot I'd put on the side of Marco's head. My own headache disappeared instantly once the Lansings were gone.

About an hour after the deputies had arrived, things were organized enough for them to take statements. I had just started my description of events when Lang and Carson came in. The Park County guys didn't mind having them there as observers, especially when they heard about the possible connection to burglary and homicide cases in Denver, and about my report of the kidnapping earlier that day. Thanks to Lang and Carson's corroboration, I was soon out of cuffs and standing by the table next to Wilson Warner.

"You son of a bitch," he said, "you saved me from some more of these crazy white people. Now I owe you again."

Eventually we were all brought down to the sheriff's station. Robert and Marco were still in cuffs, while Warner and I were unbound in the back of another deputy's SUV. As we left the house, Warner's parcel and the shards of the smashed jar were being gathered up and labeled by crime-scene investigators. The box still contained the third Lacalma peace jar.

As we drove I turned to Warner, who sat with his eyes closed.

"Sorry we had to break that jar," I said. "You okay with it?"

"I'm thinking it might have been better to let that kid shoot you, if it would preserve me from stupid questions," Warner said.

I smiled but didn't say anything else. A few minutes later Warner spoke again.

"I told you before, once they were in your hands, in your system, the jars were not ours anymore. They were not the same. Those jars were important, and they were old, but they were not the first jars. And it would be stupid to think they would be the last. You did what you had to. My people made those, and my people will make new ones."

I thought about Andrew Twofires Gregory and how he had said something similar, but I didn't mention that to Warner.

At the station Warner and I gave formal statements and answered questions. I avoided details like how Cindy had helped me track the kidnappers' car, and what the jars were really all about. Detective Lang might be open-minded on the subject of psychic talents, but I wasn't ready to count on that from the good folks of Park County.

After three more hours Warner and I were free to go. Lang and Carson drove me and Warner back to my car where I'd parked it on Greene Valley Road, and then they started back toward Denver where they would drop Warner at a motel. I'd offered to let him stay the night at my place, but he had politely declined with some creative comments about my likely hygiene deficiencies. I drove home alone, with brief calls to let Melissa know that I was okay and that things should soon be looking up for Fielding. She promised to spread the word to Cindy, Mark, and the others.

The next day was spent meeting with Lang, Carson, Liz Duncan, and two people from the Denver DA's office, plus an agent from the Colorado Bureau of Investigation. I'd also spent some time at my local print shop, placing a special order.

Now, two days after Warner was kidnapped, I finally had time to see Melissa and fill her in on the details.

"The scene at the cabin, and the statements Warner and I gave, were enough to get warrants for both of the Lansings' Colorado homes, plus the Vicar and Blake offices," I told Melissa. "The police found papers, phone messages, and other evidence about the conspiracy to buy the jars, and about tracking down Wells and Vargas after their theft ruined Lansing's plans. Looks like Lansing and her people will be facing changes for murder, fraud, conspiracy, maybe more."

"Including her son, the guy who followed you?"

"Definitely," I said. "He was picked up in Phoenix, trying to get on a flight to Mexico. From what I hear he might plead out and agree to testify against his mother and her other guys."

Melissa nodded and sipped her tea. "And what about Eleanor? Lansing's daughter? She wasn't involved, was she?"

"No, no sign of that. She's being given whatever help is possible," I said.

"I wonder what help is possible for her," Melissa said. "Sounds like her mother already tried everything medicine could do."

"Seems like she did. But Wilson Warner hinted that he might be able to help the girl. Send her some of his kind of medicine."

Melissa gaped and put down her tea. "He's going to send her a jar?"

"I don't think he can do that. But he may be able to do something."

I finished my tea and put down my mug. Melissa slid closer and lay back in the crook of my arm. She felt nice. Warm.

"I can't help but have a little sympathy for Lansing," I said. "I mean, what she did was terrible. But to see your mother driven to madness, to struggle against it yourself for a lifetime, and then to see your daughter face the same thing. I don't want to guess what lengths I'd go to."

Melissa turned her head toward me. "Do you ever think about it?"

"What?"

"Having children."

I gave her a gentle squeeze. "I suppose it occurs to me now and then. I think about a lot of things."

Melissa was silent. She stayed that way for a minute, and I could feel her stiffen.

"Hey, you okay?" I asked.

"I'm okay," she said. "I just think about it sometimes too. I wonder if I should ever have children. Whether it's a good idea for me. Considering ... everything."

"Oh, hey, I'm sorry. I never meant to upset you."

"No, no. It's not you."

"I think you should decide whether to have children based on everything that matters. But not about whether it's hereditary."

"My disability?"

I smiled and stroked her hair. "It doesn't seem to be much of a disability."

"Okay, then, my talent?"

"Right. Your talent. One of many talents you possess."

She was quiet again for a moment, then relaxed into my arm once more. "You're right. There is no normal."

Another pause.

"And what about yours?" she said.

"What?"

"Your talent."

And there it was.

I'd finally put it together myself over the past few days, while I worked through the details of everything that had happened.

I had always known that I met an unusual number of people with psychic talents. I figured it was just a quirk of my profession. But in truth, there was something else going on. I don't think I consciously sought them out, but I was drawn to them.

And what's more, I could recognize them. I could pick them out in a crowd. There was always something about them, and something about my own reactions. The distracting magnetic pull I felt at the hospital when I saw Arthur Keith and Hugo Farmer. The pressure at the back of my head when I was around Fielding or Mark Baxter. The headaches when I was around Lansing and her daughter — the headache that had gone away when the jar was activated, and had come back like a pickax when the jar was suddenly smashed and the psychic effects flooded back in.

And the warm, delicious bloom in my chest whenever I was around Melissa?

No. I refused to believe that was only because she was psychic. Or because we were both psychic.

"I'm still coming to grips with it myself," I said. "Apparently I'm a talent detector."

Melissa gave a musical chuckle. "The Talent Scout."

I laughed too. "Not bad, if I hadn't given up on nicknames for you people."

Melissa stiffened again.

"I mean, to us —"

Melissa sat up straight, pulling away from me. "No, I understand. It will take some time for you to adjust to the idea of being 'one of us.'"

"Hey, no, that's not —"

She continued in a quiet voice. "You're so used to being over there, a 'normal person,' with us, the odd ones, off to one side. The people who are different. Who should be so grateful for your help."

"Listen, Melissa, I didn't mean —"

"I do understand," she said. "It must be such a shock for you to learn which side of that line you've been on all along."

"Melissa, I'm sorry."

We sat in silence for a minute. Melissa picked up her tea mug and held it. I ground my teeth and wished I could have the last five minutes back.

"Don't you have to pick up Fielding?" Melissa said. "He's being released in forty-five minutes."

I looked at my watch. She was right, of course.

We said good-bye. Melissa continued to frown at me, but she did allow a kiss on her cheek. I told her I would call her later, to let her know how Fielding was.

IN LIGHT of the new evidence from the Lansing warrants, Judge Carp had agreed to a new hearing to assess Fielding's status. That had taken place a couple of hours earlier. I'd wanted to be there, but Liz Duncan had asked me to stay away. She thought things would go more smoothly if I were not there, especially since reports of the events at the Lansing cabin had hit the news the day before. Fielding was briefly mentioned in one of the TV news pieces as an associate of "local so-called psychic detective Martin Rodak," and was said to be awaiting formal charges that related to the Lansing investigation.

In reality, no one had any more plans to charge Fielding on anything related to Vicar and Blake or the Lansing events. With the DA bringing no further charges, and the courts and Causeway House backlogged, the judge had agreed to Fielding's release.

I drove back down Santa Fe Drive to Causeway House and walked into the simulated motel lobby. Just inside the door a couple was hugging, a young black-haired woman and a man who looked as if the hug were all that was keeping him from collapsing. Three other people fidgeted in the puffy vinyl armchairs.

The woman at the reception desk and the uniformed guard in the security booth looked up as I entered. I was about to identify myself and ask about Fielding when I heard my name from across the lobby.

"Over here, Marty." Liz Duncan was standing by another cluster of chairs behind me. "Your friend will be out in a minute."

I walked over to join her. "So the hearing went well?"

"About as well as I'd hoped," Liz said. "Deferred charges on the contempt. Recommendation of continued private psychiatric evaluation, and treatment if called for. But nothing he'll be held on. He can go home, and if he stays out of trouble for a year the slate will be clean."

I let out a breath. "Thanks, Liz. I appreciate your helping him. If I were in trouble I'd want you representing me."

"Ha!" Liz barked out her clipped laugh. "If I'd have you for a client. Anyway, you haven't been in that spot yet. Knock wood."

A buzzer sounded somewhere down a hallway. Then I heard footsteps approaching, and an orderly ushered Fielding into the lobby. I crossed the room and put a hand on his shoulder.

"Good to see you, pal," I said.

"You too, Martin."

"You okay?"

"Just tired. I'd like to go home."

"Sure. Let's go. Though you're welcome to stay at my place for a while if you want."

Fielding offered a weak smile. "Thank you, Martin. But I think I'd rather be at home. With my books. It's been a long week."

I nodded. Fielding turned toward Liz. "Thank you, Elizabeth," he said. "I appreciate your help, and your getting me out of here."

Liz nodded. "I just wish it had been sooner. Wish I'd been able to make it easier on you."

Fielding tried on another thin smile. "You did a great job, considering how I behaved in the court."

Liz barked another laugh. "Ha! I've dealt with worse." Then she hoisted her giant purse-briefcase hybrid onto her shoulder. "Now, if you boys are okay, I need to go see another client. I'll talk to you soon." Then she was gone out into the parking lot.

Fielding and I left as well. Once he was tucked into my passenger seat, I got behind the wheel and drove us toward his place.

"Do you want to stop for something to eat?" I asked.

"No, thank you," Fielding said. "I'd just like to be at home for now."

"Okay. I'll bring something in for you later."

Soon we were at Fielding's place. He took a shower while I cleaned up a little. There was not much to do, as Toni and Alison had come by earlier to undo the damage left by the break-in and by Detective Carson and his team. Soon everything was in its place, including Fielding in his reading chair with a glass of Diet Coke and a book.

"Thank you, Martin," he said. He patted the book on his lap. "This is old, but it's one of my favorites. It has a fine illustration of Crusoe's meeting with Friday." He actually looked like the man I'd known for years. It was good to see.

I checked my watch. "Look, Fielding, I have to go run a quick errand. Then I'll be back soon, with something decent to eat. You going to be okay for a little while?"

"I'll be fine," he said. "You go along." He'd already drunk half his soda and opened to the first chapter of his book.

I smiled and went out. Twenty minutes later I was at the print shop, checking out their overnight work and putting the stack of boxes in my car. On the return trip to Fielding's, I picked up two of the chicken queso burritos I knew he liked.

Back on his cul-de-sac I waved to his neighbors across the street as they loaded two kids and some baseball equipment into their SUV. I parked in front of Fielding's house and went up to the door with the bag of food in one hand and one of the boxes from the printer under my arm.

Fielding had poured himself another Diet Coke and was watching *Jeopardy* on the tiny television that usually lay hidden behind a cupboard door at the bottom of a bookcase. I sat and watched with him while we ate our burritos.

"They mentioned us on the news," he said during a commercial. "Before I changed the channel."

"Anything new?"

"Not really. They mentioned I got out of jail. And that a judge thought I might be crazy. Though they didn't use that word."

"Sorry that happened," I said.

"Me too," he said. "But it's not your fault. I like working with you. I was practically in jail when we first met, remember? And now I'm not."

When the show was over, Fielding turned off the TV. He got up to shut the cupboard, then went back to his chair to drink some more soda.

I picked up the printer's box from where I'd left it next to the sofa. "I like working with you too," I said. "And I have something for you." I handed him the box.

He opened it, and pulled out a little card. "Your business cards?" He looked up at me. "I don't understand."

"Look more carefully," I said.

He looked back at the cards. He seemed more confused for a moment, but then he smiled.

The card looked a lot like the "Martin Rodak, Investigations" cards I'd been using since I started my business. But this one said:

RODAK ASSOCIATES

Below that was Fielding's name, and then

Investigative Consultant

"I hope you like it," I said. "I got them for the others too — Mark, Toni, Alison."

"And Melissa?"

"Yes, Melissa too." I did wonder if she would accept it, after our last conversation.

"Even Cindy," I added. "She never goes out, but she can give one to the guy who delivers her groceries."

Fielding smiled and looked at the card some more.

"The point is, you're not just a bunch of people I know. Not just people who help me do my work. We're a team."

Fielding looked up at me again. "Thank you, Martin." He wiped at the corner of his eye.

"And we're a real company," I said. "I'll work out the details, but you'll all have a say in the cases we take and the way we run things."

Fielding rubbed at the corner of his eye.

"You're not going to get weepy on me now, are you?" I asked.

Fielding laughed. "No, no, won't do that."

I laughed as well. "Good!" I got up and clapped him on the shoulder, then went to get him another drink, and something for myself.

AUTHOR'S NOTE

This is a work of fiction. All characters and events are the product of my imagination, or are used fictitiously.

There is not really a private investigator in Denver working hand-in-hand with a group of psychic friends. Not that I know of, at least.

As for locations, I tried to capture something real about Denver and the surrounding areas, but I also adapted these realities as needed for the sake of the story. So at times I inserted fictional businesses, or moved things from one place to another, or brought back things that may no longer exist where and how I describe them.

Finally, a note about the Lacalma Nation. This is a fictional indigenous nation, created for this story. Because I was creating a fictional history, and connecting that to the psychic abilities that exist in the story, it seemed inappropriate to use the name of any actual nation. I did strive to portray Lacalma characters with respect and sensitivity, and I engaged in research and valuable discussions as part of that effort. But any mistakes in that regard are entirely my own, and I hope they will be excused.

ABOUT THE AUTHOR

Matthew Porter is a lawyer, writer, and media creator. With his son Ian he co-hosts the Inter-Millennium Media Project podcast, which can be found at www.IMMProject.com. Matthew lives in Colorado with his wife, a sizable collection of coffee brewers, and an alarming number of Tarot decks.

For the latest updates about his work, and to sign up for Matthew's newsletter, please visit www.ByMatthewPorter.com.

bsky.app/profile/bymatthewporter.com

mastodon.social/@ByMatthewPorter@mastodon.social

youtube.com/@bymatthewporter

9 798994 540701